THE RUNAWAY

VALKYRIE
THE RUNAWAY

BY KATE O'HEARN

ALADDIN

New York London Toronto Sydney New Delhi

ALADDIN

An imprint of Simon & Schuster Children's Publishing Division
1230 Avenue of the Americas, New York, New York 10020
First Aladdin hardcover edition January 2017
Text copyright © 2014 by Kate O'Hearn
Published by arrangement with Hodder & Stoughton, Ltd
Originally published in 2014 in Great Britain by Hodder Children's Books
Jacket illustration copyright © 2017 by Anna Steinbauer
All rights reserved, including the right of reproduction
in whole or in part in any form.
ALADDIN and related logo are registered trademarks of Simon & Schuster, Inc.
For information about special discounts for bulk purchases, please contact
Simon & Schuster Special Sales at 1-866-506-1949 or business@simonandschuster.com.
The Simon & Schuster Speakers Bureau can bring authors to your live event.
For more information or to book an event, contact the Simon & Schuster Speakers
Bureau at 1-866-248-3049 or visit our website at www.simonspeakers.com.
Jacket designed by Karin Paprocki
Interior designed by Mike Rosamilia
The text of this book was set in Goudy Old Style.
Manufactured in the United States of America 1216 FFG
2 4 6 8 10 9 7 5 3 1
Library of Congress Cataloging-in-Publication Data
Names: O'Hearn, Kate, author.
Title: The runaway / Kate O'Hearn.
Description: First Aladdin hardcover edition. | New York : Aladdin, 2017. |
Series: Valkyrie ; 2 | Originally published in London by Hodder Children's Books in 2014. |
Summary: "Freya and Archie are sent back to Earth by Odin in order to locate a banished Valkyrie
and bring her back to Asgaard. But Brunnhilde has built a life for herself on Earth
and has no desire to return. And what Freya learns about that life, changes her
understanding of her own family"— Provided by publisher.
Identifiers: LCCN 2016009715 |
ISBN 9781481447409 (hardcover) | ISBN 9781481447423 (eBook)
Subjects: | CYAC: Valkyries (Norse mythology)—Fiction. | Mythology, Norse—Fiction. |
BISAC: JUVENILE FICTION / Legends, Myths, Fables / Norse. |
JUVENILE FICTION / Action & Adventure / General. |
JUVENILE FICTION / Girls & Women.
Classification: LCC PZ7.O4137 Ru 2017 | DDC [Fic]—dc23
LC record available at https://lccn.loc.gov/2016009715

DEDICATION

This book is dedicated with much gratitude to my MONSTERS (those special guys who dress up in really uncomfortable, hot costumes and do events with me so I can show you some of my characters in live action)! If you want to see them, please check out my website and look at the photos.

Kevin—the Minotaur (even if he did fire me . . . No, wait, he made me redundant!)

Frank—the Turtle (my very own Florence Nightingale)

Ollie—the Blackbird (a rising star who will shine the brightest)

Romin—the Dragon Knight (mobile obsessive, but sweet beyond measure)

And David—the best brother in the world and . . . Lord Dorcon, Malek, Dark Searcher, & Dragon!

I love you all—especially the "Elevator Slam-Dancing"!

THE NINE REALMS CHALLENGE

LONG BEFORE TIME WAS MEASURED, DEEP IN THE depths of the cosmos, there came into being a magnificent tree.

This Cosmic World Tree is known as Yggdrasil.

Surrounded by billions of stars and rumored to have a hideous dragon called Nidhogg guarding its roots and a powerful eagle protecting the top, Yggdrasil contains nine separate realms within its leafy branches and deep roots.

Living in each realm are populations of every conceivable size, shape, and power—from the largest frost and fire giants to the Norse gods; from humans to trolls; elves to faeries; and everything in between.

The residents of these realms can visit each other only by using the Rainbow Bridge, Bifröst. There are rumors of secret tunnels within the root system of Yggdrasil, though they have never been proven, and with Nidhogg protecting the roots, it is doubtful anyone would survive the attempt to use them should such a system even exist.

Long ago, however, despite each world's connection through Yggdrasil, peace did not reign. War within the realms was common. The residents in the lower worlds viewed the upper worlds with envy and jealousy. Often they would invade in the hopes of claiming the upper realms for themselves.

So violent and destructive were these wars that Yggdrasil itself was suffering and in grave danger of being destroyed. But if Yggdrasil died, so would all the realms.

Finally Odin, leader of the highest realm, Asgard, summoned the kings and rulers of the lower realms together to forge a lasting peace. But with jealousy and anger still prevalent, the peace they forged was as delicate as a spider's web, and just as easily broken.

To ensure a continued, peaceful coexistence within Yggdrasil, and as a way of working out their frustrations and squabbles, the leaders of the realms came up with a solution.

Thus, the Nine Realms Challenge was born.

Every ten cosmic years, and moving from world to world, the Challenge is held. Here the realms can compete against each other in a show of power and strength without the risk of starting another war.

During the Nine Realms Challenge, any animosity

between the worlds is suspended and an armistice declared. The anger between the frost giants and the people of Asgard is put aside, just as peace is declared between the Light and Dark Elves.

But with so many different and combative species competing in the Nine Realms Challenge, Odin knew that this peace would be unstable. So he and the other leaders agreed on the creation of a special group of "Enforcers of Justice." These enforcers are also known as the Dark Searchers. They do not compete; nor do they favor sides. During the Challenge, the Dark Searchers remain neutral and dole out harsh punishments to anyone endangering the delicate balance of peace.

When not working for the Nine Realms Challenge, the Dark Searchers are fiercely loyal to Odin and do his bidding. Though they serve only Odin, they do not live in Asgard. They have their own keep, protected inside Utgard in the realm of Jotunheim, land of the frost giants—and only leave their keep when summoned.

The Nine Realms Challenge has kept the peace for thousands of years. But it is a fragile peace that can easily be shattered. When that happens, the final, devastating war, known as Ragnarök, will begin, and not even the Cosmic World Tree, Yggdrasil, will survive it. . . .

1

AS DAWN ROSE PINK IN THE SKY, THE HEAVY
footfalls of visitors arriving in Asgard shook the ground.
High up on a hill, far from Bifröst, the Rainbow Bridge
and entrance to Asgard, stood the home of Eir, the head
Valkyrie, and her daughters.

Servants of Odin, and also known as his Battle-Maidens,
the Valkyries work hard to bring the most valiant of the
dying soldiers from the human world to Asgard.

But for one Valkyrie there is no reaping of soldiers. Still
on probation for leaving the realm without permission, Freya
is forced to work twice as hard as the others as punishment—
spending her mornings working in the stables of the Reaping
Mares, cleaning and caring for the winged horses, and afternoons in full battle training with the other Valkyries.

At the end of each day Freya returns to her bed exhausted and craving much-needed rest.

But today she was awakened extra early by loud pounding on her bedroom door.

"Gee, get up!" Archie called, using his pet name for Freya.

Archie was her best friend and companion, and seemed to always have limitless energy, while Freya was perpetually exhausted. She moaned sleepily and started to doze off again.

"C'mon, Gee and Maya," Archie called through the door. "You're missing it!"

Freya sat up, remembering what day it was. From outside the window came the sound of rumbling thunder as the ground beneath their home started to quake. She looked over at her sister's bed. Maya was lying on her side and facing away from her, sleeping soundly.

"Maya, wake up." Freya tossed a pillow at her sister. "The giants are here!"

Maya mumbled softly and rolled onto her stomach. She yawned, stretched, and extended her white wings up into the air. Folding them neatly on her back again, she mumbled a few more incoherent words and drifted back to sleep.

"Gee . . . ," Archie repeated. "Are you up?"

"*She is,*" Orus cawed loudly. Freya's raven companion sat on a perch at the base of her bed and kept watch while she slept.

Maya's own raven, Grul, had his head tucked under

his wing and was sleeping as soundly as Maya.

Freya took one final look at Maya and sighed. "I'm coming," she called as she climbed from her bed and started to get dressed. Moments later they stood on an open balcony high above the streets of Asgard.

"Cool!" Archie pointed to a long line of impossibly tall giants stomping through the narrow streets of the city. Each step caused the ground to rumble and buildings to shake. In the distance they heard the sound of breaking glass as windows shattered from the giants' heavy footfalls.

"I never thought they'd be so big. Are they the frost or fire giants?"

"They're frost giants," Freya explained. "You can tell by the color of their skin. Frost giants are silvery gray like ice, and their eyes are almost white to reflect the glare of snow from their realm. They have long, streaky black-and-white hair. Fire giants have bright-red skin, blazing-yellow eyes, and flaming-red hair."

They followed the long line of frost giants lumbering toward Valhalla, Odin's Great Heavenly Hall, where the opening ceremonies to the Nine Realms Challenge were to be held. The giants' shoulders and heads rose high above the roofs of the buildings in Asgard. Their expressions were at best unfriendly, with some looking hostile and even threatening.

"Frost giants hate us," Freya said matter-of-factly. "Fire giants aren't much better."

"Why?"

She shrugged. "I'm not sure. It goes way back to when there used to be a lot of wars—they nearly destroyed the realms." She paused and then pointed. "Look down there. The trolls are here too!"

Squat, round creatures were strolling along the street. They were dressed in rough-hewn clothes, so it was difficult to tell the women from the men. Occasionally they would throw a stone or spit at the people of Asgard.

"That's gross," Archie said. "Do they always spit?"

"They're trolls—what do you expect?"

Archie spotted more new arrivals. "Whoa, what are they?"

Freya looked down at the lovely line of creatures streaming through the streets. They were of slight build and seemed to float more than walk. They had pale complexions that looked like moonlight, and their soft, spider's weblike clothes billowed in the gentle breeze. "They're the Light Elves."

"They're so beautiful."

"They are," Freya agreed, "but, Archie, you have to be careful around them. They can be very dangerous, especially to humans. They love to keep them as pets. If one approaches you, do anything you can to get away as quickly as possible. Don't talk to them, or they may try to enchant you and take you away to Alfheim."

"Alfheim?" Archie repeated.

Freya nodded. "That's their realm. It's higher than Midgard but lower than Asgard."

"Does it matter where they are?"

"To them it does," Freya said. "That's why there have been so many wars. The lower realms claimed the upper realms had the most beautiful and fruitful lands. So they attacked us and tried to drive us out to take it for themselves."

"But you always won?"

Freya nodded. "There are more of us in Asgard than in the other realms. The last war was long before I was born."

They stood on the balcony watching more competitors arrive. Archie was completely mesmerized by the dragons, demons, Dark Elves, Light Elves, and dwarfs heading toward the battlefields at Valhalla.

"There's a lot more to come," Freya said. "They'll be competing here for twelve days. I wish we could go see them." She sighed. "I was just a child the last time the Nine Realms Challenge was held—back then it was in Utgard. This would have been the first time I could actually compete."

Freya's older sister Skaga had appeared on the balcony. She was taller than Freya, with blazing-white wings and pale-gray eyes. Her expression was disapproving. "You would've been allowed to compete this time if you hadn't run away and caused all that trouble in Midgard. You're both lucky Odin didn't do more to you. I can think of worse fates than cleaning out the stables."

"I know," Freya said. "But I only went to Earth to help. How could I know that Odin would send the Dark Searchers after us?"

"You broke the rules, Freya. What did you expect?" Skaga said. "Now you and your dead human are paying for it."

"Archie." Archie glared at her.

"What?"

"My name is Archie," he said. "Use it! Don't call me a dead human."

Freya's family still hadn't accepted Archie's presence in the house. But since Freya had reaped him and given him her real name, they didn't have any choice. Whether they liked it or not, Freya and Archie were bound together.

Skaga inhaled, about to retort, but Freya interrupted. "Look at everyone down there! I really hate to miss it."

She turned to Archie. "Maybe we can sneak away from the stables to watch some of the opening ceremonies. If we're careful, Odin will never know."

"*Oh, no you don't!*" Orus cawed from her shoulder. "*Freya, don't even think about it. That's the sort of thing the Dark Searchers will be looking for. We're banned from the games and they know it!*"

"Listen to Orus, Freya," Skaga warned. "If the Dark Searchers catch you, they'll hand you over to Odin. I'm sure he'll cut off your wings this time. Just do your work at the stables. There will always be more Challenges."

Archie nodded. "If I never see another Dark Searcher again, I'll be happy. Come on, let's get to work and let everyone else get on with the Challenge."

Freya's eyes lingered on the Light Elves as they drifted through the streets. She wanted so much to see the Challenge. Sighing, she finally let Archie draw her away from the balcony. Walking through the streets of Asgard was almost as exciting as watching from the balcony. Streams of visitors clogged their way. They had to stand far back on the pavement while a tall line of fire giants strode past.

"I smell smoke," Archie commented, looking around.

"It's them," Freya explained, pointing at the giants. "Can you see their clothes smoldering? In their own realm, their clothes burn. When they come to Asgard, they have to wear special garments that don't set fire to everything. If we're lucky, a fire giant will get angry—then you can watch their clothes burst into flame!"

"*Freya,*" Orus warned. "*Must you always look for trouble?*"

"I'm not looking for trouble," Freya said innocently. "I'm just explaining to Archie, that's all." But there was a twinkle in her eye that let them know she'd have been quite happy to watch the fire giants start to burn.

Behind the fire giants was a gathering of creatures wearing dark-green cloaks. Their faces were obscured by black masks and they were silent as they drifted past.

"Those are Dark Elves," Freya whispered. "Outside of

their realm, they keep their faces hidden. I've heard they're hideous. But I don't know for certain."

"Dark Elves are even uglier than trolls," Orus commented.

The nearest Dark Elf heard the comment and stepped closer. It pointed a gloved finger at the raven, hissing. The elf remained still, as though waiting for a challenge. When Orus said nothing, the creature hissed once more before walking away.

"Watch out for them as well," Orus warned Archie. *"Light Elves keep humans as pets. Dark Elves eat them with berry jam."*

"I'm not sure I want to meet any of them," Archie said. "They're really interesting to look at, but I think I'll stick with you two."

"Coward," Freya teased, punching him in the arm.

"I'm not a coward. I'm just not crazy. Let's see if I got this right." He started to count on his fingers. "The giants will either step on me or set me on fire if I'm not careful. Light Elves want to abduct me, Dark Elves want to eat me, and trolls just want to spit at me and hit me with rocks. This world takes a bit of getting used to."

"Don't forget the faeries," Orus added.

"Faeries? In Asgard?" Archie asked.

"Light Faeries, just like Light Elves, also come from Alfheim. They'll steal anything shiny that you're wearing, so be extra careful around them. Look over there. . . ."

The road had cleared and they were finally able to cross.

Up ahead, they spied a swarm of glowing Light Faeries using their little daggers to pry several jewels out of a sign over a jeweler's shop.

"*See what I mean?*" Orus cawed. "*They'll keep at it until they get all the jewels.*"

Archie stood very still, enchanted by the tiny figures doing all they could to free rubies from the sign. "They almost look like dragonflies, only more beautiful. Look at their tiny hands!"

"They're thieves, that's what they are." Freya ran over to where the faeries were swarming on the sign. Her wings flashed open, and she launched into the air. "Get away from there!"

The Light Faeries cried out with voices that sounded like tiny bells as they scattered. But the moment Freya landed on the ground, they went right back to work on the sign. She jumped at them again, and once more they scattered only to return when she was back on the ground. Their soft laughter rang out, and the tiny faeries stuck out their tongues and blew raspberries at her.

Freya shook her head and walked away, calling to Archie to follow her. Farther down the street, they slipped between two grand buildings to take a shortcut to the Reaping Mares' stables.

From behind them came the sounds of cheering as the crowds swelled to greet the new arrivals to Asgard. "We should be there," Freya complained, kicking a pebble away. "Not shoveling out dirty stalls."

"At least we don't have to train during the Challenge," Archie said. "I might actually go a day without a fresh bruise or cut."

"I thought you liked battle training?" Freya asked.

"I do. But the warriors at Valhalla have more experience than I do. Crixus tries to make it easy for me, but he used to be a gladiator."

"Crixus is your instructor?" Freya asked, awestruck. "He's the best warrior at Valhalla! How did you get him?"

Archie shrugged. "He saw me training and then offered to teach me. He believes in learning through pain and defeat." He paused. "But I rock at sword fighting. Soon I might even beat you!"

Freya smiled. When she first met Archie, he was being bullied and beaten at school by a vicious gang. Now every afternoon he was being taught by the very best of humanity's warriors, reaped from Earth's battlefields. He was learning hand-to-hand combat and fighting with many sorts of weapons. He had been accepted by the warriors of Valhalla.

"You think you can beat me?" Freya teased, shoving him. "Ha! I dare you to try!"

They reached the stable, and as soon as they opened the doors, the mares nickered to greet them. Freya went straight to her own mare.

"Good morning, Sylt." Freya stroked the horse's smooth muzzle.

Archie pulled an apple from his pocket. "Did you miss us?"

While Sylt munched the apple, Archie looked at the stalls. "Maybe if we finish quickly, we can watch from the balcony as the other competitors arrive. We can't get in trouble if we're watching from home."

"Great idea," Freya agreed as she reached for a pitchfork and they began to clean the stalls.

It wasn't long before Archie paused shoveling soiled straw out of a Reaping Mare's stall and leaned heavily on the shovel handle. His brows were knitted together in a frown. "Gee, I still don't get how this works. Are you sure I'm dead? I mean, Skaga always calls me a 'dead human,' but I just don't feel dead."

Freya forked fresh straw into a cleaned stall and looked over at her best friend, puzzled by the randomness of his question. "I'm sure."

His frown deepened. "But if I'm a ghost, why can I lift up this shovel? Or carry a sword and train with the warriors at Valhalla? And eat? I've never been so hungry. All I do is eat! You say the Light Elves would keep me for a pet if they caught me. But would they keep a dead person? And how could the Dark Elves eat me if I'm already dead?"

Freya stopped working to carefully consider her answer. It was obvious he had been thinking about this for some time.

"Here in Asgard, things work differently from the human world. You're dead, but also alive. You have an Asgard body that people can see and touch, and it can be hurt. It's just like the dead warriors at Valhalla—they were killed in Midgard battlefields and brought here. In the human world they would have no substance, but here, you've seen how they spend their days fighting and their nights drinking and singing in Valhalla. If you returned to the human world it would be different."

"So I'd be a ghost there?"

"*Yes.*" Orus flew off a stall door and landed on Archie's shoulder. "*And there, I couldn't do this to you.*" He nipped Archie's ear and cawed in laughter.

"Hey! That hurt."

"See?" Freya said. "On Earth you wouldn't have felt that."

Archie rubbed his earlobe and grimaced at the raven. "You didn't have to bite me to prove it. You could have just told me."

"Where's the fun in that! Besides, now that you're dead, you can understand me, and that alone was worth dying for!"

Archie chuckled for a moment, but then became pensive. "But I don't remember . . ."

Freya wondered about the sudden change in her friend. He'd been so happy watching the competitors arriving and had laughed at her for trying to shoo away the faeries. But now something was troubling him.

"Archie, what's wrong? What don't you remember?"

"Dying," he answered. "I can't remember how it happened."

"What can you remember?" Freya asked.

Archie frowned. "Not a lot. You and Maya were wounded and in danger, and I needed to get back to you. But that's it."

"You really don't remember?" Orus cawed. *"You don't remember taking Freya's sword to fight off the Dark Searcher?"*

"I did what?" Archie cried.

Freya nodded and stepped closer to him. "You fought the Dark Searcher for me. You nearly cut off his hand when he held me by my broken wing. I was so grateful to you."

Archie's frown deepened. "How did I die?"

Freya knew she had to approach this carefully. "I was badly hurt, but the Dark Searcher wouldn't stop. You tried to get me to run with you, but I couldn't because my leg was cut. Then you took my sword and attacked him—"

"It was really dumb but very brave," Orus cut in. *"He was bigger and much stronger than you."*

A sudden memory seemed to flash across Archie's face. "Wait—I remember something. . . ." He looked down and rubbed his stomach where the Searcher's sword had cut into him. "He stabbed me here. . . ."

"That's right. What else do you remember?"

Archie looked up at her in wonder. "I don't remember the pain, but I remember you. He was going to kill you, so I had to stop him. But then he stabbed me." Archie's eyes grew wide. "Wait, now I remember. Gee, you were crying."

"No, I wasn't," Freya huffed. "I just had something in my eyes."

"*Liar!*" Orus teased. "*You're not such a tough Valkyrie after all, are you? You knew Archie was going to die, and you didn't want to lose him. Then the floods arrived.*"

"I didn't want to leave you either," Archie continued. "But then you gave me your name and your mark." He held up his right hand, indicating the symbol that had appeared on the back of his hand the moment she'd told him her true name and reaped him. "You saved me, and I'm so glad you did."

Freya looked at the ornate gold and black symbol blazoned on the back of Archie's hand like a strange tattoo. Every Valkyrie had a unique pattern, which appeared on the hands of those they gave their true name to. In Asgard it was a great honor to be marked by a Valkyrie, and these chosen ones were the envy of those who didn't bear such a mark. With it, Archie was safe from anyone who might trouble him, because he had a Valkyrie's protection.

"Most of the warriors I train with are jealous that I've got your mark. Crixus says I'm really lucky. But I just think it's cool!"

"You do?" Freya asked. "It doesn't bother you that it means you belong to me?"

Archie shrugged. "Nope. I'd be with you anyway, with or

without the mark. Besides, it means that you belong to me too. So we're even."

"Yes, we are," Freya agreed softly.

The turn in the conversation was making her uncomfortable, and she fumbled to change the subject. "We'd better get these stalls finished if we want to see anyone else arriving."

Freya lifted a forkful of clean straw and heard Archie chuckle. Before she could question why, she was struck in the back with a shovelful of smelly, soiled straw.

Spinning round, Freya saw Archie laughing as he bent down and picked up handfuls of straw and threw them at her.

"*Straw fight!*" Orus cawed as he swooped off his perch, caught straw in his claws, soared higher, and dropped it on Freya's head.

"Hey! You're going to pay for that!" Freya threw down her fork and hurled handfuls of straw at Archie.

The barn erupted into a full-on war as neatly stacked bales of straw were torn open and used as ammunition. Archie ran across the barn and tried to avoid Freya's projectiles while gathering up more to throw at her.

Freya opened her black wings and launched into the air. She reached Archie in two wing beats and knocked him into a large pile of clean straw.

"Using wings is cheating!" Archie laughed as he rubbed handfuls of straw into Freya's dyed-red hair and into the feathers of her wings. Lost in fits of hysterics, they were soon covered in dry, golden shafts of straw. Freya pinned Archie down and hovered above him. "Do you surrender?"

"Never!"

Freya pulled a large stack of straw down onto him and shoved it into his face. "Now do you surrender?"

"No!" Archie cried, spitting out straw. "It's you who's going to surrender." With a quick wrestling maneuver, Archie spun Freya around and was soon pinning her down in the straw. "Do you give up?"

Freya cried, "Who taught you that?"

"Crixus," Archie answered. "He said if I'm going to stay with you, I'd better learn how to fight properly so I can protect you."

"Crixus said that?" Freya asked. "How does he even know me?"

Archie shrugged. "Don't know. He just does. Now do you give up?"

"Archie, I'm lying on my wings," Freya protested.

"Then you'd better tell me quickly!"

"Let me up!"

"Not until you say 'uncle' and give up!"

Freya was laughing too hard to use her Valkyrie strength against him. Instead she lay in the straw, looking up into his beaming face, and saw that it was true. Archie had no regrets that she had reaped him and brought him into her life here in Asgard.

A familiar voice rose from behind them. "Is this what you two call cleaning the stables?"

"Azrael?"

Freya rose and flew at the leader of the Angels of Death.

Azrael received her in his open arms and wrapped his white wings around her tightly until she could no longer be seen in his angelic embrace.

"I'm glad to see that Odin's been keeping you busy." He released her and chuckled softly as he picked straw from her tousled hair.

Archie walked forward and bowed his head. "Hello, sir."

Azrael smiled. "And how's my favorite human?"

"Not too bad, thanks."

"What are you doing in Asgard?" Freya asked.

"I'm here for the Challenge. I've been speaking with Odin, and we both feel it's time for my realm to join in the competition. We're the Tenth Realm."

"The Tenth Realm?" Freya asked.

Azrael nodded. "Heofon. My angels will be arriving shortly."

"I really wish we could watch," Freya explained sadly. "Odin has forbidden us from competing in any Challenge or visiting Valhalla during the events. We're even banned from watching."

"Yes. About that . . . ," Azrael said. "I've been speaking with Odin and asked if your punishment might be suspended, just for the Challenge."

"You did?" Archie asked.

The tall Angel of Death nodded and plucked another piece of straw from Freya's hair. "I did. And Odin has agreed. So if you two would like to get cleaned up, we can head over to the opening ceremonies. You will be competing with your sisters and the other Valkyries. But you'd better hurry if you want to join them in the opening parade."

The parade wound its way through the crowded streets of Asgard. Freya was thrilled to be riding her Reaping Mare, Sylt, beside Maya. Seated tall and proud on her own Reaping Mare, Maya glowed with excitement at being part of the opening ceremonies. As the most beautiful of all the Valkyries, Maya held everyone's attention. But Freya wasn't jealous. She adored her older sister and was honored to ride beside her.

They were following their mother, Eir, who was leading the Valkyries upon her tall Reaping Mare and waving the Valkyrie banner proudly up ahead.

But the noise, colors, and crowds ebbed away as Freya felt a sudden chill running down her spine that caused her to look back. More participants had joined the parade directly behind the Valkyries.

Dark Searchers.

As Freya's eyes passed over the dark-cloaked, armored creatures, her blood ran cold when she noticed one Dark Searcher in particular staring directly at her.

Knowing he now had her attention, the Dark Searcher opened his black wings and raised his right arm. He made a cutting gesture across his wrist with his left hand. Then he pointed at her and shook his head slowly. The message was crystal clear. This was the Dark Searcher that Odin had sent to find her in Chicago. The same one Archie had cut with her sword. He had not forgotten—nor forgiven—what they had done to him.

"Maya, look," Freya said tightly to her sister. "Dark Searchers."

Maya refused to turn back. She shivered. "Mother warned me they were coming. They're the 'Enforcers of Justice.' It's their job to keep everyone from fighting and to deal with any troublemakers. She warned us not to antagonize them."

"*Us*, antagonize *them?*" Freya cried. "The one that killed Archie just threatened me. He's going to try something. I just know it."

"*He's definitely going to do something,*" Orus cawed.

"He can't. Odin has declared an armistice, which includes the Dark Searchers. Just ignore him. I'm sure we won't see them again after today," Maya said.

"*Ignore him? Are you kidding?*" Orus complained.

"Have you forgotten Chicago so soon?" Freya asked.

"No, I haven't. But it's over now. They are here to watch over the games and keep the peace. Not cause trouble for us. That Searcher can't do anything to you."

"*Did you tell him that?*" Orus finished.

"*Don't be such a scaredy-bird,*" Grul, Maya's raven, cawed. "*Maya and I aren't frightened of a few Dark Searchers.*"

"You're not smart enough to be scared," Orus insulted.

"Orus, that's enough." Freya stroked her raven and stole a glance back to the Searcher. The tilt of his visored head suggested he was still staring directly at her. Freya shuddered and turned to face the front, determined not to look at him again.

When the parade ended, the competitors moved into their training areas. Archie joined Freya as the Valkyries gathered in a large, brightly colored tent that flew their flag.

"Now, remember." Her mother addressed all of them, but her pale, disapproving eyes landed on Freya. "Each and every one of you represents the honor of the Valkyries. We must not bring any more shame down upon us."

"I think she means us," Archie whispered to Freya.

"I know she does," Freya agreed.

"Shhhh . . . ," Maya warned. "You don't want Mother to get any angrier."

"*I hardly think that's possible,*" Orus added.

"All the realms have drawn lots," Eir continued. "The Valkyries are participating in a total of eleven Challenges. We will be in three races—two on the ground and one in the air. Plus four different battles, and a challenge of strength, swimming, tracking, and then hunting. Finally, we'll all participate in the tug-of-war against the Angels of Death. I will assign each of you the Challenge you are to compete in. Come forward as I call your name."

"I hope I get the Moat Race Challenge, I love that one," Maya whispered to Freya as her mother began calling up the Valkyries one by one. "And I'm sure Mother will pick you for the races. You'll definitely win—you're the fastest out of all of us."

"Especially flying," Archie added.

Freya blushed under the compliment. "I'm just happy to be here."

They watched their mother call more and more Valkyries up to the front, but still none of their names were announced.

"I thought Azrael said we were going to get to participate," Freya whispered to Archie.

"Not everyone's been called yet. It will be your turn soon."

They continued to wait and watched the last of the other Valkyries walk to the front.

Soon everyone had been called, apart from Freya and Maya. But Eir turned to address them all as if she were finished. "Sisterhood of the Valkyries, this is our moment to shine. We are strong and we are powerful—let's show the other realms just what we can do! Will you give me your best?"

The Valkyries opened their wings and raised their hands to cheer. All except Freya and Maya. Both girls stood at the back, crushed, knowing they had been excluded from the games.

"It's all right," Archie said brightly. "I know how strong you both are. You don't need to prove it to anyone."

Freya was grateful to him for trying, but this cut deep. She had been desperate to participate in the Challenge.

"I don't care," Maya said lightly. But her eyes spoke differently. They were downcast and her lips held a pout. She couldn't hide that she was deeply hurt at being cut from the Challenge.

Eir climbed down from her dais. "Freya and Maya, because of your punishment you are forbidden from officially taking part in the Challenge. However, your punishment will be lifted for one event only. The tug-of-war against the Angels of Death. You are only allowed to participate because Azrael has lobbied for it. You are very lucky to have such an influential friend."

"What about Archie?" Freya asked.

"What about him?" her mother said sharply. "If Archie wishes to compete, he may join the warriors at Valhalla, as they represent Midgard—he's been training with them; let him stand with them."

"Crixus won't let me compete," Archie said. "He says I'm not ready yet."

"He's right," Eir agreed. "You have only started to train. You need more time."

"But he's with me," Freya insisted. "He should compete with us."

Her mother's eyes blazed. "Your pet human is not a Valkyrie. He may not compete with us."

"Archie is not my pet!" Freya cried. "He's my friend. If he can't compete, I won't."

"It's okay," Archie insisted. "I don't want to compete anyway. Your mother is right. I've only just started to train. I'm not ready to go up against frost giants or dwarfs or anyone."

"But—"

"It's okay," Archie repeated. "I've caused enough trouble for you already. I really would prefer to watch. Next time I'll be ready, but not now."

Eir's eyes bored into Archie. "Tell me, child, how old are you?"

"I'm fifteen," Archie said.

"Fifteen," Freya's mother repeated. "Before you died, did my daughter warn you that once she reaped you, you will forever remain that age? That even though she continues to age and grow, you will be stuck as you are? You will watch her mature and perhaps have children of her own, and still you will remain a child."

"Archie will always be my friend, no matter what!" Freya replied.

Archie faced Eir. "Crixus and I have already talked about that," he said respectfully. "And just like I told him, I'm grateful to Gee for bringing me here. Whatever happens in the future will happen. But for now we are friends."

Eir's back stiffened. "Why do you insist on calling my daughter 'Gee' when you know full well her name is Freya?"

"Mother," Freya protested.

"No, let him answer. He is in Asgard now. He should use your proper name."

"I am sorry if it upsets you," Archie said. "But for so long, I only knew her as Gee. Yes, I know her real name is Freya, because she gave it to me. But everyone here calls her that. For me to call her Gee reminds us both of our special friendship and where we've come from."

"Your special friendship?"

"Yes, friendship," Freya agreed. "I like it that he calls me Gee."

"Mother," Maya put in. "It might be hard to understand, but Archie is my friend too. He will remain so for all time."

Eir's eyes softened as she looked at them. "You all feel the same?"

"Yes," Freya agreed. Archie and Maya nodded.

"Time alone will tell," the tall, elegant Valkyrie said. "For now, Archie, if you will not compete with the Valhalla warriors, you may remain with Freya and help her prepare for her Challenge." Just as she was leaving, she paused and turned back. "Also, I am sorry, but you are all restricted to watching only one event per day. So choose wisely."

"One?" Freya protested. "That's not fair!"

Her mother charged back and pointed a shaking finger in Freya's face. "Running away to Chicago without permission was wrong. You must be punished. This is the price you will pay! Be grateful I don't ban you from watching all Challenges!"

2

"HURRY UP," FREYA CALLED TO ARCHIE AS SHE struggled to clean the stable as quickly as possible. "We don't want to miss the Troll Racing Challenge!"

Up before dawn, they cleaned all the stalls faster than they had ever done before. Just as they finished, Maya arrived.

"Perfect timing," Freya said sarcastically as she wiped sweat off her brow. "You show up just as we finish all the work."

"I would have come sooner, but Heimdall wanted to chat." Maya was spending a lot of time with the Watchman of the Rainbow Bridge. "He's asked me to go with him to the closing ceremonies."

Archie grinned. "Ooh, Maya's got a boyfriend."

"I do not!" Maya blushed. "He's just . . . very nice."

"*Nice or not, hurry up!*" Orus cawed. "*I want to see the races!*"

"*Don't tell Maya what to do!*" Grul snapped. "*We'll go when we're ready.*"

"And we're ready now," Freya said impatiently as she hung up her fork and brushed off her soiled tunic.

"Please tell me you're going to get changed first." Maya looked at her in disgust. "Look at your hair! When did you brush it last? I won't even mention how you smell or the state of your feathers."

Freya looked down at herself. "I'm fine. Now, let's go."

It was Archie who convinced Freya to get cleaned up before heading over to Valhalla to watch the Troll Racing— much to Maya's relief.

The open battlefields outside the Heavenly Hall had been transformed into a massive arena encircled with high bleachers. At ground level, with the best view of the field, were the two thrones for Odin and his wife, Frigg. Beside their thrones were seats for Thor, his brother Balder, and the other high-ranking officials from all the realms.

Changing rooms had been constructed near the entrance to Valhalla, and a large score-keeping board had been built. An exceptionally tall frost giant used a huge piece of chalk to enter the teams and their scores.

The first competitors entered the field, and Archie frowned. "Frost giants? I thought you said this was Troll Racing."

"It is Troll Racing," Freya said. "Keep watching."

A line of frost giants gathered at the starting point, just in front of Odin's and Frigg's raised thrones. Once they were in position, the squat, round trolls entered the arena. They each took a place in front of a frost giant and then bent down and tucked themselves into tight balls. When Odin gave the signal, the frost giants pulled back their legs and gave the trolls mighty kicks.

The trolls soared high over the heads of the cheering crowds toward the highest bleachers and out of the arena. As they sailed through the air, they unfurled, reached into their hidden pouches, and pulled out handfuls of rocks. Without losing momentum in the air, the trolls started hurling the rocks down at the crowds below.

"Why do they always bring rocks?" Maya ducked aside just as a rock the size of her fist whizzed past her head. "I know it was you, Skull!" she howled, and waved a threatening fist in the air.

The sound of troll laughter filled the sky above them. Archie was stunned. "That is Troll Racing?"

Freya nodded. "They search the trolls before the race, but somehow they always manage to bring rocks to throw at us."

"That's insane!" Archie protested. "You call that sport? Those giants are kicking the trolls!"

Freya shrugged. "And the troll that lands the farthest away wins. What did you expect?"

"I expected the trolls to run a race. Not get beaten up."

"You've seen them. They can't run. They can barely walk. Making them race would be cruel. Trust me, they like it. If they didn't, no one could get them to do it."

"What they like is hitting us with rocks!" Orus complained as a smaller pebble rained down and struck him in the beak.

"But it's barbaric!" Archie cried.

"No, it's the Ten Realms Challenge. What were you expecting, Earth games?"

"Yes," Archie cried. "Running, swimming, track and field, gymnastics, maybe even soccer, like the Olympics."

"We do have swimming," Maya offered. "Well, kind of. There's the Odin's Falls Challenge, where frost giants freeze Odin's Falls. Then competitors jump off the top, and those that don't crash through the ice at the bottom win."

"What happens to those that break through the ice?"

Freya shrugged. "They drown and get washed away under the ice."

"What?" Archie cried. "They die?"

"Only for a little while. They come back to life later."

"Then there is the Moat Race," Maya added. "That's the one I really wanted to be in. It's where the Valkyries race the Dark Elves. We swim eight laps in the deep moat surrounding Valhalla."

"What's the danger there?" Archie asked. "Because it seems to me all these Challenges are dangerous."

"There's no serious danger," Maya said.

"Except for the water dragons in the moat," Freya added. "They bite really hard!"

"And occasionally eat a competitor," Orus added.

"What?" Archie cried. "And you call these games?"

"These aren't games," Freya said. "They are Challenges. And they're here to keep peace in the realms. So there has to be an element of danger."

A second line of frost giants and trolls were taking their place on the starting line. The trolls balled themselves up and were kicked by the frost giants and, like before, as the trolls flew into the air, they pulled out more rocks and fired them into the crowds below.

"Argh—every time?" Maya ducked but not quickly enough, and she was struck in the shoulder with a rock.

Freya couldn't help but laugh at Archie's reactions as nothing was as he expected. Least of all the Drinking Challenge, which took place on the second day. For this Challenge, Thor and his brother Balder competed against the dwarfs to see who could drink the most.

Thor had a reputation of being the biggest drinker in all Asgard. So to keep the competition fair, instead of his favorite drink, mead, Thor was forced to drink what he hated most—apple juice.

The brothers stood on a raised dais beside twelve dwarfs. A bell sounded and they each made a grab for the nearest tankard and began to guzzle down the drink. "Look at Thor's face!" Freya laughed, pointing. As he drained tankard after tankard of apple juice, his pinched face grew greener and greener. He looked as if he were about to be sick.

Soon only the brothers and three dwarfs were left, until Balder drained another tankard of mead, gave a foolish grin to Thor, fell backward off his chair, and passed out.

Another three tankards were consumed before the last dwarf surrendered and Thor won. When he came forward to receive his medal, he belched with enough force to blow the judges off the field, and the stench of his breath sent the crowds running and screaming to get away.

But it was when Odin joined the games on the fifth day that things started to get interesting. Climbing onto his eight-legged steed, Sleipnir, he took his place at the starting line in the Lightning Race. For this Challenge, Odin would team up with eight Valkyries against eight Light Elves.

While the speedy Light Elves raced around the outer wall of Asgard four times, the Valkyries tried to slow them down by pulling on their cloaks or darting in front of them, and Odin would fire lightning bolts at them. If Odin struck a Valkyrie, she would be disqualified and removed from the race. But if he struck all eight Light Elves before they made it around Asgard four times, Odin and the Valkyries would win. If just one Light Elf remained untouched, the Light Elves would be declared the winners.

"Whoa—talk about complicated . . . ," Archie mumbled when Freya finished explaining the rules.

"What? It's simple."

Archie shook his head in disbelief and tried to keep up with the race.

Despite Odin and the Valkyries' best efforts, the Light Elves won the Challenge. But Odin took the defeat gracefully and shared drinks and celebrations with the victorious Light Elves.

"Odin would have won if you'd been allowed to compete," Maya complained to Freya as they walked away from the Challenge. "Everyone knows you're the fastest flyer in Asgard."

"I asked Mother this morning if I could enter," Freya said. "She said if either of us asks her again, we'll be banned from watching any more Challenges!"

"No way!" Archie said. "She's still mad. Why is she always so angry?"

Freya sighed. "Mother has never been a happy woman."

"She used to be," Maya said. "I remember before you were born, she would laugh and play with us all the time."

"Really?" Freya said. "What happened?"

"I don't know," Maya said. "She seemed to change overnight. Now we rarely see her smile."

After their Challenge that day, Freya and Archie returned to the stables to feed the Reaping Mares.

"What's on the agenda for tomorrow?" Archie asked.

"Dragon Wrestling," Freya said as she petted Sylt. "This is one I'm really looking forward to. Normally it's fire giants versus fire-breathing dragons. This time it's the Angels of Death against the dragons. Azrael is competing."

"Now this I gotta see!" Archie said as he set to work.

The next morning the Angels of Death entered the field and took on a line of fire-breathing dragons. The Challenge was for the angels to wrestle a dragon to the ground while avoiding getting burned by the dragon's fire.

When Azrael led his angels forward, Freya, Archie, and Maya cheered loudest.

Right from the start, Freya was surprised by the power and strength of the Angels of Death. She had only ever seen their compassionate side when their paths crossed. But as Azrael took on Nidhogg, the largest and most ferocious dragon in all the realms, he showed skills of speed and guile that Freya would never have imagined possible in an angel.

The wrestling event went on for the better part of the day. Sometimes an angel would win, other times a dragon. But, as day gave way to night, Azrael and Nidhogg were the only competitors left on the field.

All other Challenges paused as every spectator and participant came down to the main arena to watch the leader of the Angels of Death do battle with the dragon. Freya couldn't watch as Nidhogg caught Azrael by the wings and hoisted him in the air. As Azrael struggled to get free, Nidhogg slammed him down on the ground.

"Azrael!" Freya cried.

But Azrael was back on his feet before Nidhogg could shoot flames from his nostrils.

It was nearly dawn before Nidhogg made his fatal mistake. He lifted his wing, intending to smash it down on Azrael. But as it made contact with him, Azrael caught hold of it and flew up into the air.

Nidhogg was caught by complete surprise and roared in fury as Azrael twisted his wing back. The more Nidhogg struggled, the harder Azrael pulled, until he managed to pin the dragon to the ground. Victory was declared.

As the dragon was corralled and taken away, Freya and Archie ran up to the edge of the battlefield to greet Azrael. Most of his clothes had been burned away and the pristine white feathers on his wings were singed black. His face was filthy, but he was grinning.

"Are you all right?" Freya cried as another Angel of Death handed Azrael a clean robe.

Azrael laughed and his bright eyes shone with excitement. "I haven't fought like that in ages! It was wonderful!"

"Whoa," Archie finally managed. "If I hadn't seen it, I'd never have believed it! You were amazing! I wish I could fight like that."

Azrael grinned. "I hear you're being trained by Crixus

and the Warriors of Valhalla. With a bit of time and practice, I'm sure you could manage it."

"Not against Nidhogg," Freya said. "I doubt even Thor could win against him."

Azrael shrugged. "Thor is much stronger than you think. Now, part of the closing ceremonies is going to be our tug-of-war." His eyes landed on Freya. "I hope you'll be ready."

"We will. But will you?"

Azrael ruffled her hair before being swept away by the other angels. "We're always ready for a fight."

As the days of the Ten Realms Challenge continued, Freya, Archie, and Maya took in as many events as they were allowed, while also training for their Tug-of-War Challenge. It was late afternoon on the eleventh day when the Valkyries were called onto the battlefield to take on the Dark Elves in the Three-Strike Sword Challenge.

From the podium, Odin called the crowd to attention. "Hear me! There has been a program change! A challenge has been laid down that I have accepted. For the very first time ever, the Dark Searchers will participate in a Challenge. The Dark Searchers will replace the Dark Elves on the battlefield against the Valkyries!"

The spectators erupted in cheers as the black-robed Dark Searchers filed onto the battleground. Everyone knew the Valkyries and Searchers hated each other. This would be the battle of the millennium.

Freya shot a look at her sister. "Did you know about this?"

"No!" Maya cried. "The Valkyries were supposed to take on the Dark Elves. The Searchers never participate in the events."

"They do now," said a voice behind them.

Freya turned to see Loki grinning. She hadn't felt or heard his approach. "What are you doing here?" she demanded of the one who'd caused her to almost be blinded, de-winged, and banished from Asgard.

"I'm watching the Challenge, just like you. And just like you, I too have been banned from participating in most events. I wonder how long it will take Odin to forgive us."

"After all the trouble you caused, I hope he never forgives you," Freya cried. "You should have been banished from Asgard!"

"Temper, temper," Loki teased. "If it hadn't been for me, you and young Archie would never have met. You should thank me."

"Thank you? Are you insane?"

"Gee, calm down," Archie said. "He's just trying to get at you."

"*Go away, Loki,*" Orus cawed. "*You are not welcome here.*"

A sneaky smile pulled at the corners of Loki's mouth as he leaned closer to Freya. "Don't worry—I'll go. I just wondered how you feel about the new Challenge."

"It doesn't matter," Maya said. "We're not competing."

"I wouldn't be so sure," Loki said knowingly.

Freya pulled back her fist, ready to punch Loki in the nose. "Get out of here, Loki."

"All right, all right." He chuckled, and held up his hands. "I'll go. But before I do, I want to draw your attention to the Dark Searchers."

Freya followed Loki's gaze toward the Dark Searchers filing onto the field of battle. "Look at that last Searcher at the end of the line. Look how small he is compared to the others—his cloak hardly fits. And how he covers his wings when all the other Searchers are proudly revealing theirs. Don't you wonder why?"

"He's a Dark Searcher," Freya spat. "I don't wonder any-thing about them except why Odin tolerates them."

"Oh, child, you do make me laugh," Loki cried. "Odin does much more than tolerate them. They are his closest servants. His Enforcers of Justice. I am certain Odin would see the Valkyries banished from Asgard long before his Dark Searchers."

"Go away, Loki," Maya warned. "My sister doesn't have the tolerance I have. I don't want to see her getting into any more trouble by breaking your nose."

The smile faded from Loki's face and his dark eyes grew hard and stormy. "I don't appreciate empty threats, Valkyrie, not from you or anyone. You would be wise to remember that."

Maya's wings opened as she advanced on him. "And I don't make empty threats. Now, go!"

A dangerous silence fell as Freya, Archie, and Maya squared up to Loki. After a long moment, Loki straightened to his full height and smiled again. He focused on Freya. "This isn't over between us."

As he walked away, he almost bumped into Thor. Loki bowed respectfully, but all Thor did was grunt in response.

"Was he bothering you?" Thor demanded as he approached Freya.

Freya secretly wondered if this day could get any worse. Odin's powerful son was known to resent the Valkyries. "Not really. I just wish he would leave us alone."

"That's not his way." Thor turned to watch Loki's back. "Causing mischief is in his nature. But you would do well to stay on his good side."

"Loki doesn't have a good side," Maya said.

"He does," Thor said. "It just takes time to find it. My father has sent me to collect you. You are both to join the others on the battlefield."

Freya's heart sank. The day just got worse.

"What?" Archie cried. "No way! You can't mean they have to fight the Dark Searchers?"

Thor nodded his reddish-blond head. "I mean exactly that. Father has ordered that Freya and Maya must finish the battle they started with the Searchers he sent after them." He paused and glared at Archie. "Be thankful he hasn't ordered you onto the field with them. That Searcher hasn't forgiven you for what you did to him with Freya's sword."

"He doesn't scare me!" Archie replied. He stood up straight and puffed out his chest. "After what he did to Gee, I'd love a chance to get even."

"He was following Odin's orders," Thor finished. "You stopped him from doing his duty."

"His duty was to kill Gee!"

"His duty," Thor corrected, "was to capture her. He would not have killed her. Your involvement impeded him and forced him to be harsher than ordered."

"You weren't there," Freya cut in. "You didn't see what he did. He was going to kill me, and he's going to try it again. I'm not going to compete." Freya crossed her arms over her chest. "Not against them."

"Are you refusing Odin's command?" Thor said. "While you are still under probation?"

"*The Searchers will kill Freya and Maya,*" Orus cried. "*Odin can't want that.*"

"*Kill them dead,*" Grul added from Maya's shoulder.

"No, they won't," Thor said. "This isn't a battle to the death. Believe me, Freya and Maya will be perfectly safe." He turned back to Freya. "Now, you will join your sisters on the battlefield even if I have to drag you there myself. It's that, or face Odin's wrath."

Thor caught each Valkyrie by the arm and led them forward. His grip was firm enough to let them know there was no refusing. The crowds parted to allow them through. Freya heard their whispered excitement. Everyone knew about their trouble in Chicago and were anxious to see a live re-creation of the fight.

As they stepped onto the battlefield, Freya's mother approached them. "I am sorry, my daughters. I have tried to talk Odin out of this madness, but he refuses. He says the Dark Searchers demand justice and he will grant it."

"But we didn't do anything wrong!" Maya insisted.

"And Odin called them off," Freya added. "It's over."

"It's not over for the Dark Searchers. You didn't surrender to them. To a Searcher, that is crime enough. You must use all your skills to keep away from them. We will do all we can to keep you safe, but we each have our own Searcher to fight."

Freya, Maya, and their mother joined the long line of Valkyries on the field, facing an equally long line of Dark Searchers.

As Odin continued to address the crowds, the Searcher that had pursued Freya through the streets of Chicago bullied his way into the line so that he was directly opposite her. He raised his fist in challenge, focusing only on her.

"The rules of this Challenge are simple," Odin continued. "Each combatant will be stripped of their protective armor. . . ." He paused and corrected himself. "Though for anonymity, the Searchers will be allowed to wear their cloaks and visored helmets.

"Each of you will be given one weapon: a wooden sword. But this is no ordinary sword. It has been created and enchanted by the dwarfs so that each time the sword bearer makes a lethal strike against their opponent, it will call out. After three such lethal strikes, the sword bearer will be declared the winner and their battle will be over.

"Now, receive your weapons and prepare to fight."

Each Valkyrie was given a wooden sword from a dwarf, while across the field the Dark Searchers were doing the same. *"It's going to be a slaughter,"* Orus protested. *"Everyone knows the Searchers are stronger. Freya, you and Maya must fly away as soon as you can."*

"We tried that in Chicago, remember?" Freya said grimly. "It didn't work then; it won't work now. We must be cleverer." She gave her raven a kiss on the beak. "Orus, please go to Archie. I don't want you hurt."

"I'm not going anywhere." Orus held fast to her shoulder. *"We started this together; we're going to finish it together."*

"And don't try to tell me to go either," Grul cawed to Maya before she could speak. *"If Orus is staying, so am I!"*

On the sidelines, Archie pushed his way to the front. "C'mon, Gee, you can do it!"

Freya could barely see him as he stood among the Dark

Elves. Directly behind them were the frost and fire giants, with trolls sitting neatly on their shoulders. The tension intensified as they waited for the battle to begin. Azrael appeared beside Archie, wearing an expression that revealed his disapproval of the Challenge. He nodded an acknowledgment to Freya.

Thor marched into the center of the field between the rows of Valkyries and Dark Searchers. "On my mark, you will begin!"

The Thunder God raised his hammer high in the air, and a large streak of lightning exploded from it, followed by a booming crack of thunder. Bringing the hammer down, Thor signaled the start of the Challenge.

The Valkyries raised their wooden swords and let out their loud howls as they charged into battle. The Dark Searchers growled and roared as they ran toward them. Almost immediately most combatants opened their wings and took to the sky.

Freya and Maya remained on the ground. With memories of their flight through Chicago still fresh, they knew they could never outfly the Searchers. Their only hope was to be faster on the ground.

A chilling roar came from the Dark Searcher charging Freya. This was no game or Challenge to him. His honor was at stake, and he wasn't going to be held back by foolish rules.

They met halfway across the battlefield. Wings open and

swords raised, Freya was determined to take him on with all the skills she possessed. Their wooden swords thunked against each other as the battle began.

Though he was much bigger and stronger, Freya soon discovered that when the Dark Searcher turned his head suddenly, his hood and helmet visor obscured his vision for a fraction of a second. She learned quickly to dart from side to side, forcing him to turn his head faster than his cloak's hood would allow.

As he came down with a swing that would have broken her bones, Freya dashed to the side, away from the Searcher's sword. Using his momentary blindness to her advantage, she darted behind him and drove the tip of her wooden sword deep into his wings and back.

Her sword sounded out the lethal hit. Freya had won the first point.

The Dark Searcher roared in fury and swung around swiftly. The tip of his wooden blade whooshed past Freya's face, missing her by a fraction.

Other battles being fought around and above her were forgotten as Freya focused fully on her Dark Searcher. Each swing of his wooden sword revealed his blinding hatred of her. Each growl coming from behind his visor spoke of his unrelenting rage. This wasn't a challenge or war game. It was a fight to the death.

As the Dark Searcher pressed his attack, Freya backed

into the Searcher fighting her mother. The moment they touched, Freya felt the strangest sensation—almost like an electric current shooting through her.

The Searcher must have felt it too, as he turned to her and paused. It was the short Searcher that Loki had pointed out. He tilted his head to the side in confusion.

Freya could feel his powers reaching out to her, scanning her. Then, shaking his head, he struck Freya in the side with his wooden sword. It sounded out the lethal strike, causing Freya's Dark Searcher to roar in fury and charge at the Searcher who'd hit her.

The enraged Dark Searcher caught hold of the smaller one, and lifting him high off the ground, cast him viciously aside.

As the smaller Searcher opened his wings to right himself, Freya gasped. Instead of having jet-black wings like all the others, his feathers were blazing white. In all her life, she had never heard of a white-winged Dark Searcher.

But she had no time to ask questions—her attacker suddenly roared and made it clear to everyone on the field that Freya belonged only to him.

In response, the other Searchers moved away.

Freya stood before her Dark Searcher. He was tall, imposing, and dripping with rage. She was sure that if she could see under his visor, his eyes would be glowing with unrestrained hatred. All she could hear were his deep breaths and his growls.

"Freya, move away from him," her mother called. "This isn't a game to him!"

"She knows that!" Orus cried. He flew off Freya's shoulder and tried to catch the Searcher's hood to pull it over his face. But with each swoop the raven made, the Searcher's sword flashed, barely missing him.

In a desperate attempt to protect her, Eir ran in front of Freya, but the vicious Dark Searcher knocked her away with a bone-crushing blow.

"Mother!" Freya cried as she tried to run after her. But the Dark Searcher's arm shot out and caught Freya by the wing. Squeezing it painfully, he dragged her back and brought his sword crashing down on her head. The sound of the wood striking Freya's scalp mixed with the cry of the sword announcing the Searcher's lethal strike.

Freya was driven to the ground with the blow. Her head spun and blood from the cut trickled into one of her eyes. She could feel more than see that he was raising his sword to hit her again. Instinctively she raised her weapon and plunged it deep into the Searcher's midsection.

"That's for Archie!" Freya shouted as her sword announced its second lethal strike against him.

Knocked back, the Dark Searcher shrieked in rage

Dizzy and half-blind from her head wound, Freya knew she only had an instant before he recovered and came at her again. Gaining her feet, she dashed forward. Ducking under the Searcher's swinging sword, she opened her wings and leaped into the air. But instead of flying away, she turned in the sky and flew directly at the Dark Searcher. Raising her wooden sword, she let her own momentum drive her straight into her surprised opponent.

They both crashed to the ground in a tangled heap of arms, legs, and wings. Being lighter and more agile, Freya gained her feet first. She lifted her sword high and brought it crashing down on the Searcher's neck. Had the blade been real, the blow would have severed his head from his body.

"Third lethal strike—winner!" her sword announced. Suddenly it turned from wood into a blazing gold sword, with a blade shaped like a flame.

"It's over!" Freya shouted breathlessly to the Dark Searcher. But although the Challenge was over, the fight wasn't. The creature threw aside his weapon and charged forward.

Before she could run, fly, or even raise her new golden sword, the Searcher caught hold of Freya and drove her to the ground. His massive weight pinned her down as he wrapped his gloved hands around her neck and started to squeeze.

Kicking and thrashing couldn't stop him from tightening his grip. Fighting with all her strength, Freya only managed to pull one of his fingers away from her throat. With her air cut off, she felt herself growing weaker. She punched desperately at his hooded head and managed to break part of his visor. But as he pressed harder, her vision started to fade. The last thing Freya saw was the Dark Searcher's cold blue eyes boring into her. The final thing she heard was his harsh cruel laugh as her life ebbed away.

3

IT WAS SO LOUD. EVERYONE SEEMED TO BE SHOUTING. There was movement all around her. The earthy smell of trolls filled the air, and she could hear the soft, tingling voices of Light Elves.

Freya opened her eyes and saw Archie leaning over her.

"Gee, talk to me. Are you all right?" He waved his hand in front of her face, holding up two fingers. "How many fingers can you see?"

She had never felt weaker than she did at that moment. She was lying on a narrow cot and found it too much effort to turn over, even though she was lying uncomfortably on her wings. She couldn't lift her head. Freya tried to speak, but nothing came out of her parched mouth. She could see that she was in the treatment tent where all wounded or defeated participants were taken to be healed. Beside her, an old troll was snoring loudly. Across the tent, Light Elves were visiting a wounded elf sitting up with her arm in a splint.

Twelve, she weakly mouthed.

"Twelve?" Archie cried. "Gee, I only have ten fingers! Boy, he really did a number on you!"

Orus was standing on her chest. *"Don't try to move. Just rest."*

"Wha-what happened?" she rasped.

"That Dark Searcher killed you . . . ," Archie said. "Everyone tried to pull him off, even the other Searchers. But he wouldn't let you go. Finally Azrael tackled him. There was a big fight, but Azrael won." Archie's face was flushed with concern.

"Killed . . . ," Freya struggled to say.

Orus nodded. *"You have suffered your first death. But you weren't gone long. Your body recovered quickly."*

Everyone who lived in Asgard was vulnerable to injuries. But if they were killed or wounded, they rose the next day as if nothing had happened, which was why the human warriors fighting at Valhalla could do so without fear.

Freya knew this and had even witnessed it herself. But she had never wanted to experience it. Now that she had, she never wanted to go through it again.

"I feel awful. . . ."

"That's the trouble with dying," Orus remarked. *"It hurts when you come back to life."*

Archie knelt down beside her bed and stroked her forehead. "I guess that makes us even—one death each."

"*And both caused by the same Dark Searcher,*" Orus added. "*But he won't be bothering you ever again. He got what he deserved.*"

When Freya frowned, Archie explained. "Odin promised your mother nothing would happen to you or Maya in the Challenge. But when the Dark Searcher killed you, your mother went ballistic. She demanded justice from Odin. He agreed and made a big deal of punishing the Searcher in the center of the arena, in front of everyone. Odin cut off one of his wings and banished him from Asgard. He can never come back here and from now on is stuck in Utgard."

"*All of the Dark Searchers have been sent home in disgrace. They cannot participate in the closing ceremonies,*" Orus added.

"Sent home? No, they can't be," Freya protested.

Archie frowned. "I thought you'd be happy about that."

Freya shook her head. "No. I'm glad my Searcher was sent home, but . . ." She tried to lift her head. "Archie, did you see him?"

"Who?"

"The small Searcher. He was fighting my mother. I backed into him, and when we touched, I felt so strange. I know he did too. Then I saw his wings. They were white!"

"All I saw was you fighting that monster. But what does it matter what color his wings were?"

"Don't you see? Dark Searchers have black wings. Valkyries have white!"

"So? You've got black wings," Archie said.

"Yes, and that's what makes her different," Orus said. *"So that other Searcher is as different from his kind as you are from the other Valkyries."*

"It's more than just the color of our wings," Freya insisted, struggling to get her muddled thoughts together. "I think I know him."

"How can you know him?" Archie asked.

A healer approached Freya's cot. "You two have been here long enough." She was short and built like a dwarf, but, instead of skin, her face was covered with fine green scales layered neatly over each other. "It's late. This Valkyrie needs her rest if she is to be well enough to attend the closing ceremonies tomorrow. Go home now. Let me do my work. You may come back in the morning."

Orus cawed in protest. But the healer wouldn't be put off. She put her hands on her hips and stood, tapping her foot impatiently. Her golden eyes blazed. "Am I going to have a problem with you? You don't want me to lose my temper, do you?"

Freya knew this healer. She was small but fierce. Her mother was a dragon and her father was a dwarf. She had inherited amazing strength from her mother and all the stubbornness and temper from her father.

"I'll be fine, Orus. You and Archie go home. I'll see you tomorrow."

Archie nodded and reluctantly rose. "We'll go. Sleep well, Gee. We'll be here first thing to see you."

Orus hopped up to Freya's chin and gave her a gentle peck on the lips. *"We'll be back at dawn, and no one is going to stop us."* The raven glared at the healer. *"No one!"* He flew up onto Archie's shoulder and cawed loudly.

When they were gone, the healer chuckled softly, crossing her scaled hands over her chest. "Not even a frost giant could pry those two away from you. One of the Light Elves over there tried to enchant your human friend, but his concern for you overpowered the elf's magic. He even threatened her."

"Archie threatened a Light Elf?"

The healer nodded. "He showed her your mark on his hand and claimed his place among the Valkyries. He said he was training with the warriors at Valhalla and that he'd kill anyone who tried to separate the two of you. I believe he truly frightened the elf. You should be very proud of him."

Freya could just imagine Archie doing that. "I am." She smiled.

The healer knelt down beside the cot, lifted Freya's head, and brought a wooden cup to her lips. "Here, drink this. It will put you to sleep and take away the pain while you recover."

Taking a deep draft of the sweet liquid, Freya was about to ask the woman to help her turn over and take the weight off her wings. But the moment she swallowed, she felt herself drifting off into a deep, peaceful sleep.

"Freya, wake up!" Orus cawed.

Freya awoke to find the raven standing on her chest again. "I thought the healer told you to go," she mumbled groggily.

"That was last night," Orus said. *"I told you we'd be back at dawn. Now, get up—the closing ceremonies will be starting soon. You need to get changed."*

"It's dawn?" Freya frowned.

Archie nodded. "It's still early, so there's time to get you home and dressed to compete. Remember, the tug-of-war is today."

Freya closed her eyes and took stock of herself. She was in no pain apart from the stiffness from lying on her wings too long. She climbed to her feet and yawned, then stretched and extended her wings fully. Everything felt back to normal.

"Ah, I see you are up!" The healer peered into Freya's eyes. "Good, good, all better. You may go. But try not to get killed again too soon. Next time will hurt more."

Freya smiled at the kind healer. "There won't be a next time!"

As the healer walked away, she called over her shoulder,

"That's what they all say—" Suddenly she shrieked in anger. "Put that down!"

A large swarm of tiny Light Faeries were trying to lift a golden sword and carry it out of the tent.

"I said drop it!" the healer shouted. She opened her mouth and a blazing dragon flame came shooting out. The faeries shrieked as their tiny wings were singed from the heat. They dropped the sword and fled out of the medical tent.

"Filthy faeries!" the healer muttered. "I have lost so many supplies to them." She collected the sword and handed it to Freya. "You don't want to forget this. You've earned it. This is your prize."

Freya took the magnificent enchanted sword. "It's beautiful."

"And it's all yours." The healer grinned. "Dwarf gold is very precious. You're lucky. This blade can never be used against you. It is yours and yours alone."

"Hey, Gee, since you've got your new golden sword, can I have your old one? The one Crixus gave me is chipped and bent."

Freya grinned, admiring her new blade. "Sure. With this, I don't need it anymore."

Her mother and sisters were waiting for her outside the tent. The harshness had left her mother's face and she was beaming with pride. Maya dashed forward and embraced her tightly.

"I'm so sorry we couldn't stop the Searcher," she cried. "We tried to pull him away, but he was too strong."

"They're all too strong," complained her eldest sister, Gwyn.

Freya held Maya tightly. "No one could have. He was determined to kill me, and nothing was going to stop him."

After her sisters had each embraced her, her mother opened her arms to receive Freya. "You fought bravely, my daughter. I couldn't be more proud of you."

Maya nudged her mother. "Go on and tell her."

"Tell me what?"

Her mother chuckled softly. "You are among a small handful of Valkyries who won their Challenge. You may count yourself among the elite."

"Mother won too," Freya's second-oldest sister, Skaga, said happily, pointing to the golden sword at their mother's side. "I was knocked out almost at the start."

"You didn't really try," her mother scolded. She looked at all her daughters. "None of you did, except Freya."

Maya shook her beautiful blond head. "I'm not crazy. I'd already gone up against my Searcher in Chicago. I didn't want to do it again, so I let him win." Maya paused. "To be honest, he took it easy on me. When he knocked me down, he actually helped me get up again."

Grul was seated at Maya's shoulder. *"Your beauty has once again charmed even the coldest Dark Searcher's heart."*

Freya looked at Orus, expecting him to make some sarcastic remark, but her raven remained quiet. "I'm just glad it's over. Maybe now he'll leave me alone."

"I fear you have made a powerful enemy," her mother warned. "He is called Dirian, and he was one of the highest-ranking Dark Searchers. He has been stripped of his rank and grounded in disgrace. I just hope you need never venture to Utgard and the Keep of the Searchers. I doubt even Azrael will be able to help you if you two ever meet again."

"I have no reason to go there," Freya said. She frowned and gazed around. "Where is Azrael? I want to thank him for helping me."

"He's in a meeting with Odin," her mother explained. "He said he was looking forward to seeing you today at the tug-of-war."

Maya grinned. "He also said that you shouldn't expect any mercy from him. He and his angels intend to win, regardless of you being killed."

Freya laughed lightly. "He can intend all he wants. We're going to beat them."

Her mother gave Freya a gentle kiss on the cheek. "Go prepare yourself. Dress in your best outfit and polish your armor. The closing ceremonies will begin right after the tug-of-war, and we are all to be in the final parade." As her mother walked away, she called back, "And don't forget your helmet. You'll be wearing that, too."

Freya had never been happier to bathe and get cleaned up. She wanted to scrub away her battle with the Dark Searcher and was grateful she'd never have to see him again.

Archie arrived from his quarters, dressed in his best new clothes, with Freya's old sword attached to his hip. He helped her into her armor. "Now, wait here. We've got a surprise for you."

He disappeared for a moment and returned, carrying her helmet. But something was different. The wings on her helmet had new feathers on each side. Jet-black feathers.

"What happened to my helmet?"

"Frigg did it." Archie explained how Odin's wife said that Freya had earned the change in her helmet and status. "These are feathers taken from the Dark Searcher's severed wing. She said it is to remind everyone of your win."

Freya looked at her helmet in disgust. "These are Dirian's feathers?"

Archie nodded. "I tried to tell her you wouldn't like it. But she insisted."

"But I didn't win. Dirian killed me."

"*Not before you got your third lethal strike against him,*" Orus corrected. "*Those feathers are a great honor, Freya; you must wear them with pride.*"

Freya didn't see them as an honor. They were a reminder of a lifelong enemy she had made.

"*Now, put on your new sword and let's go.*"

* * *

Freya, together with her mother, sisters, and Archie, marched to Valhalla, showing off the golden swords won by Freya and Eir.

"Loosen up a bit, Gee. You're a hero," Archie said proudly, taking his place beside her. "Savor the moment."

Freya smiled uncomfortably at everyone who cheered her along. "I think I preferred it when they ignored me."

"Are you ever happy?" Orus teased. *"First you think everyone hates you because you've got black wings. Now that everyone loves you, you don't like it either."*

Freya looked up at her raven and smiled. "The only thing that makes me happy is flying with you and Archie."

Orus puffed up his shiny black feathers and stood taller.

"Oh, please," Grul complained from Maya's shoulder.

They soon joined the large parade of competitors filing through the streets of Asgard. Heimdall caught up with Maya and took her hand as they continued onto the battlefield at Valhalla.

The whole arena had been decorated with brightly colored ribbons. Flagpoles rose high in the sky, encircling the field and proudly displaying the flags of the ten realms. In the center of the arena, a long stage had been built with tall poles erected at either end. Odin and Frigg sat together in thrones at the front of the stage. As more and more crowds arrived, they rose to greet everyone.

"Welcome, one and all!" Odin said. "As we draw the Ten Realms Challenge to a close, there is one more Challenge yet to be won. The tug-of-war. Will the Angels of Death and the Valkyries please come forward?"

This was the first-ever friendly competition between the Valkyries and the Angels of Death. There had always been a simmering of resentment between the two winged species because of their similar jobs in the land of the humans. While the Angels of Death guided the souls of humanity to their afterlives, the Valkyries reaped selected souls of brave warriors who died on Earth's battlefields to bring them to Valhalla. It was a subtle but important difference that at times caused friction.

"This is it," Freya said. She caught Archie by the hand. "C'mon, let's show Azrael what we can do."

Archie stayed put. "I'm not a Valkyrie."

For the first time since he'd arrived in Asgard, Freya's mother put her arm lightly around his shoulders and smiled warmly at him. "We would be honored if you would join us, Archie." She paused. "Just this once."

"Really?"

When she nodded, Archie grinned and walked with Freya and the other Valkyries up to the thick rope that had been laid out the length of the field. He looked up at the poles rising high into the sky at either end of the stage.

"What are those poles for?"

Freya grinned. "We've all got wings, Archie. You didn't think this tug-of-war would stay on the ground did you?"

His eyes flew from Freya up to the very tops of the poles. "We're going to fly up there?"

She nodded. "So you'd better hold on tight!"

The Angels of Death were already waiting on one side of the ribbon that had been tied around the center of the rope.

Azrael smiled brightly at Freya. "How are you feeling?"

"Much better, thank you," Freya responded. Then she laughed. "In fact, I'm feeling strong enough to beat you!"

"Powerful words." Azrael chuckled. "But can you back them up?"

Her grin broadened. "You bet I can!"

Odin jumped down from the stage and approached the competitors. "Take your positions!"

Eir indicated that Freya should take the lead position, with Archie behind her in second place.

"But you're the head Valkyrie," Freya protested. "You must take first position."

Her mother whispered in her ear. "Azrael has asked for you and Archie to be lead. He's almost as much of a trickster as Loki. Don't be surprised if he tries something." Her mother straightened and then winked at Azrael as color came to her cheeks.

"Did your mother just blush?" Archie cried.

Freya nodded. "Azrael is very handsome and his wings are

beautiful. Half the Valkyries have a big crush on him. The other half have fallen in love with all the other Angels of Death."

"What about you?" Archie teased. "Do you have a crush on Azrael?"

Freya was saved from having to answer as Odin's voice boomed out, "Competitors, pick up the rope. The first team to drag the center ribbon past one of the poles at the end of the stage will win. On my mark, you will begin."

Odin raised his spear high in the air. As he brought it down, he shouted, "Go!"

Immediately the slack on the rope pulled tight. Within seconds, the competitors on either side opened their wings and started to flap.

Archie struggled to hold on as the Valkyries and Angels of Death lifted up into the air, taking the rope with them.

Freya pulled as hard as she could, beating her wings to help her balance while she heaved. Directly across from her, Azrael and his angels were doing the same.

"Pull!" her mother shouted from the back of the line. "Pull!"

The ribbon marking the center hardly moved as the teams pulled and dragged on the rope. The crowd erupted in cheers.

"Pull!" Odin roared from the stage. "Valkyries, pull!" Even Thor and Balder were cheering on the Valkyries. Raising their tankards of mead, they laughed and cried encouragement.

Frost giants charged forward and stood at eye level with the tug-of-war as the teams struggled to move the ribbon past the pole at their end.

It was soon clear that the Valkyries and the Angels of Death were too evenly matched and at this rate the Challenge would take all day.

As Freya strained to pull as hard as she could, Azrael leaned forward with a playful glint in his eye. "Freya, I meant to tell you . . . ," he called over the grunting of the angels behind him. "Alma Johnson sends her love. She has been reunited with her son, Tyrone. He says hello too."

"Alma?" Freya cried. Loosening her grip, she remembered the kind old woman she'd met in Chicago. Her son, Tyrone Johnson, had been the first soldier she'd ever reaped, and it was he who had set her on the path to Earth.

"Alma is dead?" Shocked and saddened by the passing of the old woman, Freya's thoughts immediately turned to her granddaughters, Tamika and Uniik. Freya and Tamika had become close friends and she missed her dearly.

Distracted by the news, Freya released the rope.

"Gee, no!" Archie cried behind her. "Don't stop!"

With his lack of wings, Archie was now doing more harm than good to the Valkyries' side, as he simply hung on to the rope to keep from falling. Without Freya's efforts, the Valkyries were being dragged closer to the pole at the opposite end of the stage.

"Freya!" her mother called. "Pull!" But it was too late. By the time Freya realized what she was doing, the ribbon was too close to the Angels of Death's pole for her to make a difference. Her heart sank as she watched the ribbon slip past the marker.

"Winner!" Odin boomed from the ground. "The Angels of Death win!"

Freya swooped down to the ground and charged at Azrael. "You cheated! You knew I cared about Alma and used that against me to win!"

The tall leader of the angels was shaking hands with his people and patting them on the wings in congratulations. Turning to her, he put his hand on his heart. "You wound me, Freya—such accusations! An Angel of Death never cheats." He burst out laughing. "Well, maybe I did cheat a little, but I wasn't lying. Alma has joined her son. She asked me to tell you she is out of pain. She often checks on the girls, and they are doing well."

Her mother came up and offered her hand to Azrael. "I knew you were up to something when you asked for Freya to be put in lead position. That was naughty of you."

Shaking the Valkyrie's hand, Azrael turned on his charm. "Perhaps next time you'll take the lead and we can do this again."

Her mother grinned like a shy schoolgirl. "Yes, next time, Azrael."

* * *

After the tug-of-war, the full closing ceremonies began. There was a party on the battlefield as the realms joined together to celebrate another successful Challenge.

The singing, dancing, eating, and drinking continued into the night. Trolls laughed with the warriors of Valhalla. Frost giants and Light Elves danced together, and the Dark Elves played with the dragons and fire giants. The Valkyries danced and sang with the Angels of Death. Only the Dark Searchers were missing. Freya knew she should have been grateful for their absence. But she wasn't. She was haunted by the memory of the Dark Searcher with the white wings.

For three full days the celebrations continued, until, little by little, the competitors drifted away from Asgard and returned to their own realms.

4

IT DIDN'T TAKE LONG FOR NORMALITY TO RESUME
in Asgard. Freya and Archie returned to their daily routine
of mornings spent cleaning the stables and afternoons in
training—Archie at Valhalla with Crixus and the human
warriors and Freya with the Valkyries.

But as a new day dawned, after only an hour of work,
Freya's mother burst into the stables. The scowl had returned
to the tall Valkyrie's beautiful face.

"Freya, have you done something I should know about?"

Instantly on her guard, Freya shook her head. "I don't
think so."

Her mother frowned. "Then can you tell me why you and
Archie have been summoned to Valhalla? You are to meet
Odin there."

"Odin?" Freya cried. "Why?"

"I was hoping you could tell me."

"We haven't done anything," Archie said. "I swear."

"If you have done nothing, you have nothing to fear. Come. I will escort you there myself."

Freya put down her shovel and they followed Eir out of the stables and down the steep hill to Valhalla. Little was said on the way. But as they walked beside the battlefield, now stripped of flags and filled with dead warriors who had resumed their daily fighting, Freya asked, "Do you think we're in more trouble?"

Her mother paused. "I really don't know. I had your sisters keep a close eye on you during the Challenge and they haven't told me about anything you did wrong."

The tall, wide doors of the Great Heavenly Hall were always open. Freya and Archie followed Eir through the long chambers and finally into the grand banquet hall.

Odin sat at the end of the hall in his raised chair. He was lightly stroking the heads of his two pet wolves, which were sitting before him. Frigg sat beside him and waved them forward.

"Come," she called. "Come closer."

Freya was surprised to see Azrael standing next to Odin's chair. He was back in his official robes and smiling gently. Freya, Archie, and her mother all bowed as they approached their leader.

"You summoned us, Great Odin," her mother said formally.

Odin rose and stepped down from his chair. With Azrael at his side, they approached Freya. Odin grasped her chin lightly in his large hand. He inspected her face closely with his one piercing blue eye. As always, the other eye was covered with a gold patch. Freya often wondered if he actually had traded his eye for wisdom. And if so, what was he like before the trade?

"You have recovered from your unfortunate ordeal with Dirian?"

Freya was almost too terrified to speak. The last time she had been this close to Odin, he was preparing to cut off her wings and banish her from Asgard.

"Yes," she mumbled.

"Thank you, Odin . . . ," Orus whispered softly in her ear. *"Say 'thank you, Odin.'"*

Freya corrected herself. "Yes, I am fine, thank you, Odin."

"Good, good." Odin paused and glanced over to Azrael before focusing on her again. "I have a mission for you."

"Me?" Freya said timidly.

"Actually, for you and Archie," Azrael added, coming closer.

Freya could feel her mother stiffening beside her. Her voice was distinctly uncomfortable as she said, "Great Odin, if it is an important mission, perhaps we should send one of my other Valkyries. One who is more experienced than Freya? I can recommend—"

"No!" Odin boomed. The sound seemed to echo throughout all Valhalla. "I need Freya and Archie for this. She has spent time living in Midgard and has experience with humans of this age."

"And with Archie as her guide, there is little that can go wrong," Azrael added.

"Forgive me, Odin," Freya's mother said, bowing deeply. "I meant no disrespect. Just that Freya is so young and still on probation."

Odin focused on Freya again. The intensity of his stare was making her very uncomfortable. She didn't need her powers to know that Odin was troubled by something.

"Azrael has reminded me that my punishments can be too harsh and are not always just."

Freya lowered her head away from his penetrating eyes. "Sir, if you are speaking of our punishment . . ."

"Your punishment was just," Odin said quickly. "I am speaking of another. One who was banished a very long time ago. One whom I de-winged and blinded, leaving her to wander the World of Man alone."

"Do you mean Frigha?" Freya asked timidly, recalling the name of the only other Valkyrie ever to defy Odin and run away from Asgard.

Odin nodded. "Her true name was not Frigha but Brünnhilde. It is time to bring her home."

Freya's mother cried out and pulled her hands to her mouth.

"Hush!" Odin commanded. "Eir, if you cannot contain yourself, you may go. But do not speak of this to anyone. Do you understand me?"

"Yes, Odin. As you command." Eir bowed, nodded once to Freya, and then hurried out of the banquet hall.

Freya turned to watch her mother's retreat and noticed that Eir was trembling. She wondered what could have upset her so greatly.

A heavy hand pressed down on her shoulder. "Freya," Odin said, drawing her attention back to him. "You will leave here now. You will not return to your home. You will not speak to anyone about this or tell anyone where you are going."

"Where are we going?" Freya asked timidly.

"Midgard," Frigg said. She reached down beside her chair and pulled out Freya's golden sword. Stepping down beside her husband, she handed it to Freya. "I had this retrieved from your home earlier today. A Valkyrie must never venture to Midgard without her weapon. We want you to find Brünnhilde and bring her back to Asgard. It is time her banishment ended and she returned home." Frigg pulled out from her pocket a small glass vial. "Give this to Brünnhilde. My husband's punishments can be harsh, but they are not always permanent. When Brünnhilde drinks this, her eyesight will be restored."

"What about her wings?" Archie asked.

"There is nothing we can do about that," Frigg said softly. "She will remain grounded."

Freya was trying to process what she was asked to do. Frigha, or Brünnhilde, was a legend, a story told to all the Valkyries to frighten them into obedience. It had never occurred to her that Brünnhilde was still living on Earth somewhere.

"If it's been so long, she may not be alive," Archie said.

"She lives," Odin said. "She cannot be permanently killed unless I allow it."

Frigg smiled at her husband and her eyes sparkled. "Don't let Odin's gruffness fool you. He may have a foul temper, but he would never allow permanent death to claim one of his Valkyries. She lives still."

"What foul temper?" Odin's red eyebrows came together in a frown as he turned to his wife. "I don't have a temper."

Frigg smiled warmly and stroked her husband's cheek. "No, of course not, my beloved—though at times you can be a little difficult. But it makes me love you all the more."

Freya was stunned at the sudden blush rising in Odin's face. She could feel his deep emotions toward his wife. In all Asgard, Frigg was the only one who could calm him.

"Perhaps I can be a bit harsh," Odin admitted softly. "But it is necessary to maintain order."

"And so you must," Frigg teased. She turned back to

Freya and Archie again. "Go to Midgard. Find Brünnhilde and bring her home."

"How will we find her?" Archie asked.

Azrael answered for Frigg. "The same way Maya found Freya that first time in Chicago. You will take Brünnhilde's Reaping Mare. She will lead you to her mistress."

"Her Reaping Mare is here?" Freya asked, finally finding her voice. "Where? All the Reaping Mares at the stables belong to the Valkyries."

"She is not at the stables," Frigg answered. "She has been kept in a quiet pasture behind our palace. I have cared for her well, but she still pines for Brünnhilde."

Odin's voice softened. "It is my command that you find my missing Valkyrie, Brünnhilde, and bring her back to Asgard. If you are successful in this endeavor, I will end your probation and you may return to your full duties as a Valkyrie."

"What if we are unsuccessful?" Freya asked.

Odin's brows knit together in a deep frown. "You are a Valkyrie on a formal mission; you must not fail. To do so would bring shame on the sisterhood of the Valkyries. There will be repercussions for all of us, should that happen."

"That's not fair," Archie said.

"What?" Odin shouted. "You accuse me of being unfair?"

Archie took a step back. "No, sir! I just mean, what happens if we get there and Brünnhilde doesn't want to come back?"

"She has no choice. Should she refuse my command, then I shall return to Midgard to collect her myself. And you remember what happened last time. . . ." Odin turned back to Azrael. "Your angelic friend here will not be able to help you a second time."

Frigg put her hand on Odin's arm to calm him. "Freya, you must understand. To maintain order, Odin's commands must be obeyed. Otherwise those in the other realms, especially the frost and fire giants, will see this as weakness and move against us."

"Do you mean attack us?" Archie asked.

Frigg nodded. "Peace has a delicate balance. It won't take much to tip that balance against us."

Odin's eyes flashed a warning to his wife. "Enough talk. You and Archie have two Asgard days to find Brünnhilde and bring her back. That should be plenty of time. Any longer, and I shall have no choice but to consider this a defiance of my command."

He placed his hand on Freya's head. "I restore to you all your powers. Now, Brünnhilde's Reaping Mare, Jonquil, has been taken to Bifröst and is waiting for you there. Heimdall is aware that you are on this mission and will allow you to cross the bridge without question. Go now and return my missing Valkyrie to Asgard."

Freya paused before Odin, delighting in the feeling of all her restored powers. She hadn't missed her reaping ability, but being without the full power to sense people's intentions, or to feel the approach of danger, was like a constant ache. As if a piece of her was missing.

Finally she bowed her head. "As you command, Great Odin, we will bring Brünnhilde home."

5

FREYA DREW HER SWORD-BELT AROUND HER WAIST
as she walked to Bifröst with Archie and Azrael. The angel
looked deeply troubled and spoke very little. While he had
been with Odin, he'd kept his manner light and friendly, but
the moment they left Valhalla, he became withdrawn.

"Is everything all right?" Archie asked.

Azrael paused, gazing around them as though searching for someone. "I can say nothing here, but once we cross
Bifröst, we need to talk."

"That doesn't sound good," Orus muttered softly to Freya.

Freya didn't press him for information, but there was
something about his manner that troubled her. Instead,
she warned Archie that once they crossed the Rainbow
Bridge he would become like a ghost. "You'll only be able

to touch people and objects from our world."

"I'll be able to speak, right?" Archie asked in alarm.

"Of course," Azrael answered. "But only Freya, Orus, and those of the ethereal plane will be able to hear or see you. You will be silent and invisible to most humans and animals."

"Most?"

Azrael nodded. "Some may be able to see you, but they will be uncomfortable in your presence."

"Don't worry, Archie," Orus said. *"I'll take care of you."*

"What about me?" Freya said.

"I'll take care of you, too," Orus cawed.

"That's not what I meant. I was going to take care of Archie."

"I can take care of myself, thank you very much," Archie said. "I haven't trained all this time at Valhalla to let you two babysit me. I can fight now, you know."

"You can all take care of each other," Azrael pressed. "Now, please, we must go. We don't have a lot of time."

"Time for what?" Freya asked.

Azrael paused and stared at her, but said nothing.

As promised, Heimdall was waiting at Bifröst with Jonquil. The ancient Reaping Mare was magnificent. She was the tallest horse they'd ever seen and as black as midnight. The feathers on her wings shone in the light as brightly as Freya's and Orus's wings. Frigg was right; she had taken good care of the Reaping Mare. Freya tilted her head to the side as they drew near. "From here, she looks a bit like Sylt, doesn't she?"

"I guess so," Archie agreed. "But she's much bigger."

"That's because she is much older," Azrael said.

"Freya and I can fly, but you should ride Jonquil. It's been some time since someone rode on her and it will do her good."

At their approach, the Watchman of the Bridge came forward and held up his hand.

"Greetings, Heimdall," Freya said, nodding and giving the formal address. "We come in the service of Odin."

"Greetings, Valkyrie," Heimdall responded, bowing deeply. "Be welcome and cross in peace."

With the formalities out of the way, Heimdall grinned and patted Jonquil's neck with his huge hand. "I haven't seen this beauty in an age. Does this mean Odin has finally forgiven Frigha?"

Freya nodded. "We've been sent to find her and bring her home. But we mustn't tell anyone yet. Not even Maya or my other sisters can know."

Heimdall winked. "You know you can trust me. Maya could torture me, and I still wouldn't tell."

Freya grinned, imagining her beautiful, finely boned sister trying to take on the massive Watchman. The only way Maya could threaten him would be to tickle him into submission. Despite his size and terrifying demeanor, Heimdall had proven to be a great and trusted friend. He had let Maya slip across Bifröst more than once to protect Freya and had even testified on their behalf when they'd returned to Asgard in disgrace. Recently he'd been spending a great deal of time with her sister at Valhalla.

"Do you know how long you might be?" Heimdall asked.

Freya answered. "Odin's given us two days. But I'm worried that isn't enough time."

"Especially if she's made a life for herself on Earth," Archie added.

"I am sure Odin knows what he is doing. If he has set that deadline, there must be a reason."

"Indeed," Azrael agreed.

The Angel of Death's dark expression troubled Freya as she helped Archie up onto the Reaping Mare.

"She is big," Archie said as he tucked his feet under her neatly folded wings and caught hold of the reins.

"Journey well!" Heimdall called as he escorted them on to the Rainbow Bridge. "I will be waiting for you."

As they made their way over the bridge, Freya wondered why Azrael was accompanying them. She was glad for his presence, but she knew he was needed elsewhere. At the other side of the bridge they took to the sky, following Jonquil's lead.

The Reaping Mare held her head high and whinnied in excitement—it was obvious that Jonquil was happy to be flying in Midgard again. It wasn't long before she picked up a scent that made her put on more speed.

"I think she knows the way!" Freya called over to Archie.

Orus was struggling to keep up beside her. *"She's much faster than Sylt!"*

"Come here and let me carry you." Freya opened her arms and held him tight as they followed closely behind the Reaping Mare.

For half a day they flew. Freya recognized that they were flying across the Atlantic Ocean and once again heading for the United States. Reaching the eastern coast, they continued west.

On and on, Jonquil led them. But after a time, Azrael took the lead. With his smooth, even wing beats, he took them lower in the sky. Soon they were flying over tree-covered mountains.

"Let's land here for a bit," Azrael called, soaring smoothly toward a tall, rocky mountain.

They touched down on the mountaintop. Stunning views surrounded them: far below, a lush forest of trees encircled a sparkling, sapphire-blue lake. "It's amazing!" Archie called, still on Jonquil's back. "Where are we?"

"Idaho," Azrael answered.

With all of her powers and senses returned, Freya could feel deep concern coming from the angel. "All right, Azrael, we're out of Asgard. Now will you tell us what's wrong?"

The Angel of Death settled his large white wings on his back. "We're all in big trouble, Freya, and I can't see an easy way out of it."

She wasn't sure what she'd expected, but it wasn't this. "What do you mean?"

Azrael looked as if he were struggling for the best way to explain. He kicked a branch off the top of the mountain and watched it fly across the sky. He turned back to her. "I haven't been completely honest with Odin, and if he finds out the truth, he will be furious and not accept our help."

"Help with what?" Freya asked.

"The war," Azrael said flatly.

"What war?" Archie cried, sliding down from the mare. "With who?"

"All the realms."

"What?" Freya demanded.

Azrael sat down on a boulder and dropped his head in his hands—he seemed to be carrying the weight of all the realms on his shoulders. Finally he looked up. "You know there has been tension in the realms almost from the very beginning of life. The lower realms want to possess the upper realms. The middle realms don't care either way, but will side with the winner."

"That's why we have the Nine Realms Challenge," Freya said. "To keep the peace."

"Ten Realms," Archie corrected. "The Angels of Death are competing now."

"True," Azrael agreed, looking up. "But our involvement was about more than just wanting to unite our realms. We've heard rumblings that someone is stirring up the frost giants and trying to unite them with the fire giants. Together, the giants will be powerful enough to wage war against Odin and claim Asgard. We came to the Challenge to see what we could learn. The giant clans have always been enemies, which made them easy to defeat. There's no way they would work together unless someone else brokered the deal."

"And?" Freya asked.

"And it's as we feared. From their behavior at the Challenge, it seems the frost and fire giants have formed a secret alliance—an alliance that could move against Asgard at any time."

"How do you know all this?" Archie asked.

"We are not part of the nine realms," Azrael explained. "Living outside them means we can study them without taking sides. Throughout time we have watched the various petty squabbles between the realms. No real damage has been done because none of the realms worked together long enough to defeat another. But this time it's different. If the giant clans can stay united, they will be powerful enough to defeat Odin and take Asgard."

"Does Odin know?" Freya asked.

Azrael nodded. "Of course. He's not a fool. He has suspected this for some time—though he has no idea who is behind it all. I fear it could actually be someone from Asgard."

"You're saying there's a traitor in Asgard?" Freya cried.

Azrael nodded. "But they are being very clever. I still haven't discovered who it is."

"So why are we here?" Archie said. "We should be in Asgard helping to prepare for war."

"Odin has sent you here for a good reason. He put on a brave face during the Challenge, but he is deeply concerned. And although he may not show it, he cares for all his people. If trouble is coming, he wants everyone safe in Asgard, under his protection—including Brünnhilde. But more than that, he wants to see if anyone will follow you. He suspects there may be more than one traitor in Asgard. You are here as the bait to draw them out. If the giants learn that you have come here, then he has confirmation of more spies."

"Why didn't he tell us?" Freya asked.

"He doesn't want you to behave any differently. You are both young and inexperienced with the politics of war. If you knew, you might give something away. But it's because of your youth and inexperience that he specifically chose you to go. Odin knows he's being watched. He's hoping that the giants will interpret your mission here as him finally forgiving Brünnhilde and not anything more suspicious."

"Like trying to find out who the spy is," Archie said.

"Exactly," Azrael agreed.

"Why are you telling us if Odin didn't want us to know?"

"Because I need your help," Azrael said. "And because you deserve to know. If you are going to be pawns in war, I think it's only fair that you should be told. You are both old enough to understand what's at stake."

"How can we help you?" Freya asked. "What have you done?"

"I have been protecting a Midgard family that I shouldn't have. It wasn't my place to get involved, but I knew what Odin would have done. Now it's too late for any of us."

"Azrael, I don't understand," Freya said.

The Angel of Death stepped up to Jonquil and stroked the Reaping Mare's neck. His wings drooped and he sighed.

"A very long time ago," he started, without turning around, "a young Valkyrie defied Odin and fled Asgard. She was beautiful, feisty, and loving. I cared deeply for her and tried to help."

"You mean Brünnhilde?" Freya asked softly.

Azrael nodded. "But the betrayal was greater than even Odin knows. She was with child. But not just one; she was going to have twins."

"Twins?" Freya repeated in shock.

"So?" Archie said. "Women have twins all the time."

"Women do, but Valkyries don't," Freya explained.

"Exactly," Azrael agreed. "But Brünnhilde was carrying twins. . . ." He paused and turned to Freya. "A girl and a boy."

"That's impossible!" Freya cried. "Valkyries don't have boys."

"Really?" Archie asked. "No boys, ever?"

Freya shook her head. "Babies born of Valkyries are always female."

"That's not entirely true," Azrael said. "It's very rare, but sometimes boys are born to Valkyries. But the newborn is taken from his mother and delivered to Utgard . . ." Once again Azrael paused. "To the Keep of the Dark Searchers."

"Why?" Archie asked. "What do the Dark Searchers want with them?"

It took a moment for the information to sink in. The idea was too terrible to consider. But the more Freya thought about it, the more it made perfect sense. Their wings, their incredible strength, hiding their faces . . .

"Dark Searchers are the boys born to the Valkyries," Freya gasped.

Azrael nodded. "That is why Odin keeps them close. The males aren't needed on the battlefields. Though they are strong and powerful, they don't possess the power to reap like the female Valkyries. So Odin turns them into his Enforcers of Justice, the Dark Searchers."

"*And that's why Odin trusts them,*" Orus added.

Azrael nodded again.

"Do the Valkyries know that the Dark Searchers are their sons?" Freya asked.

"I don't think so," Azrael said. "Valkyries' natural fear of the Dark Searchers means their recognizing senses don't work. Most believe their sons have either been killed or sent to another realm. It is a secret that has been kept from the very beginning."

"But you knew," Freya said.

Azrael nodded. "I told you, we've been watching the nine realms for a very long time."

"Wow . . . ," Archie murmured.

"So what happened to Brünnhilde's babies?" Freya asked.

"The twins were not her first children. Her first child had been male. According to Odin's law, the baby was taken away from her the moment she gave him his name. She grieved for a very long time. When she found out she was with child again, she discovered that she was having twins and that one of them would be a boy. She couldn't bear the thought of losing another son. Just before she gave birth, she flew from Asgard and fled to Earth.

"She found a small village here and bore her twins. She tried to keep them safe, but Odin would not tolerate her disobedience. He sent a Dark Searcher after her. Brünnhilde managed to hide her son with an elder from the village before the Searcher caught her. When Odin arrived, her new baby daughter was taken away and returned to Asgard to be raised by another Valkyrie. Then Odin de-winged and blinded Brünnhilde. After that, he released the Midgard Serpent to punish the village that had sheltered her."

"*What happened to the baby boy?*" Orus asked.

"Nothing," Azrael said. "The village elder survived the Midgard Serpent and returned him to his mother. Knowing what fate awaited them if Odin were ever to learn the truth, the elder suggested that the child's wings be removed. That child grew up knowing he was immortal like his mother, but he had no idea he was a Dark Searcher."

"How much of this does Odin know?" Freya asked.

Azrael shook his head. "About the boy? None—if Odin had known, he would have ordered the family destroyed, and because of my involvement he would have never spoken to me again."

"What did you do that was so wrong?" Freya asked.

"I was the village elder who shielded Brünnhilde's son from the Dark Searcher and protected him from the Midgard Serpent."

"You?" Archie cried. "Did she know?"

"No. I came in disguise, and Brünnhilde was too frightened for her son to recognize me. Then, after her eyesight and powers were removed, she couldn't see or sense me. But I was the one who carefully cut off her son's wings—I hated to do it, but it was the only way to keep him safe. I also advised her not to give him a name that might lead back to Asgard.

So she called him Giovanni—these days he's called Vonni."

Orus cawed. *"Why would you risk Odin's wrath?"*

"Were the twins yours?" Archie asked.

"I am not their father," Azrael said. "I did it because I don't agree with Odin's law and because of the love Brünnhilde felt for her children. That Valkyrie sacrificed everything to protect her child. Seeing that, how could I not help her?"

Freya now understood. "You're frightened that Odin will learn of the son's existence and your involvement."

"It's much worse than that, I'm afraid." Azrael started to pace. "Everything was fine. Brünnhilde and Vonni lived among humans for thousands of years, always on the move, never staying in one place long enough to draw attention to themselves. Male Valkyries don't develop reaping powers, so I knew there was no danger. I left them alone, just keeping a distant eye on them.

"But the one thing I never counted on was Vonni falling in love and marrying a human woman."

"He did what?" Orus cawed.

"I told Brünnhilde that this must never happen. And for thousands of years she has kept Giovanni from forming relationships. But love can't be denied, no matter how hard any of us try."

"So he got married? So what?" Archie said.

Azrael smiled gently at Archie. "I don't think you grasp the importance of what has happened. Vonni is the first ever

Dark Searcher to grow up among humans. I don't know what Brünnhilde told him to halt his curiosity about himself, but whatever it was, it wasn't enough to stop him from marrying a woman and having a daughter. No Dark Searcher has *ever* had children. And now a Valkyrie male has produced a child with a living woman."

Orus cawed in understanding. *"You don't know what they have produced—human or Valkyrie. What realm do they belong to?"*

"Exactly," Azrael agreed. "Their daughter was born without wings, so I had high hopes that she was human. But now that she is approaching maturity, she is showing signs of great strength, speed, and agility. I fear she is becoming a full, wingless Valkyrie—a Valkyrie that doesn't know what she is or how deadly she will soon become."

Freya inhaled sharply. Her own strength had increased right before her reaping powers arrived.

"But worse still," Azrael continued, "Vonni's wife, Sarah, is with child again. I already know this child is a boy with wings."

"How could you know that?" Archie asked.

Azrael sighed and looked at Freya. "You aren't the only one with powers to sense people. I've been keeping an eye on Vonni's wife, Sarah, from afar and can sense the baby—he has wings. Very soon a living human woman will bear a Dark Searcher. No realm is prepared for that—war or no war."

Freya walked up to the cliff edge, gazing out over the

tranquil valley and trees. Learning that there were tensions of war brewing in Asgard was too awful to consider. But now, hearing about Brünnhilde's family and the danger they were in complicated everything.

Azrael continued. "Odin will never tolerate in Asgard children born in Midgard to a living woman—especially if war is brewing. But he certainly won't allow them to remain here. Not if they carry Valkyrie blood that could be used against him."

"Surely he wouldn't harm them," Freya insisted.

"He may. If war does come, he can't risk any Asgard blood being left in Midgard. If the giants were to learn of the family's existence, they may use them as hostages against Odin."

"We must help them," Freya insisted. "Runaway or not, Brünnhilde is part of the sisterhood of Valkyries. Her children are too. We can't leave them to the mercy of the frost giants or Odin."

"I do have a plan," Azrael said. "But I need your help for it to work."

"Tell us," Freya said.

"I need you to speak with Brünnhilde and let her know the danger her family is in. She must tell her son what he is, and what his children are, and send them into hiding. Then you must ask Brünnhilde to make the ultimate sacrifice to protect her family."

"What's that?" Archie asked.

"She must leave her family and return to Asgard alone and pretend they never existed. That's the only way Odin will never learn the truth."

Freya started to shake her head. "There has to be another way. How can I ask Brünnhilde to abandon her family?"

"There is no other way. Believe me, I've been thinking about this for ages. You must get her back to Asgard alone."

"What about you?" Archie asked. "If you come too, Brünnhilde is sure to understand and agree to this."

"I've already caused enough damage." Azrael paused and gazed around. "If there is a spy following you, he might tell of my involvement. That alone may be the trigger that starts the war."

"If there is a spy following us, we'll lead them to the family!" Freya said.

"It is a risk," Azrael agreed. "But we have no choice. I can't feel anyone around us at the moment. If you move quickly, there may be time to hide the family before my involvement is discovered."

The Angel of Death stepped away from them and walked over to a large boulder. He lifted it aside as if it weighed nothing. There was a hole cut into the solid rock. Azrael reached inside and pulled out a large package wrapped in brown paper.

"Here," he said. "You'll need these."

Freya opened up the bundle. Inside were human clothes

in the Steampunk style she had adopted when she was last in the human world: a full-length skirt, a large men's shirt with slits for her wings, and a long, burgundy velvet coat. "My coat?"

"Not quite. I couldn't find one exactly like your old one, but this should cover your wings just as well. There are gloves in the pocket. Now that you've got your powers back, we can't risk you touching someone and reaping them."

Freya held up the velvet coat. It was covered in copper chains with copper and brass leaves and Steampunkesque pins, including a pair of old welder's goggles. Pocket watches were sewn to the arms and the lapels at the front.

"I love it!"

Azrael chuckled softly. "I thought you might. Though your Asgard clothes are very fetching, they're not appropriate for Earth. Not that Steampunk is much better. This is Idaho, after all."

Freya looked down at her short, rough-woven tunic and her fur-lined boots. Odin hadn't given them time to change, and she and Archie were still wearing their stable-cleaning clothes. She pulled the velvet coat on. "Thank you so much. It's beautiful! But how did you know we'd be coming?"

"I didn't know for certain, but I'd hoped Odin would take my advice and ask you." He paused. "There is one more thing I must tell you. The girl baby Odin took away from Brünnhilde was actually your mother."

"*What?*" Orus cawed.

The angel nodded. "Yes, Eir is Brünnhilde's daughter. Vonni is your mother's twin brother."

"That mean's Brünnhilde is your grandmother. Now we've really got to help them—they're family!" Archie exclaimed.

"Exactly," Azrael said. "And I know you, Freya. You are so very much like your grandmother—you will fight to protect your family. You and Archie are the only ones who can save them."

"Does my mother know?" Freya asked softly.

"I believe she knows that the runaway Valkyrie was her mother. I could see by her reaction when Odin said the name. But there is no way she could know about the existence of her twin brother or the danger they face."

"It all makes sense now," Freya said.

"*What does?*" Orus asked.

"How many times have you heard me ask Mother about our family? Who is my father, and who is her mother? She wouldn't tell me."

Azrael nodded. "Your mother has worked tirelessly to restore her family's reputation with Odin. That is why she is always harder on you than your sisters. She sees in you a wild spirit—the same wild spirit that she has fought to contain within herself. The wild spirit she inherited from her real mother . . ."

Azrael stopped speaking and stood tall. He looked around, as if hearing something on the wind that Freya couldn't. "I wish I could stay and help you through this time," he said sadly. "But I must go. Jonquil will take you the rest of the way. It's not far. Just over that ridge you will find her ranch. I suggest you wait here until sundown."

"We will," Freya agreed.

"Good." He stood before Freya and rested his hands on her shoulders. "Now, Freya, listen to me. Brünnhilde is bitter and angry at what Odin did to her. She is going to be very difficult, if not impossible, to convince. But you must make her understand what is at stake. She must send her family into hiding and return to Asgard alone."

"I understand," Freya said solemnly.

"She can never know it was me who saved Vonni. There is too much risk if others learn the truth."

Freya nodded at the tall Angel of Death.

"And remember, there is at least one traitor in Asgard. Be on your guard. Spies may have followed you here—so always be aware of who is around you. I am never far away. Call me if you get into serious trouble. But only if there is no other way. If I am discovered—"

"It could start the war," Archie finished.

Azrael nodded. He kissed her lightly on the head. "Good luck. We are all counting on you."

Freya and Archie stood back as Azrael opened his wings

and leaped gracefully into the air. He soared down the sharp mountainside and then vanished into a shaft of sunlight.

When they were alone, the silence seemed oppressive. The soft wind was all they heard at the top of the craggy mountain.

"Are you okay, Gee?" Archie asked softly.

Freya opened her wings and sat down heavily on a large boulder, feeling the weight of responsibility. She looked up at Archie. "How could Odin do it?"

"Do what?"

"Host the Ten Realms Challenge knowing that someone in Asgard was betraying him and uniting the frost and fire giants against him. He smiled the whole time, knowing the truth."

"He's a great leader. He has to protect his people. He couldn't show anyone what he was thinking. It must have been very hard."

"Yes, he is a great man," Freya agreed. "But he can be so cruel. Every time I heard him tell the story of Frigha, the runaway Valkyrie, I used to stop listening and think of anything else. But it wasn't Frigha he was talking about. It was Brünnhilde, my grandmother. He cut off her wings and blinded her just because she wanted to protect her children."

"And now it's our turn to protect them and end that terrible story."

"Yes, but if Odin finds out the whole truth, it will be even worse for all of us."

"*Has fear of Odin ever stopped you before?*" Orus asked.

Freya shook her head.

"*Then why should it concern you now?*"

"Because before, it was only us that I was putting in danger. Now if we fail, it could start a war."

"Then we'd better not fail," Archie said.

6

MAYA ENTERED THE REAPING MARES' STABLES, humming to herself. "Freya, I'm here to help." But as she walked the length of the long building, she saw that although all the mares were in their stalls, only half of them had been cleaned. Her own Reaping Mare, Lutna, nickered softly when she walked past.

Maya stopped and kissed her softly on the muzzle. Beside Lutna's stall was Sylt. Freya's chestnut mare with the brown and black wings was munching on hay. Maya gave her a friendly pat. "Have you seen Freya and Archie?" Sylt nickered and nudged Maya, inviting another stroke. Maya gazed around and saw that one of the stalls opposite was in the process of being cleared. The pitchfork and shovel had been left leaning against the wall.

"*Maybe Orus talked them into going somewhere,*" her raven, Grul, suggested. "*He can get Freya to do anything.*"

Maya shook her head. "It's not like Freya to leave a job half finished—especially while she's on probation with Odin. And even if she wanted to, Archie wouldn't let her."

Giving Sylt a final pat, Maya left the stables, opened her fine wings, and leaped up into the sky.

She landed on the flight balcony of their beautiful palace. Inside Maya found her mother sitting in the lounge. Eir's head was down, her wings drooped, and she was weeping softly. Three of Maya's sisters were sitting around her, begging her to tell them what was wrong.

"Mother, what is it?" Maya cried in alarm. "What has happened?"

"Maya," her mother cried. "We are all in such terrible danger."

Seeing her like this tore at Maya's heart. Her mother was the strongest woman she knew. She hadn't seen her weep in a very, very long time. "What is it?"

"Now that you are all here, I can tell you. It's Freya . . ." Her mother was unable to continue as she broke into sobs again.

"Freya?" Gwyn, the eldest, demanded harshly. "What has she done now?"

Their mother rose and started to pace the long lounge. "She has done nothing."

"What's happened to her?" Maya asked. "She and Archie aren't in the barn. I can't get a sense of Freya anywhere."

"She's not here. They've gone back to Midgard."

"What?" Maya cried. "Odin will kill them!"

"Odin sent them!" her mother said, as she started to shake.

"Mother, please, you're speaking in riddles. Tell us what's happened," Skaga demanded.

Eir took a seat and indicated to her daughters to do the same.

She took in a deep breath and let it out slowly. "You all know the story of Frigha the runaway Valkyrie," she started. "But what you don't know is that Frigha was not her true name. It was Brünnhilde. . . ." She paused. "She was my mother."

"What?" the sisters cried as one.

Eir nodded. "I was not born in Asgard," she continued. "I was born in Midgard. Not long after the Dark Searcher captured my mother, Odin arrived. I was ripped from my mother's arms and brought back here to be raised by another."

"And then Odin punished her?" Gwyn asked.

"Yes," Eir said. "She was de-winged, blinded, and banished. This is why I have fought so hard to please Odin. After the shame my mother brought down on our name, I have had to work twice as hard to gain back his faith."

"Mother, I don't understand," Maya said. "What does this have to do with Freya and Archie?"

"Everything," Eir said. "I am sure Azrael thought he was being kind, but he has been our undoing. He has convinced Odin to forgive my mother and allow her to come back to Asgard. Odin has just sent Freya and Archie to collect her."

"But this is wonderful!" Maya cried. "How can you not be happy?"

Her mother shook her head. "For many, many generations, I have known about my mother and why she did what she did. But if Odin were to find out the truth, it will mean disaster for all of us."

"What truth?" Gwyn asked.

"My mother didn't run away to Midgard to protect me from Odin or to escape Asgard. She did it to protect my twin."

"You have a twin?" Maya cried.

Eir nodded. "Many, many hundreds of years ago, I was on a reaping in France. I was just about to collect my intended on the battlefield when I felt something—a tug in my chest—that made me turn around. And there he was, carrying his friend away from danger. I know he felt me too because he stopped and stared at me. I was in my helmet and should have been invisible to the human eye, but he could see me. It was like looking at myself. I reached out with my senses and I knew. He was my twin. I have a brother—he is living in Midgard as a human."

"Did anyone else see this?" Gwyn asked.

Eir shook her head. "No. He called to me and started

to approach, but I held up my hand and warned him back. There were Valkyries and Angels of Death all around us; the danger of exposure was too great. I reaped my warrior and flew away.

"Ever since that moment, I have felt him and yearned to be reunited with him. But as long as I stayed away, as long as I stayed silent, he remained safe. Until now. The moment Odin finds out, there will be no stopping his rage."

"Does Freya know any of this?" Maya asked.

Eir shook her head. "How could she? She and Archie believe they are going to Midgard to find the runaway Valkyrie and bring her home. But what they are going to find is my mother and brother. What will happen then? To fulfill Odin's command, Freya will have no choice but to expose him."

"No, Mother," Maya said. "You must trust Freya. She would never betray this family."

"She would," Eir said. "After all the harsh things I have said to her, all the demands of loyalty to Odin I have placed upon her, she will betray them. And when she does, it will mean my brother's life!"

7

FREYA AND ARCHIE REMAINED AT THE TOP OF THE
mountain all afternoon. Jonquil whinnied constantly, trying
to break free so she could go to Brünnhilde.

"*She must be close,*" Orus commented as he perched on a
boulder, watching the Reaping Mare.

"Sylt is the same with you," Archie commented. He was
stroking the mare to calm her. "This is so freaky." He combed
his fingers through her black mane. "I can touch Jonquil, but
I can't pick up a tiny rock."

"You'll get used to it," Freya offered. She rose and walked up
to the edge of the cliff. A strong wind was picking up and whip-
ping her hair back. Freya lifted her head, closed her eyes, and
opened her arms and wings. Standing on her toes, she savored
the sensations of the wind blowing through her feathers.

"What are you doing?" Archie asked.

Freya looked back at him. "Wind dancing. It helps me relax. There is something special about the wind. It calls to me and makes me want to leap off the cliff and take to the sky."

"But you can do that anyway."

"I know," Freya said. "But this feels so good."

"I don't think I'll ever understand you."

Freya smiled. "That's because you don't have wings."

She continued wind dancing until the sun started to dip on the western horizon. When it had faded completely, Orus took to the air. *"Come on, you two, we don't have all night."*

Freya helped Archie climb back up onto Jonquil and untied the reins. As soon as she was free, the Reaping Mare opened her wings and leaped off the top of the mountain.

Freya did the same and followed closely behind the mare. The moon was rising and shone its light down on the dense woodland below.

"Jonquil, slow down!" Archie fought to stay on the mare's back.

Nothing was going to stop the Reaping Mare from returning to Brünnhilde. They soared lower over a beautiful, moonlit valley. To her left, Freya saw a massive three-story house. Lights gave the home a warm, welcoming glow. Freya could smell horses and other animals and saw large barns close by.

They glided silently over the barns, and Freya sensed the

presence of a being. They continued ahead until Freya saw a flat wooden platform rising high in the air. A lone figure was standing at the top. It was a woman, with her head thrown back and arms open to the wind.

Jonquil started to circle the platform, neighing uncontrollably.

"Jon?" the woman called. "Is that you, my Jon?"

The woman spun around, trying to follow the sounds of the Reaping Mare, but she turned too quickly and lost her balance.

"*Brundi, be careful!*" a raven cawed, trying to stop the woman from falling.

"No!" Freya howled. Throwing down her new coat, she tucked in her wings and dove at the platform. Landing hard, she caught hold of the woman just as she was about to fall over the side.

"I've got you!" Freya said as relief washed over her. "You're safe."

The woman turned. Even in the darkness, Freya could see her mother's face in the older woman. The only difference was her eyes. This woman's were pearled with blindness.

"Brünnhilde?"

The woman was breathing heavily as the large raven landed on her shoulder.

"I have not gone by that name in a very long time." She reached out and felt Freya's face, then her shoulders.

Finally her shaking hands went down to the wings on Freya's back. "Valkyrie?"

"Yes. I'm Freya. What are you doing up here?"

"I may have lost my wings, but that doesn't mean I can't wind dance. It is one of the few pleasures I have left." Her expression hardened. "Is Odin here? Has he finally come to apologize for what he did to me?"

"No. But I've come with my raven and my friend—and, of course, Jonquil—to find you. She led us to you."

"Jonquil, where is she?" Brünnhilde tilted her head to the side to listen for her horse.

"She's on the ground with a dead boy," the raven said.

"That's Archie," Freya corrected. "Please come down. Your Reaping Mare has missed you."

When Freya offered to help, the woman swatted her hand away. "I don't need a Valkyrie's help. I have managed quite well by myself."

Azrael was right. Brünnhilde had become bitter over the years of banishment. Freya stepped aside, and her grandmother walked confidently to an opening in the floor of the platform where a ladder led to the ground.

Freya leaped off the side and glided down to follow.

"Go easy on her, Freya," Orus warned as he settled on her shoulder. *"She has lost so much. No matter what she says, don't lose your temper."*

Before Brünnhilde was even halfway down the ladder,

Jonquil raced over to meet her. She pawed at the ground, waiting for Brünnhilde to reach the bottom.

"Is she okay?" Archie asked.

Freya shook her head and spoke softly. "Azrael was right, she's very bitter. This isn't going to be easy."

They stood back and watched the reunion between the older Valkyrie and her Reaping Mare.

"How long have they been apart?" Archie asked.

"I don't really know," Freya answered. "It must be thousands of Midgard years." She felt her throat tighten at the waves of joy emanating from her grandmother as she held Jonquil.

When Brünnhilde stepped away from the mare, she called for Freya.

"I'm still here," Freya responded, approaching the older Valkyrie. "I have something else for you. I think you should drink it before we talk."

"What is it?" Brünnhilde demanded as Freya put the glass vial in her hands. "What new punishment is this?"

"It's not a punishment. It's a gift from Frigg. She says that Odin's damage to your eyes isn't permanent. If you drink this, your sight will be restored."

Brünnhilde shook her head. "I don't want it. I've got along fine without my sight. I don't need it now, and I refuse to be in debt to Frigg."

"Please," Freya said. "This valley and these mountains are beautiful. Don't you want to see them?"

"I know they're beautiful. I can smell them. That's enough for me."

"If not the mountains, don't you want to see your granddaughters?" Archie asked.

Brünnhilde inhaled sharply. "What are you talking about, boy?"

"Archie, no," Freya whispered. "Not yet."

"Freya is your granddaughter," Orus blurted out. *"The daughter of your only daughter."*

"My daughter?"

"Yes, it's true," Freya said. "Please, drink the medicine so we can talk properly."

"How do I know this is not a trick?" the old woman demanded.

"Drink it, Brundi," Brünnhilde's raven said. *"She's telling you the truth. I can see Freya. She looks very much like Mims. They could be sisters."*

"Mims?" Archie asked. "Is that your other granddaughter?"

Brünnhilde's expression darkened. "How much do you know about me? Does Odin know I have a human granddaughter?"

"Not yet," Freya said. "But your Midgard granddaughter isn't human. She's a Valkyrie, just like me and you. Please, trust me and drink."

"What else do you know?" Brünnhilde demanded.

"Everything," Freya said. "Including the fact that your

son's wife is going to have another child. But this time it will be a boy—and he has wings."

Brünnhilde whispered, "How can you know all this?"

"Drink and we'll tell you," Freya promised.

Brünnhilde's hands shook as she felt for the stopper at the top of the vial. She pulled it out, brought the vial to her lips, and took a long draft of the liquid. Her eyes rolled back in her head, and she started to collapse.

Freya caught her before she hit the ground. She lay her down carefully and looked up at Archie in alarm. "Frigg didn't say this would happen."

Brünnhilde's raven settled on the older woman's chest. *"Healing potions always do this. She is safe. When she wakes, her eyes will be restored. Before she does, tell me, child, is Brundi in danger?"*

Freya knelt before her grandmother. "Yes. We all are. We're in terrible danger that could lead to war in the realms."

The raven checked on Brünnhilde, examining her closed eyes and the gentle rise and fall of her chest. *"It's Azrael, isn't it? Odin has discovered what he did for us."*

Freya inhaled sharply. "You know about Azrael?"

"Brundi was blind and powerless after Odin's punishment," the raven said. *"But I could see it was him. He disguised himself as an elder, but he couldn't hide from me."*

"Did you tell her?" Archie asked.

The raven cawed. *"There was no point. She had suffered enough already. I wasn't about to tell her that, on top of everything, she owed a debt to an Angel of Death. Now, tell me, what has happened?"*

"I think we should wait to tell Brünnhilde," Freya said.

"But we're not to mention Azrael. He thinks it would upset her too much."

"Brundi, not Brünnhilde," the raven corrected. *"She never uses her true name anymore. It reminds her too much of what she's lost. Just as I have changed my name. You may call me Pym."*

Freya nodded. "In Midgard I use the name Greta."

"I'm just Archie," Archie shrugged. Orus cawed and cleared his throat.

"And this is Orus," Freya introduced her raven.

On the ground, Brundi began to stir. They watched in silence as she opened her eyes. The white was gone. Her healed eyes were the same arctic blue as Freya's mother's and were slowly focusing on what was around her.

"I can see!" She sat up. "Pym, I can truly see!"

The older Valkyrie reached for her raven and gave him a tight hug. "My old friend, you're just as handsome as I remember! You haven't changed a bit."

The raven cawed. *"That's not completely true. I have a few white feathers now."* He opened his large wings to show three white flight feathers on each wing.

Freya helped her grandmother climb to her feet. When the older woman's eyes settled on her, she asked, "Are you truly my granddaughter?"

Freya nodded. "I am. And I have four sisters."

"Your mother, what did they call her?" Brundi said sadly.

"Eir," Freya answered.

"Is she happy? Has she had a good life?"

Freya nodded. "She is the head of the Valkyries and is greatly respected in Asgard."

A shadow crossed Brundi's face. "Does she know what happened to me?"

"I think so," Freya said. "But she has never spoken of it. I could tell from her reaction to Odin's command that I find you."

"Odin sent you here?" Pym asked. *"Why?"*

"Gran?" A new voice sounded in the distance. "It's time to come in for dinner."

"That's Mims." Brundi hushed them. "You are welcome to join us for dinner, but you must hide your wings. No one knows the truth about me or where I come from."

"But she must be told," Freya insisted. "She will have reaping powers soon."

"Mims is human!" Brundi insisted. "I don't want her to be part of my old life."

"Denying the truth won't change it," Archie tried. "She's a Valkyrie. You must tell her before she accidentally kills someone with her touch."

"You're wrong!" Brundi glared at them. "Now, hide your wings or fly away from here. I don't care which. But you will not reveal yourself. Do you understand me?"

"Put on your coat," Orus suggested. *"We can talk later."*

Freya retrieved her coat and pulled it on over her wings. "What are you going to tell her about Jonquil and Archie?" she asked Brundi.

"Mims will understand."

"About a ghost and a flying horse?" Archie asked.

"She is human," Brundi repeated. "Only those of us from the other realms can see the dead. She won't be able to see you." She paused and frowned at Archie. "Why are you here? You should have ascended or remained at Valhalla."

"Archie is my friend," Freya retorted. "He protected me from Dark Searchers—they were hunting me down in Chicago."

"There were Searchers in Chicago?" Brundi cried. "Let me guess . . . the disaster there last year. Did that have anything to do with you? They said it was a terrorist attack, but people claimed to have seen monsters and a dragon tearing through the city."

"It wasn't terrorists," Orus explained. *"It was Odin, Thor, and the Midgard Serpent."*

"Jormungand was back in Midgard? I knew there was more to it!"

Freya nodded, but before she had a chance to explain further, Mims had appeared. She was almost as old as Freya and bore a striking resemblance to her. They had the same sharp nose and sculpted eyes and looked more like sisters than cousins. Her hair was dark, however, not like other Valkyries, who were always blond.

"Gran?" She halted when she saw her grandmother had company. Her eyes momentarily settled on Archie. She frowned and then looked back to her grandmother. "Gran, Mom sent me to get you. . . ." She stopped. "What's happened to your eyes?"

"They've been healed . . . ," the older Valkyrie said as she gazed upon her granddaughter for the very first time. She smiled. "My sweet little girl, you are just as beautiful as I always imagined you."

"I—I don't understand," Mims stuttered. "How can you see?"

"I know this will seem impossible, but I brought medicine for Brundi's eyes." Freya took a step toward her and raised her hand in a half wave. "I'm your cousin Greta."

"But I don't have a cousin," Mims said.

Brundi caught her by the hands. "Actually, you do. Greta is the daughter of your father's twin sister. They were separated at birth. Greta has only just found me."

"Dad has a sister?"

"Yes, though your father doesn't know about her," Brundi said. "I didn't think I'd ever see my daughter again, so I never told him he had a twin."

"Hi, Mims," Archie said, not giving Mims any time to process this bombshell. "I'm a friend of Greta's. This is a cool place you live in."

Mims's mouth hung open as she stared at Archie. "What the . . . ? You—you're fuzzy around the edges. What's wrong with you? You're not like the others. . . ."

"Take his hand," Freya suggested. "See if you can touch him."

Mims looked scared but allowed Archie to take her hand. There was no doubt about it—if she could touch him, she was a Valkyrie.

"No." Brundi hushed as she put her hands on Mims's shoulder and turned her to face her. "No, no . . ." She began to moan.

"Gran, what's wrong?"

The older Valkyrie looked to Freya.

"I told you," Freya said to Brundi. "She's one of us, and you know what that means when she reaches maturity."

"One of who?" Mims insisted. "Who are you?"

"*I think it's time we told her,*" Pym advised.

"Pym? You can talk?" Mims cried, staring in disbelief at the raven on her grandmother's shoulder.

The raven cawed, "*Yes, child, I have always been able to, but Brundi forbade me to speak in front of you.*"

Mims started to back away. "Gran, what's happening here?" She bumped into Jonquil and turned around. She gasped. "But . . . It's . . . it's got wings?" She staggered backward and fell to the ground.

Brundi knelt down next to her granddaughter and her voice grew stern. "Mims, look at me. Stop being so foolish. There is nothing to be frightened of. Jonquil is mine. I haven't seen her in many, many years. But your cousin Greta brought her to me."

Mims's wild eyes were looking at everyone. "From where?"

Freya opened her mouth to speak, but her grandmother held up a warning hand. "From very far away," Brundi finished. "Now, I need you to be brave. We can't put Jonquil in the stables—someone will see her. Let's move her to the far shed. No one ever goes there. Then we'll go into the house and act like everything is normal. We don't want to upset your mother, not in her condition."

"But what about when she sees it?" Mims pointed a shaking finger at Archie.

"I'm not an 'it'—my name is Archie!" He looked back at Freya. "Why is it so hard for everyone to say my name?"

"Your mother won't be able to see him," Brundi said. "Neither will any of the others."

"But what's wrong with him?"

Archie grinned. "Well, if you must know, I'm a little bit dead."

"*Actually, you're a lot dead!*" Orus cried, cawing in laughter.

"You can talk too?" Mims cried.

"*Of course. And if you had your own companion, he'd talk as well.*"

"Orus, that's enough," Brundi warned. She turned back to Mims. "Yes, my beloved. Archie is a ghost, but he won't hurt you. Have you ever seen others like him?"

Mims nodded weakly. "But not exactly like him. They weren't so clear—they were more like floating clouds. Archie almost looks real." Her voice was a whisper. "I've never told anyone because I thought you'd think I was crazy."

"I wish you had told me," Brundi said. "On my side of the family, we see the dead. Your father can too. We both thought it best if we didn't mention it to your mother. We had hoped you wouldn't be able to."

"I've always seen them, even when I was small. I thought something was wrong with me."

Brundi brushed back a lock of her granddaughter's long dark hair. "There's not a thing wrong with you. You're my perfect girl. And you're brave. So we're all going to go in and act like nothing has changed. I'll tell everyone that Greta and Orus have come for a visit. We don't have to mention Archie or Jonquil."

"Brundi, we really need to talk," Freya warned. "Now more than ever."

"I know," her grandmother snapped. "But not now. I need time to think."

"Mims? Brundi?" a deep voice called. "Are you out there?"

"Coming," Brundi called back. "That's John. He helps manage the ranch. Let's get Jonquil settled and then go in."

"Wait," Archie called. "What are we going to tell everyone about your eyes? You were blind, now you can see; they're going to notice."

Brundi paused and rubbed her chin. "Good point."

"*I know,*" Pym said. "*Why don't we tell them you fell down from the platform? Everyone has been terrified that you'd fall— they've tried to stop you from climbing up there.*"

"It's a bit weak," Brundi said. "Who'd really believe a fall restored my sight?"

"*Have you got a better idea?*" Pym countered.

"No."

"We could tell them I gave you something?" Freya suggested.

Brundi shook her head. "No, that would cause too many questions. As it is, I'm going to have a hard time explaining your presence. Let's not add to it." She gave Pym a gentle stroke. "A fall it is then. Besides it will make John happy to know he was right when he warned me about the dangers of climbing that ladder. I don't think I'll hear the end of it."

"Or," Freya said, "we tell them the whole truth."

"No!" Brundi insisted. The tone of her voice made it clear it wasn't open for discussion. "We'll tell them I fell. Case closed. Now let's put Jonquil away before they come out looking for us."

For the short time Freya had known Brünnhilde, she had seemed angry and bitter. So when they entered her home, they were unprepared for the number of people the older Valkyrie called her "family."

The reactions to the story of Brundi's fall and then restored eyesight were loud and filled with emotion. Some cried with joy, claiming it was a miracle, while others cheered and greeted her anew now that she could see them all. Whatever the reaction, they all had one thing in common. Everyone cared deeply for the old Valkyrie.

They gathered around a long oak trestle table with bench seats. A large wagon-wheel light fixture hung down from the ceiling, and the red-and-white-check tablecloth gave the dining room a real country style. The table was bursting with food, and the room was full of laughter.

Brundi sat at the head and offered Freya a seat directly beside her. Freya turned the chair around and straddled it so she wouldn't have to sit on her wings. It wasn't comfortable, but it was the only way to sit. Archie stood behind her and smiled every time Mims stole a nervous glance in his direction.

Freya counted over twenty people around the table, including Sarah, Mims's mother. She was a beautiful woman with a kind and generous nature and seemed thrilled to meet another member of her husband's small family. She was heavily pregnant, but still insisted on helping to serve the food.

Freya was overwhelmed by the warmth of the people around her. They varied in age and background. She could sense that they had all found refuge here with Brundi, and with each other, and she wondered what it was that had brought each of them here. They all shared a deep, protective love for Brünnhilde, that was for sure.

"So tell us, Greta," Sarah said from the other end of the long table. "How far have you traveled?"

"Tell her you're from Lincolnwood," Archie whispered in Freya's ear.

"I'm from Lincolnwood, Illinois," Freya repeated, but she was distracted by a boy staring directly at Archie. He looked about eight or nine and had carrot-colored hair and warm brown eyes. He was laughing and waving at Archie. "Hello!" he called. "Hello, hello, hello!"

"Gee, I think that boy can see me," Archie leaned to whisper in Freya's ear. "What's that about? You said only people from the other realms would see me."

"Tash, what is 'realms'?" the little boy asked, parroting Archie's words.

"Gage, stop it," the teenage girl sitting next to him said gently. She was cutting up his food.

"But look at him. That boy is smiling at me." Gage was still waving at Archie. "Say hello to him."

"It's all right, Gage," Brundi spoke gently. "Settle down and eat your dinner like a good boy."

Gage calmed, though his sparkling eyes remained on Archie and his expression was full of wonder.

Freya was soon bombarded with questions from the extended family around the table. She was grateful to have Archie behind her, helping her to form human responses.

"How long can you stay?" Sarah passed around a basket of corn bread. "I would love for you to meet your uncle—he's currently on tour, but is scheduled back in three weeks. Can you stay until then? We have plenty of room, and I know he'll be delighted to meet you."

"Greta won't be here that long," Brundi said. "I'm sure her mother will start to miss her."

Freya looked at her grandmother. "Of course. This is just a short visit."

There was a loud knock at the front door.

"I'll get it!" Mims sprang from her chair and dashed out of the room.

Freya could sense she was glad to get away. Fear and mistrust poured from her young cousin. She had lived such a normal, human life. Freya regretted what must now happen to this wonderful family.

Mims returned, and Freya's heart pounded at the sight of the visitor. Archie gasped and Orus cawed loudly.

"Everyone, look," Mims called excitedly. "Uncle Loki is here!"

Loki's eyes sought Freya. They shone with pure mischief.

He looked every inch a human in his faded jeans, checked shirt, and cowboy boots. He couldn't have looked less like the Norse god that he was. He pulled an old cowboy hat off his head, and Freya saw that his dark hair was tied back.

"It's been too long!" He laughed aloud. "But it looks like I've arrived just in time for a family reunion." He walked over to Brundi and gave her a warm embrace. "Brundi, how wonderful to see you again. My, my, your eyes are looking stunning tonight!"

"It's a miracle," Sarah said. "Brundi fell off that ladder on her platform, but somehow, it restored her vision. We're all so thankful she wasn't hurt and that she can see again."

Loki looked at Brundi and then to Freya as his eyebrows rose into his hairline. "Really? A fall restored your eyes? That's the story you're going with?" He started to laugh again.

"Loki . . . ," Brundi warned.

"Fine, if everyone is happy with that, who am I to argue?" Undeterred, Loki walked to Sarah and patted her bump. "So how is my little godson?"

"Kicking up a storm," Sarah said. "And we don't know for sure it's a boy. It could just as easily be a girl."

"Of course it's a boy," Loki said. "I can feel him from here. He's going to be extra special."

"We're just sitting down to dinner," Brundi said quickly, taking Loki by the hand. "Please, join us. There is always room for you at our table."

"Don't mind if I do," Loki said casually. He approached Freya and offered his hand. "Howdy. I'm Loki. May I sit beside you?"

Freya was lost for words as she stared at Loki's offered hand. She couldn't comprehend what was happening as her worlds collided. Loki on Earth and visiting Brünnhilde? How did he get out of Asgard with Odin on high alert? And why was everyone happy to see him and treating him like family? But the bigger question remained—was he the spy Azrael had warned her about?

Trouble was brewing; she could feel it. But Freya realized she had to respond to Loki. She shook his hand. "Of course," she said tightly. "I'm Greta."

"Greta?" Loki said—giving her hand a squeeze so tight it would have broken human bones. His eyes narrowed. "Lovely name but, if I'm honest, you don't look much like a Greta to me. Maybe more like a Maya or even Frey—"

"Stop!" Freya shot. "I—I mean, my name is Greta." She used her own Valkyrie strength to squeeze his hand even harder until he winced and pulled free.

"Of course it is," Loki said, eyes teasing. "So what brings you to our humble home?"

"Our?" Archie cried incredulously.

Loki stole a quick look at Archie before turning to the others. "Did anyone feel that? It's like a cold chill in the room. Almost like a ghost has just walked past."

"That's enough, Loki," Brundi said. "Sit down and we can begin."

As Loki took a seat beside Freya, he touched the cuff of her coat. "Isn't it a little warm to be wearing such a heavy coat? And gloves, too? We're all family here. Why don't you take them off and get comfortable?"

"I'm fine." She looked at her grandmother. "How long have you known Loki?"

Brundi's eyes sparkled as she gazed lovingly at Loki. "We've been friends forever. He's helped me through some very difficult times."

Archie leaned forward and whispered to Freya, "I think we'd better get out of here before things get out of hand. We can talk to Brundi later."

"There's that cold breeze again," Loki said as his eyes bored into Archie. "Brundi, I think the house might be haunted."

"Loki, behave," Brundi said, though she was smiling. "Now, let's eat."

Freya had never sat through a more awkward meal. As she watched the others at the table, she could sense that none of them had a clue who or what Loki really was. She was no longer sure who Loki was herself! Brundi certainly had some explaining to do. . . .

8

"HOW LONG HAS LOKI BEEN COMING HERE?" FREYA asked Brundi. They were taking a walk away from the ranch so that they could talk in confidence. "He's dangerous. If he tells Odin . . ."

Brundi stopped. "Freya, enough! It doesn't take a genius to know there's tension between you two, but that stops now. Loki has been a good friend to me all my life. He found me right after Odin de-winged me. He helped keep me and Vonni safe as we wandered the Earth, blind and alone. It was Loki who helped us build Valhalla Valley many years ago, and he's helped make it the wonderful place it is. Loki is family."

"Valhalla Valley?" Archie asked.

"*This ranch is called Valhalla Valley,*" Pym cawed from Brundi's shoulder. "*Our home.*"

"After Odin banished me from the real Valhalla, Loki helped me create my own, here in Midgard. Instead of being for valiant warriors, this ranch is a safe haven for anyone who seeks it. We turn no one away and that includes animals too. Valhalla Valley is a sanctuary to all."

Freya was almost too stunned to speak. "Loki did all that? Why? He's just a troublemaker. He never does anything nice. Not without a personal motive or something to be gained."

"Loki didn't have to help us!" Brundi barked. "But he did. I was already defeated by Odin. He could have gloated and made my life miserable. Instead he showed great compassion and kept me safe. He helped me build a life for myself and my family. I never asked why, and he's never told me. But Loki has been a truer friend than anyone in Asgard ever was." The Valkyrie paused. "It is you who are endangering everything, not Loki."

"We aren't endangering; we're trying to save you and your family. I wish there were another way to do it, I really do," Freya said. "But war is coming to the realms. Odin wants you back to protect you. He doesn't know about your family. But he won't allow anyone with Asgard blood to remain in Midgard when it starts. You must tell your family and then hide them so deeply that not even Odin or the frost giants can sense them."

"War?" Brundi cried. "How?"

"I don't know," Freya admitted. "We suspect there's a

traitor in Asgard who's been stirring up the frost and fire giants."

"Hey," Archie cried. "Maybe Loki is the spy."

"No!" Brundi snapped. "That's not possible."

"But he's trouble," Archie insisted. "It would be just the sort of thing he'd do!"

"It's not Loki!" Brundi shouted. "And I'm not going anywhere. My home is here."

"But your family . . . ," Freya cried.

"My family will be fine. I can protect them," Brundi insisted.

"No, you can't," Freya replied. "You've seen frost and fire giants. Imagine what they could do here. Just one could destroy Valhalla Valley without effort. A few, and this world would fall. If there is a war, your family will be at risk. Mims is changing. With your powers gone, you can't sense it. But I can. She is becoming a Valkyrie, and Sarah's unborn child is a Dark Searcher with wings. If I can feel them, others can too. They must be hidden, far away from Odin and the giants."

Hardness came to Brundi's eyes. "I won't go back. If a war is coming, so be it. I will suffer the same fate as my family. Let the frost giants come. Let Odin come. I don't care. But I won't abandon them in their greatest time of need."

"Odin only gave us two days to find you," Orus cried, fluttering his wings in anger. *"If we don't bring you back, he will come after you."*

"Let him," Brundi said defiantly. "A very long time ago, Odin took everything from me. I'll not let him do it again. I will fight him with everything I have."

"*And you will lose,*" Orus cawed. "*Valhalla Valley, your family in there—everyone will be destroyed.*"

"You're wrong," Brundi said.

"We're telling you the truth," Archie insisted. "Odin nearly destroyed Chicago because he thought Freya had run away. There's no telling what he'd do here if he learns of Vonni's and Mims's existence—especially if a war is coming."

Brundi shook her head. "I am just one powerless old Valkyrie. What should he care if I am here or there when the war starts? I'm too old and weak to fight. He doesn't need me."

"*But it's not just you now, is it?*" Orus cawed. "*Your family could be used against him. Odin won't allow that. Brundi, you must return to Asgard if you want to protect your family here.*"

They had reached the shed where they were hiding the Reaping Mare. When Brundi opened the door, Jonquil nickered and trotted out.

"I have waited a lifetime to see you again, my love," she said softly. She pulled carrots from her pocket and offered them to her mare. "Will you fly with me?"

Brundi removed the blanket on Jonquil's black wings and hopped up onto her back. "I'm sorry, this is all too much. I can't decide right now. I need time to think what is best for my family. I am going for a flight—don't follow me."

"Don't take too long," Orus cawed. *"Every moment is crucial."*

"Don't tell me what to do!" Brundi snapped as she directed Jonquil away from them and they disappeared into the night.

"You didn't handle that very well. . . ."

Freya and Archie turned and saw a large raccoon ambling up to them.

Before their eyes, it changed into Loki. "Brundi is stubborn. She has struggled long and hard to build Valhalla Valley into what it is. She won't give it up too easily."

Orus cawed, *"Get away from here, Loki!"*

Freya frowned at the trickster. "Is it you? Are you the traitor who is betraying Odin?"

"What are you talking about?" Loki said. "What traitor?"

"We've heard there's a traitor in Asgard uniting the giants against us."

"And you immediately thought of me," Loki challenged. "Well, isn't that nice! No, Freya, I am not the traitor, and your special senses should tell you that."

"Then why did you do it?" Freya asked.

"Do what?"

"Help Brundi and Vonni."

"Would you rather I ignored them and let them suffer, blind and alone in Midgard?"

"No," Freya said softly. "But why would you help them, when you tried to have me killed?"

"Ah, is that it?" Loki challenged. He started to walk around her like a predator stalking his prey. "You're jealous that I chose to help Brundi and not you."

"What?" Freya cried. "No, of course not. I just don't understand. You like to cause trouble. Yet you've helped Brundi and everyone here. They all adore you."

"You really don't see it, do you?" Loki peered closely at her and chuckled. "The answer is right before your eyes, and yet you are blind to it."

"I bet there is no answer," Archie cried. "You're just setting them up for a bigger fall."

Loki turned hard eyes on him. "Silence, ghost. That mark on your hand won't protect you here—especially from me—so tread lightly."

"I'm not afraid of you," Archie said.

"That is your first mistake," Loki said darkly. He focused on Freya. "Is it so hard to consider that I might actually care for someone? That perhaps Brundi was my dearest friend, long before you were born?"

"It's just—"

"You see me only as a troublemaker; that's fair enough," Loki answered for her. "And, granted, I do like to have a bit of fun. But not about this. Odin was cruel and unreasonable when he punished Brundi—especially as her only crime was trying to protect her son. I may be many things, but I am also a father. Had I been her, I would have done exactly the same thing and fled Asgard—unlike some Valkyries I could name, who blindly handed over their sons, never knowing or caring about their fate."

"Can you truly expect us to believe that you care for Brundi and did all this to be kind?" Orus cawed.

"I don't really care what you believe," Loki said. "When Brundi told me she was going to have twins and was planning to run because one of them was a boy, I offered her a place in my home in Utgard. But she knew that Valkyries were forbidden there except during a Challenge. I told her I would smuggle her in and keep her safe, but she refused my offer and came here instead. I found her after Odin's punishment. How could I abandon my dearest friend after that?"

Freya's sensed that every word Loki said was true. His feelings for Brundi were genuine. Had Thor been right? Did Loki really have a good side?

"Do you know what's about to happen in Asgard?"

"Gee, no," Archie warned.

"The war?" Loki said casually, ignoring Archie. He shrugged. "Frost giants have been plotting against Asgard forever. This too shall pass. I doubt it will amount to much."

"But still, Brundi must return."

"I know," Loki agreed, and a shadow of genuine sadness replaced the sly smile on his face. "It will destroy her to go back, but she will make the right decision to protect the others; it will just take her time."

As Loki started to walk away, Freya ran after him. "Loki, wait. I need to ask you one more thing."

The trickster paused.

"Back in Asgard, during the Challenge, you asked me to look at one of the Dark Searchers—the shortest one. Why? Who is he and why does he have white wings?"

"How funny that a Valkyrie with black wings should ask about a young Searcher with white wings. . . ." The smile returned to his face. "Why do you ask the question when you already know the answer?"

And with that, Loki turned himself into a fly and buzzed off into the night.

"*I should have eaten him while I had the chance,*" Orus cawed, snapping his beak shut in the air after the departing fly.

"He'd have given you indigestion," Archie said. "Gee, what was that all about? Why are you so interested in that white-winged Searcher?"

Freya remained silent and watched Loki flying away. "It's not important," she finally answered.

"What are we going to do about Brundi?" Archie asked.

"*We could always hit her on the head and drag her home . . . ,*" Orus offered.

Freya shook her head. "We've got to be patient and try to make her see reason."

"And if she doesn't?" Archie asked.

"*Then* we hit her on the head and drag her home."

*   *   *

"Don't worry. Brundi will be fine," Sarah said when Freya explained Brundi's absence when they returned to the house. "She likes to go off on her own every now and then. Now, let's get you settled in your room. Where are your bags?"

"Um . . . ," Freya started.

"Tell her they were stolen," Archie said.

"They were stolen," Freya repeated. "I only had enough money to get out here."

"How awful!" Sarah cried. "I'm sure Mims has some clothes you can borrow."

They followed Sarah through the house and into a type of playroom with a large pool table, a massive television screen, game consoles, and pinball machines.

"Cool!" Archie breathed. "Look at all this stuff! I could die happy here!"

"*You're already dead,*" Orus cawed.

Freya stroked the raven, grateful that Sarah couldn't understand him.

Inside the game room, Tash and Gage were playing pool. "Hi," Gage called, waving at Archie. "You want to play with us?"

"Hi, Gage," Archie responded, waving. "Not right now, thanks."

Freya studied the boy's face. She could sense a "knowing"

from him. Gage was definitely sensitive to otherworldly things. "Are they your family?" she asked Sarah.

Sarah nodded. "In a way, yes. Gage and his sister have been with us almost two years. Their mother couldn't handle a child with Down syndrome, so they were both put into care when Gage was very young. But they were having a really tough time until they were brought here. Brundi fosters a lot of troubled or disabled children. She has this way about her that works wonders. Children, animals, there isn't a creature alive that she can't reach."

"How many people live here?" Freya asked.

"It varies. Most times, we have almost thirty." Sarah stopped. "You should be proud of your grandmother. She and Vonni have built something very special out here. Troubled teens from all over the country are sent here to work on the ranch. After a few weeks with Brundi, these kids turn their lives around. I don't know what it is that she does, but it works."

Sarah led Freya upstairs. "There's an empty bedroom beside Mims's. If you need anything, just knock on her door."

They stopped outside a room. "Here you go. Come downstairs if you need me or want to call your mother to let her know you've arrived safely."

"Thank you," Freya said. "I should be fine for the night." Her eyes lingered on Sarah's belly.

"Just a few weeks now," Sarah said, rubbing her bump. "I can't wait. This little fellow has been kicking up a storm."

"You know it's a boy?"

"Not for certain, but I have a feeling. He's been kicking like he's playing soccer in there," Sarah said, laughing. "Gage insists I'm having a little angel. He says the baby has wings. I just don't know where he gets these crazy ideas." Freya and Archie gave each other a knowing look. "Anyway, I'll leave you to get settled."

When she was gone, Freya and Archie entered the room. It was comfortably furnished and had a television set up on a stand.

"*Great!*" Orus cawed as he flew to the bed. "*I want to see what I've missed on TV.*"

"You and television!" Archie teased. When he reached for the remote, his hand passed right through it and the table beneath. "Sorry, Orus, you'll have to do this on your own."

Freya lost no time pulling off her coat and gloves. Stretching out her wings, she massaged an ache in their muscles. "I'd forgotten how uncomfortable it is to keep them bound."

"You won't have to bind your wings for long," Archie said. "We've got to hide the family and get Brundi out of here as soon as possible. Loki may not believe there's going to be a war, but Azrael is convinced. My money's on Azrael."

Freya nodded and stepped to the window. She peered out into the darkness, feeling the weight of responsibility pressing down on her.

"It's not easy, is it?" Archie asked.

Freya shook her head. "Brundi has created something so special here. It will be a shame to destroy it."

"*We don't have much choice,*" Orus cawed.

A knock on the door interrupted them. "Who is it?" Freya called.

"It's Mims."

Freya reached for her coat. "Come in."

As soon as she walked into the room Mims's eyes landed on Archie and she looked uneasy.

"Erm, can I talk to you for a moment, Greta?" Mims asked her. "Alone."

Freya shook her head. "You must get over your fear of Archie. He's not going to hurt you. Just think of him as being alive. Talk to him. You'll see what I mean."

"I was alive not too long ago," Archie said. "I went to school and I had friends. I'm normal. Only now I'm a normal ghost."

"What happened to you?" Mims asked.

"I don't think Brundi would appreciate us telling you," Freya said. "But anything you have to say to me, you can say in front of Archie."

"*And me,*" Orus cawed.

"Yes," Freya agreed. "And Orus."

Mims sighed heavily and sat on the edge of the bed beside Orus. She wouldn't look up at Freya. "Would you please tell me what's going on here? I know there's a lot you're not telling me."

"Yes, there is," Freya admitted. "But Brundi has forbidden me from talking to you. She needs time to think."

Mims hesitated. "It's about me, isn't it? That's why you're here."

"What do you mean?" Orus asked as he hopped up on her knee.

Mims started to stroke his shiny black feathers. "Something is wrong with me. I know it. But Mom insists everything is fine. I've tried talking to Gran, but she keeps changing the subject."

"You really should talk to her again," Freya said.

"I tried, earlier tonight," Mims said in frustration. "She told me to forget about it. How am I supposed to forget about a flying horse? Or talking birds, or that your best friend is a ghost?"

"I understand," Archie said. "These things take a little getting used to. But the Reaping Mares are so cool. You should try riding Jonquil."

"I don't want to ride her. I want to understand." Mims looked at Freya. "You have wings hidden under your coat, don't you?"

Archie gasped. "How did you know about that?"

"I don't know!" Mims cried. "That's the problem. Things like this are happening to me all the time now. It's like I can read people's minds. I know what they are thinking and what they're going to do. And when I first saw you, I knew you had wings. I don't know how, but I did. I know you're not here by accident and that Gran isn't happy that you are. Something big is coming, isn't it?"

Freya nodded. "Very big. And because of it, we've come to take Brundi away."

"Why?"

"To keep you and your family safe."

"From?"

"Gee," Archie warned. "Brundi told us not to talk about this."

Freya shook her head. "Mims's powers are growing and will only get stronger." She looked back at her cousin. "Brundi is trying to ignore it, but she can't. There's too much at stake."

"Then tell me," Mims insisted. She rose and went over to Freya, and before she could stop her, Mims caught hold of Freya's bare hands and held them tightly. "Tell me now. What are you? Where do you come from? What's wrong with me?"

Orus cawed in panic, *"Freya, she's touching you!"*

Freya looked at their entwined hands. "That's the final proof."

Mims frowned. "Why did Orus call you Freya when your name is Greta?"

"Because my true name is Freya, but I can't let people know it. You must only ever call me Greta, especially in front of people."

"That's just like me," Mims said. "My real name is

Myriam-Elizabet, but Gran has forbidden me from ever telling anyone. So they only call me Mims."

Freya looked at Archie in surprise. "Deep down Brundi must have had her suspicions, even if she didn't want to admit it," she said to him. She focused on Mims. "Brundi was right. You must never tell anyone your true name."

"Why?"

"Because our names have great power. They must be protected and kept secret at all times."

Archie showed her the back of his hand. "This is Freya's mark. It appeared on my hand when she told me her true name. Now that I'm dead, it means we are bound together forever. If you give your true name to someone, they will be bound to you."

"I don't understand." Mims's eyes passed from Archie to Freya.

Freya gently led her cousin back to the bed. "You need to sit down for this, trust me."

"For what?"

"This." Freya pulled off her coat. Her beautiful black wings fell out, and the sound of rustling feathers filled the room as she extended her wings.

"I knew you had them. I just knew it," Mims gasped. "But to actually see them . . . Can you fly?"

"Yes." Freya folded her wings and reached for a desk chair. Turning it around backward, she sat down. "We can tell you everything you need to know, but it will be difficult to hear."

"*You must be prepared,*" Orus warned gently. "*This is bigger than you can ever imagine.*"

Mims was trembling, but she nodded. "I need to know. Please tell me."

Freya started. "Yes, I have wings. So do my mother and my four sisters. A very long time ago, Brundi also had wings. And so did her son, Giovanni."

"My dad had wings?" Mims gasped but then looked away, her expression becoming distant. "Dad has big scars on his back. Gran always said he had an accident when he was a baby."

"*It was no accident,*" Orus said. "*Your father's wings were removed.*"

"Why?"

"In this world, a child with wings would have been hunted down and killed. It was the only way to keep him safe," Freya said.

"But you have wings. How are you safe?"

Freya looked to Orus.

"*Go on, tell her,*" he coaxed.

"I'm safe because I don't live in this world. We all live in a place far from here, a place called Asgard."

Mims frowned. "I've never heard of it."

"Have you heard of Thor or Odin?" Archie asked.

Mims nodded. "Sure, everybody has. They're characters from superhero movies."

"*Really?*" Orus said excitedly. "*Movies? We've got to see those movies. Maybe I'm in them!*"

Archie ignored Orus. "Odin and Thor aren't just characters from a movie. They're from the Old Norse myths. But they're not myths at all. I'd never heard of Asgard until I met Gee."

"Where is it?"

"It's kind of hard to explain," Archie said. "It's in another realm. You have to cross this big Rainbow Bridge to get there."

"Bifröst," Mims said.

"Yes!" Archie exclaimed. "You do know it."

Mims nodded. "It was in the movie. But that still doesn't explain where it is."

Freya could see that none of this made much sense to her cousin. "Where it is doesn't matter. But in Asgard, we're safe."

"But, I mean, like," Mims stumbled. "If we're really cousins, and my dad had wings, why don't I?"

"I really don't know," Freya admitted. "Your mother is human. Brundi thought you were too."

"I'm not human?" Mims cried.

Freya shook her head. "No, you're not."

Mims's voice was little more than a broken whisper. "If I'm not human, what am I?"

Freya rose. "You're just like me. You're a Valkyrie."

9

"SO I'M GOING TO KILL PEOPLE." MIMS FINALLY SPOKE
after they explained everything—including Brundi's exile to
Earth, the growing tension between the realms, and the pos-
sibility of a war drawing near.

"No, you won't." Archie sat beside her. "Not if you're
careful. You see how Gee wears gloves. That's all you need to
do. Just be careful not to touch anyone skin to skin."

"Even my mother?" Mims asked.

Freya nodded. "She's human. When your full powers
come, your touch will be deadly to her."

Mims turned to Freya. "Can you stop it? Can you make
me normal again?"

"You are normal," Freya assured her. "You're a normal Valkyrie, just like me. You read people's minds, see in

the dark, and charm wild animals—that's all part of being a Valkyrie. We have enhanced senses. We are the Battle-Maidens of Odin. We reap human soldiers from the battle-field and take them to Valhalla."

"But what if I don't want it?"

Freya heard echoes of her own words spoken to Maya the day she had to reap her first soldier. She hadn't wanted to be a Valkyrie either. Freya saw so much of herself in her cousin.

"You can't change what you are," Orus said gently.

"It's like being born with blue eyes when you wanted brown. Or a hair color that you don't want. You can't change it," Archie said.

"Yes, you can." Mims wept. "You can dye your hair like Greta does, or you can wear contact lenses to change your eye color."

"And you can wear protective clothes so you don't have an accident," Archie added. "This isn't the end of your life. It's just changing."

Freya rose from the chair and knelt down before her cousin. "I didn't want to be a Valkyrie either. I was happy in Asgard before I had powers. I flew to the battlefields with my mother and sisters, but I never had to reap anybody. Then my powers arrived and I had to take up my duties. I still don't want to reap soldiers, but I must. It is what I was born to do. You are lucky—you won't have to do that. You can still live here with your family."

"But never touch anyone again," Mims said bitterly. She pulled free of Freya and walked to the window. "Why didn't Gran tell me?"

"Because you were born without wings she honestly believed you were human."

"So now what?" Mims demanded. "You take Gran away and I stay here in hiding, never knowing what I am."

"You do know what you are," Orus cawed. *"You're a Valkyrie."*

"But that means nothing to me!" Mims cried. "I have no future here now."

"You do," Freya said. "You will be needed here more than ever. Especially if the war comes. You will need to use your powers to help your family and everyone here."

"And you will be needed to protect your little brother," Archie added. "He'll be born with wings. Whether he keeps them or not, he'll need your protection."

"After everything you've just told me, you expect me to stay here?"

"Of course," Freya said. "Why wouldn't you?"

"Because I'm deadly!" Mims cried. "One mistake, just one little mistake and I could kill someone I love. I don't want this!" Mims ran toward the door. "I don't want to be a Valkyrie. I wish I'd never been born!"

"Mims, wait!" Freya reached for her coat to follow her.

"No. Let her go," Orus cawed. *"Is she so different from you?*

Look how you flew away the night before your First Day Ceremony, and you knew what you were. Imagine how hard it must be for her. In one night, her whole life has changed. She needs time to adjust."

"He's right," Archie agreed. "She needs time to take it all in."

Freya took a deep breath and nodded. She closed her eyes and tracked her cousin. "Mims has just left the house. She's run off into the woods. I'm going to follow her and make sure she's all right."

"Leave her alone," Orus warned. *"Just sit down and we can watch some television together."*

"I can't," Freya said. "Mims is confused and in pain. I don't want her doing something foolish. I won't let her see me. I'll just keep a distant eye on her."

"I'm coming too," Archie said. Then he stopped. "Gee, if I'm a ghost, does that mean I can fly?"

Freya shrugged. "I don't really know. I've never traveled to Midgard with the dead." She approached the window. "Jump out. If you fall, we'll know that you can't and I'll carry you."

Archie came up beside her and peered out. "It's a long way down to the ground."

"Don't be such a coward," Orus cawed. *"You're already dead; what more can happen to you?"*

Archie reluctantly climbed up on the ledge. "You're sure I can't be hurt?"

"Just go!" Orus cawed. The raven flew over to Archie and nipped him on the backside.

"Orus!" Archie howled as he fell out the window.

Freya peered out and watched her friend crash to the ground. Archie was lying facedown with his arms and legs outspread. She leaped out and glided down to the ground and knelt beside him. "Archie, are you all right?"

Archie moaned and turned over slowly. "Guess what? I can't fly."

"Get up. You're not hurt," Orus cawed as he landed beside Archie and pecked at him.

Archie glared at the raven. "You lied to me. You said I wouldn't feel you when we were on Earth. But I felt you, all right. You bit me in the butt!"

"Yes." Orus laughed. *"But it got you moving. Now, get up."*

Freya helped Archie climb to his feet.

"So why, if I'm a ghost, didn't I float? Gravity shouldn't work on me, but it did."

Freya shrugged. "Don't ask me. I use my wings."

"You expected to fall," Orus explained. *"You should have focused on floating. But you are still thinking like the living and believe you are bound by those rules. You expected to fall, so you fell."*

"So he can fly if he wants to?" Freya asked the raven.

"Of course," Orus cawed. *"But it will take practice and time we just don't have. Now, are we going to find Mims, or can we please go back and watch television?"*

"Let's go," Freya said. Sensing the air, she pointed. "She's gone that way."

They walked into the dark woods at the back of the house. Despite the lack of light, Freya could see perfectly well, and knew Mims would too. The air was filled with the sounds of nightlife. A fox was screaming in the distance, and with each step some unknown creature scurried away. From the canopy above they heard the hooting of an owl.

When they moved deeper into the woods, howls filled the air.

"These woods are creepy at night," Archie said nervously as his eyes darted toward the noise. "I'm sure those were wolves howling, not dogs."

From Freya's shoulder, Orus started to caw with laughter.

"What's so funny?" Archie challenged.

"*You are!*" The raven choked as he gasped to catch his breath between laughs. "*A ghost who's afraid of the dark!*"

"Orus, stop it," Freya said, though she couldn't keep the smile off her face. "Archie, you aren't afraid of wolves, are you? Odin has two—you see them all the time."

"I know," Archie said. "But those are pets. These are wild." He moved closer to Orus. "And I wasn't frightened for myself. I was thinking of Mims. What if they go after her?"

"They won't," Freya said. "No animal is dangerous to a Valkyrie. If a wolf approached her, it would be friendly. That is one of our charms."

They continued to pick their way through the dense woods. With the trees in full leaf, they couldn't see the expanse of stars above. But soon the trees thinned and then tapered off. A beautiful starlit lake spread out before them.

"There," Freya said softly. "She's over there."

Mims was sitting on a log at the water's edge. Three dogs were beside her, wagging their tails and baying for attention. When she leaned down, they licked her face.

Creeping closer, Freya smiled. They weren't dogs; they were the wolves that had been howling. "See?" she whispered softly to Archie. "Those wolves are under her spell."

"I don't believe it," Archie breathed.

"Believe it," Freya said. "That could just as easily have been bears or mountain lions. They're all the same to us." They watched the magic of Mims with the wolves until a cracking sound shattered the moment. It was followed by a loud pain-filled yelp.

"No!" Mims screamed.

"Hunters," Freya said darkly as she closed her eyes and opened her senses. "They are here to kill the wolves."

She darted into the clearing and opened her wings as a second gunshot shattered the night. "Mims is going after them. She could get hurt—I'm not going to let that happen. Archie, you and Orus stay here."

As Freya launched into the air, Archie called, "Gee, be careful. You're not wearing your armor!"

Freya rose higher in the night sky. She caught sight of her cousin and the three wolves running along the water's edge.

Orus appeared in the sky beside her.

"I told you to stay with Archie," Freya called.

"I'm not staying back there when there's a fight to be had!"

Below them, Mims was shouting at two men dressed in dark clothes. They were wearing night-vision goggles and standing over the body of a large gray wolf.

"This is private property!" Mims shouted. "You have no right to be here!"

The two hunters didn't appear surprised to see her. As she drew near, they raised their weapons. The wolves by her side lowered their heads and started to growl. Mims looked back at them and ordered them to stay.

"Step away from the wolves," a hunter ordered.

"If you think I'm going to let you kill my wolves—"

"They're not your wolves," the hunter said. "They're vermin that kill the elk. Now, stand back!"

"You don't care about the elk. You just want to kill wolves so you can hunt the elk. Get off my property!"

Freya tilted her wings and circled in the air above her cousin. She didn't want to show herself unless it was absolutely necessary. But there was no way she would let these men hurt Mims or the wolves.

"We know all about you people here," the other hunter said. "You're just a bunch of tree-hugging losers determined to stop our hunting and mining. We're doing our jobs. We're killing those predators that are eating our livestock. If you have a problem with that, call a cop. Now, step away from the wolves."

Mims called the wolves closer. "You are not going to kill any more animals. This is private property. I am warning you, leave here now before I lose my temper."

The hunters raised their weapons. "Last warning, kid. Stand back!"

"*Freya, this is getting serious,*" Orus warned.

"Orus, do as I say and stay with Mims. I'm going to take care of the hunters."

"*You're not going to reap them?*"

"Of course not!" Freya cried as she changed direction in the sky. "I'm just going to make them wish I had!"

Freya let out a Valkyrie howl and swooped down. She dove at them at full speed and caught both hunters by their shirts. Without missing a wing beat, she hoisted them off the ground and carried them away from Mims. They struggled against her iron grip.

"What are you?" one of the hunters cried, struggling to break free.

"Stay still or I'll drop you!" Freya threatened.

The second hunter maneuvered his weapon to point up at her. "You drop us and you'll be dead before we hit the ground. So take us down now or I'll shoot!"

Freya kicked him in the back. "Your threats are meaningless, your weapons powerless against me. Drop them or I'll drop you!"

Freya gave both hunters a shake. One weapon fell to the ground, but the other hunter held on to his.

"Do it!" Freya commanded as she loosened her grip. "Or learn to fly!"

Reluctantly the second hunter surrendered his weapon. "What are you?" he repeated, straining to look up at her.

"Your worst nightmare," Freya cried. "Now, don't look at me! After what you did to that wolf, I am more than happy to do the same to you. So look away now."

The hunter turned away.

Freya carried them up to the top of the same mountain Azrael had brought them to. While they were still in the air, she released them. Both hunters struck the rocky ground with a grunt.

Freya touched down and charged at them. She snatched away their night-vision goggles before they could get a good look at her and tossed them over the side of the mountain.

Standing before them, she concentrated on their minds and was chilled to discover that they were surprised by her but not frightened. They'd never seen a winged being like her before but didn't seem the least bit perturbed, only excited by what a wonderful trophy she would make.

"Just what kind of failed science experiment are you?" the hunter demanded.

"Failed science experiment?" Freya repeated. "I am the top predator in this world. I am the head of the food chain, not you." She spoke in the only language they would understand—that of the hunter. "And I'm the one that sees your kind as my prey. You are fortunate tonight; I have no desire to kill. But I will tell you this: If I ever see either of you in Valhalla Valley again, or if I ever come across you hunting anything, I won't hesitate to show you the same mercy you showed that gray wolf."

The two men remained still. Defiance poured from them.

"Valhalla Valley is under my protection," Freya continued. "You will tell the others to respect that and keep off the property, or they will face me!"

Freya moved closer. She kept her wings open wide to frighten them, but it wasn't working. What kind of men weren't frightened by the first sight of her?

"Now tell me, why are you here? It is more than just hunting wolves, I can sense it. Who sent you here?"

She received only defiant silence.

"Speak!" Freya roared as she kicked them backward. "Tell me why you're here or I will throw you both off this mountain right now!"

"Looks like you're going to have to kill us!" One of the hunters pulled a long hunting knife from his boot and lunged at Freya. As he moved forward, another blade flashed as the second man came at her from the opposite direction.

Valkyries were trained in weapons fighting from a very early age. Freya had the advantage of experience, superior strength, and full night vision. It was little work for her to duck away from their flashing blades. Drawing her sword, she flipped the knives from their grip, drawing blood from both men's hands as she did so, and left them moaning on the ground.

"You really think you can defeat me?" she challenged. Freya charged forward and placed her boot on the chest of the first attacker. "Now you listen to me very carefully. Go back into the hole you crawled out of and tell the others this property is now protected. Is that understood?"

Neither hunter said a word.

Freya threw back her head and howled the loudest Valkyrie cry she could manage. It echoed across the valley like thunder. "Must I kill you? Is that what you want?" she roared. "No one comes back to Valhalla Valley, do you understand?"

"Yes," one of the hunters spat.

Freya stepped up to the cliff edge. "Don't bother going back for your weapons. They're mine now!"

Without waiting for their reaction, Freya leaped off the cliff and glided back down to the lake where Archie was waiting with Mims. Orus was on her shoulder, and the three wolves were nearby. Mims was kneeling on the ground, stroking the dead wolf.

Freya touched down and approached her gently. "Are you all right?"

Mims nodded without looking up. "If you hadn't come, those hunters would have killed all the wolves—maybe me too." Her voice started to tremble. "This was Big Gray. He was Gran's favorite; we've known him since he was a pup. She's going to be so sad when she sees what they did to him."

"He was beautiful," Freya agreed. She looked at Archie. "I just don't understand humans. How can they keep dogs as pets but still want to hunt wolves, which are just like dogs?"

"Don't ask me," Archie said. "I've never understood hunters. What they do is disgusting. What about those two? Did you reap them?"

Freya shook her head. "No, though they deserved it. Let's just say I took them for a short flight and left them facing a long walk back. . . ." She stepped closer to her cousin. "I doubt they'll be bothering you again."

"Don't count on it," Mims said. "Hunters are always trespassing on our property. They hate that Gran attracts all the big game and wildlife. So even though we've posted 'private property' and 'no hunting' signs, they still come here to kill."

"What about the authorities?" Archie asked.

Mims shook her head. "They won't help. Everyone around here is a hunter, including the police. They call us crazy because we don't hunt and because we protect the predators."

Freya looked down at the remaining wolves. One came over and rubbed against her, and she stroked its head. "Wolves are naturally drawn to Valkyries. They come here because of you and Brundi. They know you will keep them safe."

"How can we leave here and go into hiding?" Mims said. "What will happen to all the animals and people who come for protection?"

"I don't know," Freya admitted. "But you will also be vulnerable if you stay. Those hunters are nothing compared to frost giants."

"Or Odin," Archie added.

"How will they find us?" Mims asked. "We live in the middle of nowhere!"

"I'm not really sure," Freya replied. "If there's a war, there is no reason for the frost giants not to try to take Earth. It is a beautiful world."

"*You have powers, Mims,*" Orus added. "*So does your father. They will sense them and come after you. This is why we must hide you where they can't feel you.*"

Mims shook her head. "Our property covers thousands of acres. It takes in this whole valley, the lake, and most of the mountains around us. There's even a closed gold mine. People have been trying to drive Gran and Dad off this land for years because they want to reopen the mine. But we won't let them. If those men have come this close to our house, something is up. They wanted more than to just kill the wolves. I could feel it."

Freya gazed toward the mountain where she'd left the hunters. "I know. But they kept their true intentions well hidden. I couldn't sense what they were after. Even my threats would not loosen their tongues. I'm thinking now I should have been more persuasive. Maybe I should go back up there and see if I can get the truth out of them."

"*No,*" Orus warned. "*With Brundi gone, we must stay near the house to protect it in case others come.*"

"He's right," Archie said. "We should stay until Brundi gets back."

"But sometimes she goes for days—even weeks." Mims said.

"We don't have that kind of time," Archie said. "Odin is expecting her back in Asgard. Can your father find her?"

Mims nodded. "He always seems to know where everyone is. I can never hide from him."

"That's because he's a Dark Searcher," Freya said. "No one can hide from them. Where is he? We must speak with him."

"We can't. He's on tour," Mims explained. "My dad's a singer. He was playing in Houston tonight, and tomorrow night he's going to be in Los Angeles. Then he flies to Europe."

"Then we'll go to him," Freya said. "He must be told

everything and help us convince Brundi to return to Asgard. Then he must take you all into hiding."

"Mom would never let us go. Besides, we'd need to book flights. I don't think we could get there in time for tomorrow night's concert."

Archie shook his head. "We don't need to book flights. We have our very own special way of getting there."

"What's that?" Mims asked.

Freya opened her wings wide. "Me."

10

IT WAS DEEP INTO THE NIGHT BY THE TIME THEY MADE
their way back to the house. Mims yawned as she gently
pulled the front door open. She looked back at Freya, who
was standing away from the house. "Aren't you coming?" she
whispered.

Freya shook her head. "I don't sleep very well when I'm
in this world. Just get some rest. Archie, Orus, and I will
patrol the area and make sure there are no more unexpected
visitors."

Mims nodded. "See you in the morning."

As they walked away from the house, Freya led them to
Brundi's platform. "Let's go up there for a while. It gives us a
good view of the valley."

Freya opened her wings and flew to the top of the tall

platform. She peered over the side and watched Archie on the ground. His arms were open and he was jumping in the air. She started to laugh.

"Orus, look—I think he's trying to fly."

"He's not doing a very good job of it!" Orus called down to Archie, *"Stop thinking like a living human. Focus on what you want to do. Think 'up,' and then let yourself float. Believe you can do it and you will."*

"Come on, Archie, you can do it!" Freya called as she watched Archie close his eyes and start to concentrate. He began to lift off the ground.

"Hey, I'm flying!" Archie cried. "I'm really flying!"

"That's it, Archie!" Freya encouraged. "Keep going. You're almost here."

But after a few more feet Archie cried out and crashed down to the ground.

"Well, I was flying."

After several more failed attempts, Archie gave up and climbed the tall ladder.

"I'll never figure it out," he muttered as he reached the top.

"Not with that attitude," Orus cawed. *"Do you think Freya learned to fly overnight? No. It took practice—a lot of it. Why, I can't count the number of times she took off, lost control, and fell out of the sky! One time she flew off the balcony at the house and then smashed right into a tree. We were pulling leaves out of her hair and feathers all afternoon!"*

"Thanks for bringing up a painful memory," Freya replied.

"I'm sorry, but Archie must understand that it will take him time to learn what he can do. He hasn't been dead all that long."

"It seems like forever," Archie said. He stopped beside Freya. "Whoa. You can see the whole valley from up here." Freya nodded. "I don't think Brundi built this platform just to wind dance. I think she's been using it to keep watch on the house and family."

"How?" Archie asked. "She was blind."

"Yes, but Pym isn't. And something tells me that some of Brundi's senses came back. How else would she and Vonni have managed so well over all these centuries?" She closed her eyes. "There's no one else around. But I'm certain those two hunters weren't acting alone. I'm tempted to fly back up to the mountain and have another chat with them."

"That's not a good idea," Orus cawed. *"With Brundi gone, we are all that are left to protect the house. Mims is growing in strength, but she is far from a full Valkyrie yet—and she is untrained. She may have powers, but she doesn't know how to use them."*

Panning her eyes over the dark woods, Freya recalled all the training she'd had growing up. From a very early age she'd been taught how to use her powers and how to fight with swords and all manner of weapons from across the ages. Mims's powers were emerging, but Brundi hadn't trained her at all.

"You're right," she finally admitted.

"While we're here, you could teach her," Archie offered. "Just like you did the Geek Squad back home. Show her how to use her powers and how to fight. If Brundi won't, you should."

Freya looked approvingly at Archie. "That's not a bad idea. She's going to need skills for when Brundi goes. We'll start as soon as we can."

Dawn arrived and there was still no sign of Brundi. Now that she had been reunited with Jonquil and had her sight back, there was no telling where they had gone.

"Do you think she'll come back today?" Archie asked.

"I hope so," Freya said. "If it were me, I would fly all around the world, trying to see what I'd missed. She knows big trouble is coming. She's probably trying to see as much as she can before that happens."

"But she's left the family unprotected," Archie said.

"*Brundi knows Freya is here and will protect them,*" Orus cawed. "*She may not show it, but she trusts us.*"

Freya looked over at the house. The sun was barely up, yet there was activity starting. "I'm not wearing my coat. We'd better get back inside before anyone sees me."

They just made it back up to Freya's bedroom before John, the ranch manager, was up and brewing coffee in the kitchen. Soon others joined him and started to make breakfast. Before long the house was filled with noise again.

A light knocking started on her door. Freya sensed it was her cousin and invited her in without bothering to cover her wings.

Mims looked exhausted. Dark rings circled her eyes and her hair was uncombed.

"You okay?" Archie asked.

Mims shook her head. "So much is happening, I just couldn't sleep."

"I understand." Freya approached her cousin. "Does Brundi go out a lot at night?"

Mims nodded. "She likes to spend time alone on the platform. I've asked her why, and she says she likes to do this thing called wind dancing. But lately I've sensed that she's afraid."

"Afraid? Of what?"

Mims sighed. "Last year some men came and offered her a lot of money to let them open the gold mine again. She threw them off the property. But they just won't stop bothering her. They want to get lawyers involved."

"They can't do that," Archie said. "This is private property."

"I think Gran is frightened that they can. The people who want the mine have a lot of friends in the local government. They are looking to change the law and allow mining on private land."

"*Gold isn't the big problem now,*" Orus cawed.

"We've got to get your dad back here as soon as possible and make our plans."

"He won't be easy to convince."

"Yes, he will," Freya said, "when we tell him who he really is. We'll explain why Brundi has to go back to Asgard and what he must do to protect you. I'm sure he'll come back and keep the family safe."

From downstairs came a loud clanging.

"That's the breakfast bell; we'd better go. We've got a lot of work to do today before we go to my dad."

Freya spent the day working closely beside Mims, helping to settle a large delivery of rescued horses at Valhalla Valley. Here they were cared for and found new, forever homes. If rehoming wasn't possible, the animals would spend the rest of their lives in the safety of the ranch.

By the end of the day, Freya wasn't tired like everyone else, but she was uncomfortably hot and sweaty. Her wings were cramping up from the coat and she was covered in a film of dirt. She was grateful to get back to her room, undress, and finally take a shower.

As the hot water beat down on her aching shoulders and wings, Freya leaned against the wall, feeling the weight of responsibility pressing down on her. Brundi was so desperately needed here. There seemed no way out of the problem. Other thoughts also invaded her mind—thoughts that wouldn't be put aside. Loki's final comment about the white-winged Dark Searcher haunted her: *Why do you ask the question when you already know the answer . . . ?* But she didn't know the answer. Yet it felt like she should. There was something about that Searcher. Something special that had called to her.

For the first time in her life she actually wished Loki were around so that she could ask him.

Emerging from the shower, Freya found Mims inside her bedroom, with a selection of outfits laid out on the bed.

"I thought you might like a change of clothes—especially as we're going to see Dad tonight."

Freya looked down at the lacy tops and long, colorful skirts. "They're lovely, but they won't fit over these. . . ." She fluttered open her wings to make a point.

"Sure they will," Mims said, grinning. She held up scissors. "We'll just make a few adjustments."

Freya regretted destroying her cousin's clothes, but Mims didn't mind at all. Before long, she was dressed much like her cousin.

"Perfect," Mims said approvingly. "You'll fit right in at the concert."

Freya walked over to the window. It was early evening and the temperature was finally going down. She opened her senses, searching, but could find no trace of her grandmother. Fear settled like a rock in her stomach. What if Brundi didn't return?

11

WHEN THE SUN HAD JUST STARTED TO SET, THE THREE of them walked to Brundi's platform.

"Do you know where we're going?" Mims asked.

Freya nodded. "I have a rough idea. But I'll need help when we reach Los Angeles. Where is your father performing?"

"The Hollywood Bowl," Mims said.

"Really?" Archie cried. "Wow!"

"What's so special about that?" Freya asked.

"It's huge," Mims explained. "Really famous. All the biggest acts play there, and Dad's been dreaming of it for years. Here, I printed off a map." She handed it to Freya. "I figure if we aim for the coastline, we can find it from there."

Freya studied the map. "All right, it looks like a fairly

straight route, so we should be fine." She handed back the map. "But keep this with you. We may need it again."

"Are you sure you can carry me? I'm not small," Mims said.

"She carried those two hunters away," Orus cawed. *"Don't worry. You're safe."*

Freya pulled off her coat, balled it up, and put it in a backpack. She handed it to Archie. "Would you carry this? I need my arms to hold Mims."

"Hello . . ." Archie laughed, holding up his hands. "Ghost here, remember? I can't lift anything."

"I'll take it," Mims volunteered. "Just don't drop me."

Freya was going to have to fly holding Mims in front and with Archie clinging to her back between her wings. "I'll try not to. Just tell me when you're getting tired and I'll land for a bit." She looked back at Archie, who was standing behind her. "And hold on tight back there, unless you want to try flying again."

"No, thank you!" Archie cried. "You just concentrate on not dropping Mims."

Freya felt like the filling in a very strange person-sandwich as she carefully opened her wings and leaped confidently off the top of the platform. It was the most awkward flying she'd ever done.

At first Mims held tight to Freya's arms as they climbed higher in the sky. But soon her fear turned to excitement. She relaxed and loosened her grip.

"This is awesome!" Mims shouted. She opened her arms and pretended to fly.

Freya laughed and, tucking in her wings, dove lower. Then she climbed higher in the dark sky and dove again.

Orus was flying closely at their side, calling to them and enjoying the journey.

"Tell me if you're feeling cold," Freya called.

"I never feel the cold," Mims said. "Dive again; this is amazing!"

They played the whole journey south. Freya delighted in the excitement of her cousin and Archie. Despite the awkwardness of it all, she'd never had more fun flying.

A couple of hours later Mims pulled the map out of her pocket and did her best to direct them. She pointed down. "If I'm right, we shouldn't be too far away now. Just fly west and we can head for the coastline toward Los Angeles."

The sun had set as they reached the California coastline. The great expanse of the Pacific Ocean spread out before them, with the city lights shining below. Not far away, they heard the sound of a helicopter. Freya tensed, as memories of her failed escape flight in Chicago returned to her. But she soon registered it was a tourist helicopter, and not the police.

"Okay, we're at the sea. How far to Santa Monica?" Archie called.

Mims held up the map and gazed down to follow the coastline. "Not far—it should be just ahead."

With Mims navigating, they found the point where they needed to fly east. Curious about California, Freya dipped lower in the sky.

"So this is Hollywood," Archie called. "I never dreamed I'd see it. Especially not from the back of a Valkyrie!"

The Hollywood lights blazed below them. Not far ahead, searchlights were shining their vibrant beams in the sky. "What are they looking for?" Freya shivered to herself. She didn't like searchlights—they reminded her of Chicago.

"Nothing," Mims reassured her. "They use them at premieres. There must be a new movie opening. I'm sure they're not for us."

Veering around the searchlights, Freya dipped even lower in the sky. She had heard about Hollywood from Archie and really wanted to see it. They were low enough to see people on the streets and the lines of traffic on the roads.

"I wonder what they'd do if they saw us," Archie called.

"This is California," Mims said. "Probably nothing. Hey, look . . ." Mims pointed. "There it is. That's the Hollywood Bowl!"

Freya gazed down on the large, outdoor arena, which looked like a giant seashell. Thousands of people filled the seats and were sitting on the grassy hill surrounding the shell-shaped stage. She could hear music rising up to meet them. A man's operatic voice, clear, deep, and strong, was singing to the music of the large orchestra.

"That's my dad!" Mims called excitedly.

"Vonni Angelo?" Archie cried. "He's my mom's favorite singer! She has all his albums. You never said he was your dad!"

"You knew his name was Vonni. . . ."

"Yes, but I never imagined he'd be Vonni Angelo!" Archie cried.

As she glided over the large open-air arena, Freya listened to her uncle. His voice was enchanting, and it called to her. "He has the power of the Valkyries . . . ," she mused softly. Each note, each word seemed to hypnotize her and leave her powerless. The war, Brundi, all of it was forgotten as she got lost in the music.

The song ended, and the spell was broken. Beneath them, the crowds roared with applause. Freya was able to concentrate on finding a safe place to land.

"How about down there, on that small flat bit of roof over the stage?" Mims suggested. "I can't see anyone there, and with the lights shining out from the stage, we should be able to land without being seen."

Freya followed Mims's finger and agreed. Most of the roof curved like the high slope of the band shell, but to the right was an area where she could touch down safely. She tilted her wings and descended in the sky. "Hold on, everyone. This might get messy."

With Mims at the front and Archie on her back, a

smooth landing was impossible. Just as she pulled in her wings to touch down, Mims's feet got tangled in Freya's and they lost their balance. Freya, Archie, and Mims tumbled to the roof in a heap. They lay together laughing and moaning as they untangled themselves.

"Not your best landing." Archie laughed as he rose to his feet. "I'd give it a one out of ten!"

"*I haven't seen you do so badly in a very long time!*" Orus cawed, still laughing.

"That's not fair," Freya said. "I was carrying two people and this isn't a large roof."

"*Still . . . ,*" Orus teased.

Beneath them on the stage, Vonni started to sing again. Freya lay on the roof, unable to move as she was carried away by the music. She closed her eyes and became lost in the sound. "His voice is beautiful. . . ."

"My mom wasn't the only one who liked him," Archie said. "Vonni Angelo was one of the few things we didn't fight over."

Mims didn't look impressed. "It's just my dad. He sings in the shower all the time. We have to tell him to shut up."

When the song ended, Freya shook herself again. She pulled her coat on over her wings and looked around. "There's a door over there. Let's get inside before he starts singing again."

They reached the door and found it locked. Freya stepped

forward, and with one kick the door ripped off its hinges and went flying. Mims stared at her in surprise.

"You'll soon be that strong," Orus said as he settled on Freya's shoulder.

They found a set of stairs leading down to the back of the band shell. The area was filled with people.

"It's insane back here!" Archie cried.

"It's always like this at my dad's concerts," Mims said. She stepped forward and led them through the backstage area. They reached the side of the stage, where a crowd of people were watching the performance. Mims started to push through, but Freya held back.

"C'mon," Mims called. "I want to let my dad know we're here."

Freya shook her head. "I can't. There're too many people here. Someone might touch my hair or face. It's too much of a risk."

Mims's excitement vanished. She looked at the people, then back to Freya. "I have to start thinking like that, don't I?"

Freya nodded. "I'm afraid so. As Valkyries in the human world, we have to be constantly aware of who is around us. One accident could kill."

They decided to find Vonni's dressing room and wait for him there. As they made their way through the gangs of people loitering backstage, Mims bumped into someone from her father's entourage, who pointed them in the right direction.

The dressing room was small but filled with large bouquets of flowers and boxes of chocolates. Costumes were hanging on racks, and used clothes were discarded on the floor. There was a dressing table filled with buckets of ice and bottled water. Freya smiled when she saw a photograph of Sarah and Mims in a large silver frame.

"Dad takes that with him everywhere," Mims said.

"Wow." Archie was totally starstruck. "I can't believe we're in Vonni Angelo's dressing room. This is too cool!"

Orus cawed. *"You are standing with two powerful Valkyries and yet you find this music more exciting?"*

"Not more," Archie said. He grinned at Freya. "Well, maybe a bit more."

Freya stuck out her tongue at him.

Two large speakers hung from the wall. The sound of Vonni's voice filled the room. Deafening applause followed.

"We got here just in time. That's Dad's last song. He usually does one or two encores, runs through the audience to say hello, and then he's done."

A new song started and Freya drifted away with the music. She knew a Valkyrie's voice could charm humans. But she'd never imagined a sound could enchant a Valkyrie. Every note captivated her, weakened her, and left her unable to move.

Finally the encore finished and they heard Vonni thanking everyone and wishing them a safe journey home.

"He'll be here in a minute," Mims said as she rose, ready

to greet her father. She looked back at Freya. "Just give him a few minutes to relax before we tell him, okay?"

Freya nodded as they heard lots of voices and activity fill the hall outside the dressing room. Her heart fluttered with excitement. This was her uncle. Her mother's twin brother. Her family.

When the door opened she was struck by how much Vonni looked like her mother. He was taller than she expected. His hair was dark and brushed back with sweat, and his eyes were the deepest, sparkling blue. Freya realized he was perhaps the most attractive man she'd ever seen—even surpassing Azrael.

"No wonder Dark Searchers hide their faces," Archie muttered beside her. "If they're anything like him, the Valkyries don't stand a chance!"

"I felt you arrive even before they told me." Vonni scooped Mims up in his arms. "What a wonderful surprise!"

Vonni released his daughter and his eyes found Freya. He frowned and looked back at Mims, then to Freya again. "Hello."

Freya noticed Vonni's eyes flash to Archie for a moment before settling back on her. "Do you want to introduce me to your friend?"

"Dad, this is Greta," Mims said. "And that's Archie."

He looked down on her. "Archie?"

Mims nodded. "But don't be scared; he's a friendly ghost. He won't hurt you."

"You can see him?"

"Yes, she can." Freya walked forward and offered him her hand. "It's so wonderful to meet you. We have so much to talk about."

The dressing-room door opened and another man entered. "Hey, Von, the press is here. . . ." His eyes landed on Mims.

"Hiya, squirt," he said, ruffling her hair. "When did you get here?"

"Hi, Simon," Mims said. "Not too long ago. We wanted to surprise Dad."

"Did you hear those crowds? Your dad had three curtain calls and two standing ovations. We should have been booked here for a week!" He turned to Vonni. "The reporters are anxious to interview you. Can I steal you away from the girls for a few minutes?"

Vonni's eyes went back to Archie, then to Mims. "I'll only be a couple of minutes. Will you all wait here for me?"

"Sure, Dad," Mims said.

He kissed her on the top of the head and then followed Simon out of the dressing room. Immediately the hall outside was filled with applause and people cheering.

"This is so cool," Archie cried again. "My mom would freak out if she knew I'd met him."

"He's just my dad, Archie," Mims said. But her face beamed with pride.

With her uncle out of the room, Freya shook her head

and focused. She pulled the chair out from the dressing table and sat down backward on it. "He looks so much like my mother. He's absolutely beautiful."

"Beautiful?" Mims said. "Only women are beautiful. My dad's handsome."

Freya shook her head. "No, handsome isn't the right word for him. He's more than that—he's beautiful." She paused and looked at Archie. "Do you think that's why Odin sends them to Utgard to become Dark Searchers—because they're too beautiful?"

"Maybe," Archie agreed. "Without their helmets they'd be a big distraction to the Valkyries—they wouldn't want to go to the battlefields to reap! Unmasked Dark Searchers are even more dangerous than covered ones. They're super strong, and they can fly and charm anyone with one look. I bet they could take over all the realms without anyone raising a finger against them."

Freya recalled Dirian. "Did you notice Vonni's eyes? They were the same color as the Searcher's who killed me."

Mims stood in shock. "You were killed?"

Freya nodded and then told her cousin of the Ten Realms Challenge and her battle with Dirian. "I won the Challenge and my prize was this golden sword." She held up her flaming sword.

Archie added, "Dirian went ballistic and strangled Freya to death. But she came back to life that night. She's immortal."

"If you're immortal, am I?" Mims asked.

"I really don't know," Freya admitted. "Your father is, so you could be too."

At that moment, Vonni reentered the room. "Dad," Mims started. "We have a lot to talk about."

"We sure do." A frown creased his brow. "Like, does your mother know where you are? How on earth did you get here?"

"Don't worry, Dad," Mims said. "I was safe. I was with Greta and Archie."

"*And me,*" Orus added from Freya's shoulder.

Vonni's mouth hung open. "You can talk?"

Orus cawed, "*Just like Pym.*"

"What's going on here, Mims?" Vonni demanded. "Who are these people?"

"You'd better sit down, Dad. This may upset you."

"What will?"

"Me," Freya said. "I saw you notice the resemblance between me and Mims. And you're right. We are related. We're cousins."

"Mims has no cousins. Both Sarah and I are only children."

"*That's not completely true,*" Orus said. "*You have a sister—a twin sister.*"

"Don't be ridiculous," Vonni snapped. "I don't have a sister. It's always been just me and my mother."

"Your mother and you—for thousands of years," Freya said carefully. "You've lived a very long life in hiding. Always on the move and never forming long-term relationships. Yet Brundi never told you who you really were or where you came from?"

Freya felt his doubt was mixed with anger. She continued. "Please, Giovanni, believe us. We are not here to cause trouble for you. I'm your niece and I know more about you than you do. But when I tell you, you won't want to believe it."

His eyes fell on Mims. "Believe what?"

"Dad," Mims started. "Do you know what a Valkyrie is?"

He frowned again. "From Norse mythology? Sure—you remember how you hated it when I was practicing for the role of Siegfried, from Wagner's Ring Cycle opera? That was all about a Valkyrie."

"There's an opera about Valkyries?" Freya asked.

Vonni nodded. "It's the story of Brünnhilde, a Valkyrie who disobeyed Odin and was punished. She was banished to Earth—"

"That's Gran!" Mims cried. "Dad, I can't believe it! You've been singing about Gran?"

"What are you talking about?"

"Dad," Mims said gently. "Gran was a Valkyrie, a real one. Greta is one and . . . and I am too."

Silence filled the room as they awaited Vonni's reaction. The expression on his face was one of incomprehension, and then suddenly, out of nowhere, he burst out laughing. "Okay, you got me! You had me going there for a moment. Well done." He calmed and chuckled. "Now, seriously, tell me, how did you get here?"

"We're not joking," Freya said seriously. "If you have lived an immortal life, why do you find it so difficult to believe us? Your mother is a Valkyrie."

"Yes, I have lived a very long time," Vonni admitted. "And no, I can't explain it—"

"I can," Freya cut in. "Your mother served Odin until she fled Asgard to have you. Your twin sister still serves Odin and so do I. We all come from Asgard. We are all immortal. Brundi never told you because she was protecting you."

"*And she was angry at Odin,*" Orus added.

"Don't be ridiculous," Vonni replied, rising from the sofa. "Asgard doesn't exist. Odin doesn't exist. They're all just myths and fantasy."

"Gee, I think it's time to break out the wings," Archie suggested.

Freya regretted having to shock her uncle, but she needed to make him understand. Reluctantly, she removed her coat and fanned open her black wings.

"How are you doing that?" Vonni demanded. He reached out and touched them. He flexed one of her wings up and down and open and closed. Vonni trailed his hands up to where her wings joined her back. "I don't believe it," he said in astonishment. "This isn't a game? They're real?"

Mims took her father's hand in hers. "Dad, you need to

listen to us now. You know those big scars on your back?"

He could barely draw his eyes away from Freya's wings. He nodded.

Orus flew onto his shoulder. *"You used to have your own wings. They were cut off when you were a baby, to protect you."*

Vonni stared at Orus, shaking his head.

"Don't you shake your head at me," Orus cawed. *"It's true, and deep down inside you already know it! Your senses are telling you it's the truth, even if you don't want to believe it."*

"Dad," Mims said gently. "We're in terrible danger and we don't know what to do."

"What danger?" he asked.

"The worst kind," Freya said. "War in the realms is coming. Odin sent us back here to collect Brundi so she could be safe in Asgard. But he doesn't know about you or your family. If he did, it would be disaster for all of us."

Vonni sat down on the sofa, shaking. Freya could feel that he was excited, terrified, and profoundly curious. But deep inside, she felt his strength and determination rising to the surface. He looked up at her with his piercing blue eyes.

"Tell me everything."

12

MAYA AND HER SISTERS WATCHED THEIR MOTHER WEEP softly. There was so much information to take in and so much danger coming.

"Mother, we must warn Freya," Maya insisted. "Let her know about your brother and warn her not to tell Odin."

"It's too late. She's already gone," Eir said. "We could never catch her in time. Every nerve in my body screams to go to them, to fight Odin if I must, to protect my mother and brother. But to leave Asgard is to expose ourselves and expose them. All we can do is wait and hope that Freya does the right thing."

Maya knelt before her mother. "We can't risk it, Mother. Heimdall is a friend to this family. He'll let me cross Bifröst. I'll fly to Freya and warn her. She loves this family and will do anything to protect it. Together we can find a solution."

Eir shook her head. "It's too dangerous."

"Wait," Skaga said. "I know how we can get to Freya and still let Odin think we're working for him."

"How?" her sister Gwyn demanded.

Skaga crossed the room and knelt beside Maya. "There is a reaping later today, isn't there?"

"Yes," Eir said. "A small one, only a few Valkyries are going."

Skaga rose and started to pace. "Good. Mother, I want you to make sure that Maya, Gwyn, and I are among them."

"What about me?" Kara asked.

Skaga faced her remaining sister. "Kara, yours will be the hardest job of all. I want you to stay here and go about your business as you usually do. Hide your feelings deep inside. This will be very dangerous for all of us, but I think for you most."

"What are you planning?" Eir demanded.

Skaga smiled slyly. "I'm planning to save this family. If it works, Odin will never know. He'll think we're serving him. It will be risky, but it's the only way to save our family."

Eir rose and wiped her eyes. Her fighting spirit was restored as she reached for her sword. "Tell us your idea."

13

"I DON'T UNDERSTAND," VONNI SAID WHEN FREYA finished telling him his story. "If there has been peace all this time, why would the frost giants move against Odin now?"

"I don't know," Freya admitted. "We've been told there's a traitor in Asgard who's stirring up trouble. There has always been tension—that's why we have the Ten Realms Challenge, because of the wars in the past."

"We don't know for certain that there will be a war," Orus cawed. *"But if there is, Odin will want us all in Asgard."*

"Everyone except us," Mims said. "We have to hide."

Vonni rose and started to pace his dressing room. "All right, if there is a war, why would it involve us? Earth, I mean. Why not just go after Asgard? What do we have that the frost giants would want?"

Again Freya shrugged. "I went to Jotunheim, where Utgard is, when I was a small child. It's nothing but a frozen wasteland. Here it's beautiful, like Asgard. Maybe the giants would want it because of that."

"This just doesn't make sense," Vonni insisted. "Why now? Why, after all this time, has trouble started?" He sat down, but his sad eyes rested on Mims. "I'm so sorry, baby."

"About what?"

"You're a Valkyrie," he said sadly. "What kind of life have I condemned you to? Mother tried to warn me not to get involved with Sarah, but I wouldn't listen. I loved her, and nothing was going to stop me from marrying her. But in doing that, I have endangered my most precious girl."

"Dad, it's going to be okay," Mims said. "I was shocked when Greta first told me, but . . . I'm getting used to it." She paused. "I even wish I had wings like her."

"*Wings aren't all that great,*" Orus cawed. "*Look at Greta. She can't wear normal clothes and always walks like she's got a huge lump on her back. She can't run properly, and you should see her trying to play soccer—*"

"Orus, stop helping!" Freya cried. "I'm sure she gets the idea."

Vonni approached Freya. "I wish I didn't believe you, but I know you're telling the truth. I have lived such a long time in hiding—never letting anyone know about me or Mother, but I never imagined it would lead to this."

He combed his fingers through his dark hair. "I can't tell you the number of times I've asked Mother to tell me what we are. How we could live so long. 'We are what we are' was always her answer. Now we're facing a war of cosmic proportions and, despite all these powers I possess, I feel helpless."

"You're not helpless," Freya said. "We're here."

"Dad, we're gonna have to tell Mom," Mims said.

"Not a chance," he said. "Especially so close to the baby's arrival."

"You don't have much choice," Freya put in. "That child she is carrying is a boy—and he has wings."

"What?" Vonni cried.

Freya nodded. "There is no telling what might happen if anyone here finds out."

Archie agreed. "If the doctors discover his wings, they will take him away for research. With you and Mims too."

"They could try, but they'll never get past me. No one will ever dare touch my family."

They saw Vonni's Dark Searcher nature surface—strong, adamant, and determined.

"Calm down, Dad," Mims soothed. She looked at Freya. "He's got a really short temper."

"I do not!" Vonni fired back.

"He's a Dark Searcher all right," Archie said.

"A what? I am not a Dark Searcher—whatever they are! I am just a man."

"No, you're not just a man," Freya insisted. "You are the son of a Valkyrie. You were born to be one of Odin's enforcers, a Dark Searcher. Only Brundi's sacrifice saved you from that fate. But I feel the same power from you I felt from them. I bet you are amazingly strong and fast, right?"

"Perhaps," Vonni reluctantly agreed.

"And you've got powerful senses, and when you set your mind to something, nothing will stop you from reaching that goal."

"Maybe."

"Then you *are* a Dark Searcher," Freya finished. "And right now that's not a bad thing—if war comes, you will need all your powers to survive. But first you'll need to take your family into hiding. You must hide from Odin and possibly the giants, who could use you against him."

Vonni shook his head. "Are you sure my mother has to return to Asgard?"

"Odin expects her back. If she refuses, he will come here himself. And if he does . . ."

"He'll find out about Mims and me," Vonni finished.

"Exactly."

"Okay," he said, nodding his head. "Here's what we're going to do. First thing is I'm canceling the rest of my tour. We're going back to Valhalla Valley this very minute."

Freya looked him up and down. "I'm not sure I'm going to be able to carry you, too, for that distance."

Mims smiled her first genuine smile in days. "That's not going to be a problem. Trust me."

Freya rode with Mims, Vonni, and Archie in the back of a stretch limousine as they left the Hollywood Bowl. The progress was slow as they carefully drove through the screaming fans who were trying to catch a glimpse of Vonni Angelo through the darkened windows. Girls were attempting to open the doors while others held up autograph books.

"Is it always like this?" Archie asked, gazing in wonder at the fans.

Vonni nodded. "This, and much worse. But it's the price I pay for doing what I love."

When they arrived at the airport, Archie ran up to the private jet that was waiting for them in the center of the hangar. "Wow! Is that really yours?"

Vonni nodded and opened the airplane's hatch. "I've always had this thing about flying." He paused and gazed at Freya. "It must run in the family. I learned to fly not long after they were invented."

"You saw the invention of the airplane?"

Vonni nodded. "I've lived thousands of years. I've pretty much seen the invention of everything. Everyone, on board. We don't have a moment to waste."

Her first time in an airplane was not as exciting as Freya had expected. Many times she'd seen them in the sky and wondered what it was like. But from the moment they took off, she spent the whole flight terrified that the engines were going to fail. By the time they touched down on the private airstrip at Valhalla Valley, she wished she'd flown herself.

"Never again!" she cried as she stepped off the plane.

"I thought it was fun," Orus cawed. *"Watching you turn three shades of green was the best!"*

Freya looked at her raven. "This is why Odin gave us wings. So we wouldn't have to use those horrible machines!"

"You'll get used to it," Vonni promised as he walked beside his daughter. "Now, listen to me, Mims—you too, Greta. You are not to say anything about this to Sarah until we figure this out. I don't want her upset. I'll simply tell her that I canceled the tour because I wanted to spend time with her before the baby arrives. Is that understood?"

"Yes, Dad," Mims said.

"You'll have to tell her soon," Freya warned. "She's carrying a winged child. She must be prepared to have the baby here, not at a hospital. No doctor can ever see him."

"I know," Vonni said. He lifted his head and closed his eyes.

Freya recognized that posture. He was casting out his senses. Dark Searchers didn't have the power to reap, but they had all the other powers of the Valkyries—perhaps even more.

"That was the strangest thing. I thought I felt Mother for

a moment, but then it stopped." He checked his watch. "It's just past two a.m.; I think it's time we all went to bed."

"You go," Freya said. "I'll stay out and keep watch."

"You need your sleep, Greta," Vonni said. "The ranch is fine. Go to bed."

Freya smiled at her uncle. He was sounding every bit the father. "Here in Midgard, I don't need to sleep. I'll be fine. You go in. I'll see you in the morning."

When they were gone, Freya and Archie made their way to Brundi's platform.

"He's the coolest Dark Searcher ever," Archie said.

"He sure is," Freya agreed. She looked back at the house, envious of what Mims had in her life. She had two loving parents and an extended family that cared deeply for each other. Meeting Vonni made her long to know more about her own father. When this was over, she was going to insist that her mother introduce her to him.

The next morning Sarah was ecstatic to find Vonni home. Freya didn't need to use her senses to know how much Sarah loved him and was grateful to have him back—she could see it from the glow in her face.

It was the same for him. Freya would never have guessed that a Dark Searcher could care so deeply. As the day progressed, she found herself almost pitying the Searchers of Utgard and the lives they'd been denied.

Throughout the day, Freya worried about Brundi. There

was no time to waste—they had to get back to Asgard before Odin came after them. But as the sun started to set, there was still no trace of her.

At nightfall, Freya and Archie stood near the platform and opened her senses. "She's nowhere near us. I really hope she comes back."

"You don't think she's run away because she doesn't want to go back to Asgard?" Archie asked.

Mims and Vonni joined them. "She would never abandon us," Mims insisted. "I'm sure she's just spending some time alone with Pym and Jonquil."

"It's not just Brundi I'm worried about," Freya said. "Odin expects us back. He only gave us a couple of days. We must return soon."

"He wouldn't really come here, would he?" Mims asked fearfully.

"*Not yet,*" Orus cawed. "*But he might send someone to look for us.*"

Freya looked at the raven. "Not another Dark Searcher. He knows where we are and what we're doing. He'd have no reason to send one."

"What if I talked to him?" Vonni offered. "I know there's a danger in that, but surely he's reasonable."

"No!" Freya, Archie, and Orus shouted as one.

"That would expose Brundi's big lie," Freya continued. "I don't think he'd forgive her that—even with the war coming."

"Then we've got to find her." Vonni looked out over the dense woods. "All day I've been feeling her for a few moments, but then the feeling goes. She is near. I know it. But just when I think I've got her tracked, she disappears again. It's all very strange."

"Have you ever felt her like this before?" Freya asked.

"Never," Vonni said. "I've always known exactly where she is—where everyone I care for is, even when we're continents apart. But this is so weird."

"What could it mean?" Archie asked.

"I don't know," Vonni responded. "That's what's got me so worried."

14

MAYA CREPT INTO THE STABLE OF THE REAPING MARES
once she was certain there was no one around to see her. In
her hand she carried a small bag containing sweets that had
been covered in a powerful sleeping potion. She offered the
treats to Lutna, her mare. The large, gray Reaping Mare took
them eagerly, licking all traces off her hand. Maya stroked
her neck and leaned her head against Lutna's.

"Forgive me, Lutna," she whispered softly, giving her a
light kiss. "But I have no choice."

In moments, Lutna's eyes grew cloudy. She started to stagger
on her feet. Lutna nickered softly as she collapsed into the straw.
Maya entered her stall and took a few moments to ensure that
her mare was safe and sleeping comfortably. Then she slipped
silently out of the stables and flew back to her home.

Her mother and sisters were waiting for her, dressed in their battle armor, prepared for the reaping.

"It's done," Maya said grimly as she reached for her armor and helmet. "I hope she'll be all right. If anything happens to Lutna, I'll never forgive myself."

"It wasn't that powerful a dose. She'll be fine," Eir said before addressing her daughters. "We all know what we're doing." She turned to Kara and embraced her tightly. "We'll be back soon. Just go about your work as you normally do. We can't risk anyone becoming suspicious."

"I understand," Kara said. "Good luck, everyone. Tell Freya I'm thinking of her."

Maya finished drawing the gauntlets up her arm. "We will. We'll be back as soon as we can."

Eir crossed to the flight balcony and opened her wings. "Come, my daughters. It is time for the reaping."

They arrived at the stables of the Reaping Mares, where a few other Valkyries were already gathered and waiting for them. Mist, an elder Valkyrie, jogged up to Maya.

"Come quickly! Something is wrong with Lutna. She won't wake up."

Maya put on an expression of deep concern and followed her into the stable. She threw open the door to Lutna's stable and knelt beside her mare, stroking her neck and face.

"Mother, she is unwell," she called to her mother. "I can't go on the reaping today. I must stay with her."

"Maya, you can't stay," Eir said sternly. "You have not gone on one reaping since Odin's punishment ended." The head of the Valkyries entered the stall and inspected the sleeping mare.

"Lutna is breathing well. I'll have someone come and check on her. But you will not miss this reaping." She rose and looked over to Sylt. "For now, take your sister's mare. Freya is doing Odin's work and doesn't need her."

"But Sylt doesn't like me," Maya protested.

"She will do as you command," Eir said. "Now, come. Stop wasting time. We must go!"

Maya gave Lutna a final pat and rose. She approached Sylt's stall and freed her sister's mare. She led her out of the stables, walking beside the other Valkyries.

Mist smiled at her in sympathy. "Do not fear. I'm sure Lutna will be fine."

Maya leaned closer to the older Valkyrie. "I hope so. I just wish Mother would let me stay with her. She's always so harsh."

"You know your mother," Mist said. "It's all work, work, work. It would take a Dark Searcher to stop her from leading a reaping."

Maya nodded. "I think you're right—it *would* take a Dark Searcher." She climbed up on Sylt's back and joined the other Valkyries heading to the Rainbow Bridge. They arrived and approached the Watchman of Bifröst.

"Greetings, Heimdall," Eir said formally as she bowed in respect. "We come in the service of Odin for the reaping."

"Greetings, Valkyries." Heimdall also responded formally, bowing. He swept his arm broadly to invite them onto the bridge. "Journey well."

After her mother and three other Valkyries stepped onto the bright colors of the bridge, Heimdall approached Maya and frowned. "Where is Lutna?"

"She is unwell. Mother wouldn't let me stay with her and insisted I use Freya's Reaping Mare instead."

Heimdall gave Sylt a gentle pat and smiled up at her. "I am sure your mare will recover. In the meantime, Sylt will serve you well."

Maya shrugged. "I hope you're right." As she led Sylt onto the bridge, she pulled on her winged helmet and called back to him, "See you later."

Once they crossed the bridge, Maya had Sylt join her sisters and mother at the head of the group. Bifröst had let them off over the ocean, and they had a long flight ahead of them. This gave Maya plenty of time to consider all the ways the plan could go wrong. Her heart was pounding violently in her chest and her hands were wet with nervous sweat. Everything was riding on this, and she daren't make a mistake.

Skaga was riding her Reaping Mare beside Maya, but refused to meet her eyes. Her posture let Maya know that her sister was as nervous as she was and probably thinking the same thing. The plan was risky at best. What if Sylt didn't react properly? What if others tried to follow? How could they get away without being caught?

Eventually they approached the appointed place of the reaping. Smoke was rising from the hot, arid ground, and the sounds of gunfire rang out. The dry desert air filled Maya's nostrils as they grew closer to the battleground.

As her mother started to howl the Valkyrie cry and the others joined in, Maya carefully pulled out her dagger. Her voice rose louder and harder than her sisters' as she waited for the perfect moment to strike.

Death was all around as a terrible battle raged beneath her. But all Maya could think about was the plan.

"Wait . . . ," she ordered herself.

The Valkyries started to descend to the place of reaping.

"Wait . . . wait."

The howling increased.

"Now!"

Maya winced as she plunged the tip of her dagger into Sylt's shoulder.

Freya's Reaping Mare cried out in pain and started to buck in the sky. Maya lost her grip on the reins and caught hold of Sylt's mane. But the mare would not stop. Shrieking in pain, Sylt went wild—her wings flapped madly and she flew completely out of control.

"Maya!" Skaga cried. She commanded her own mare to

put on more speed and flew closer to her mother. "Look!" she cried loudly. "Maya's in trouble! Sylt has gone mad!"

Eir looked back at her daughter, fighting to stay on the Reaping Mare. "Go to her!" Eir called, loud enough for all the Valkyries to hear. "Help her! We'll meet you at the reaping or at Bifröst!"

Skaga directed her Reaping Mare away from the group, chasing after Maya while Sylt flew wildly across the sky.

Suddenly Maya was tossed off the Reaping Mare's back. She tumbled and somersaulted in the sky before opening her wings and regaining control. "Sylt, stop!" she cried as she chased after the fleeing Reaping Mare.

Maya stole a quick look back and saw Skaga following closely behind her. But then her fear rose as she watched Mist direct her Reaping Mare away from the battle to follow Skaga.

"No. Stay away. . . ." Maya cursed as she struggled to keep up with Sylt.

Suddenly Gwyn arrived. Her move was a masterpiece. She made it look like she was in a panic to help Maya, but instead she managed to fly her Reaping Mare directly into the side of Mist's mare. The collision was sloppy and noisy and sent both mares and Valkyries tumbling in the sky!

"Thank you, Gwyn . . . ," Maya muttered as she watched her older sister and Mist finally correct themselves and regain control of their mounts.

"Gwyn, Mist, come!" Eir commanded as she led the remaining Valkyries down to the reaping. Skaga was the only Valkyrie sent after Maya to help her regain control of the bucking Sylt.

As all the other Valkyries descended into the smoke-filled battle to do their work, Maya flew harder to catch up with Sylt. She caught hold of Sylt's reins and settled on her back once again. Reaching forward, she patted the Reaping Mare's neck. "You're all right, Sylt. Just calm down, girl."

Gazing back, she saw that Skaga was directly behind her. "Maya, go!" she called.

Maya leaned forward on the Reaping Mare and gave the command. "Sylt, find Freya!" she called loudly. "Take us to Freya!"

15

"I CAN'T PUT MY FINGER ON IT, BUT I FEEL SOMETHING IS very wrong," Vonni said. "It's like Mother keeps appearing and disappearing, but it's not clear where. I feel she is blocking me."

It was past midnight, and Freya was standing with Vonni and Archie near the platform. The house was dark and everyone had gone to bed.

"Dark Searchers are the best trackers in all the realms," Freya explained. "I can't feel her at all. Try to focus. Let your senses tell you where she is."

Vonni closed his eyes and raised his head. "I can feel her again! She's very angry. . . ." He paused. "Wait. I'm picking up something else." He opened his eyes and scanned the dark, star-studded sky. "There's something out there. . . ."

Freya felt her sisters long before she saw them. "My sisters?"

Through the moonlit sky they could make out two Reaping Mares approaching swiftly. Freya saw that Sylt was one of them, while the other belonged to her sister Skaga.

"They've got flying horses?" Vonni cried as both mares touched down.

Freya nodded. "They're called Reaping Mares. We use them to bring the dead to Asgard." She ran forward. "Maya, Skaga! What are you doing here? Is Odin coming after us?"

Maya said nothing but indicated Vonni.

Freya looked back at her uncle, then to her sisters again. "It's all right. You can take off your helmets—Vonni can already see you."

Skaga's eyes narrowed. She leaned down to Freya. "We must speak—privately."

"You really are Valkyries?" Vonni gasped as he took in the flying horses, their armor, and the winged helmets they held in their hands.

"I told you we were," Freya said.

"Yes, but, in all honesty, you don't look like one. Had I first seen you like I'm seeing them, there would have been no question."

Maya and Skaga climbed down from their mares.

"Who is this?" Skaga demanded, suspiciously eyeing Vonni. "How could he see us when we had our helmets on?"

"This is Vonni. His true name is Giovanni. He is the son

of Brünnhilde and is a Dark Searcher. He's our mother's twin brother."

"He's not a Dark Searcher," Maya insisted. "He looks nothing like them."

Freya nodded. "Trust me, he is. All the boys born to Valkyries are Dark Searchers. They're taken to Utgard to be trained. The only difference is that Vonni was raised here and not at the keep, and in order to keep a low profile, his mother had his wings cut off."

"This can't be true," Skaga cried. "There's no way we're related to the Dark Searchers. Not when Valkyries and Searchers hate each other as much as they do."

"And they shouldn't," Freya insisted. "We're all the same."

"I'm not a Dark Searcher," Vonni protested. "I keep telling you that. I'm just a man."

"*A man born of a Valkyrie*," Orus cawed. "*Thus, you are a Dark Searcher.*"

Maya and Skaga looked sharply at each other. "How did you know Mother had a twin?"

"I've known for some time," Freya said. "What's more, Vonni has a daughter, and his wife is about to have their son."

"First you expect us to believe that he's a Dark Searcher. Now you're saying he has a wife and children?" Skaga gasped. "That's impossible!"

"How many times must I say it? I am not a Dark Searcher!" Before Orus could speak, Vonni held up a warning finger. "Don't say it—I am not one of Odin's enforcers. I am me, nothing more." He turned to Skaga again. "Now, tell me, did Odin send you? Has my mother's deception been discovered?"

Maya smiled radiantly at him. If anyone could calm her angry uncle, Freya knew it would be Maya. "No. Our mother sent us to protect you. And of course you're not a Dark Searcher. They are dangerous and vicious; you are not."

Vonni stepped closer to her. "And you are?"

"Maya," she said. She turned back to her older sister. "This is Skaga. You must forgive her rudeness; we didn't expect to find you here with Freya."

Vonni frowned at Freya. "You told me your name is Greta."

"That is the name I give to humans in Midgard. I'm sure Brundi must have told you our true names have great power. We daren't share them with humans. I am Greta when I'm here. Maya is Mia and Skaga is . . ." Freya looked at her sister and shrugged.

Skaga's face softened. "In Midgard, I am called Sky."

"Please, while we're here, you must only use our Midgard names," Freya insisted.

"I understand," Vonni said. "What I don't understand is why you are here."

Freya agreed. "And how did you get past Heimdall?"

Archie grinned at Maya. "What did you promise him?"

"Look," Skaga interrupted, "we don't have a lot of time to discuss this. Mother is keeping the other Valkyries occupied while we're here, but we must return to the battlefield or Asgard before we're missed. Where is Brünnhilde?"

"Her Midgard name is Brundi," Freya said. "We don't know where's she's gone."

Archie added, "She's flown off on her Reaping Mare. She told us not to follow her."

"We have another problem," Orus added. *"Loki is here. He knows all about Brundi, Vonni, and the family."*

"Loki?" Maya cried, while her raven Grul cawed in distress. "How did he find them?"

Vonni looked at Freya and frowned. "Wait a minute. Are you saying the Loki I've known all my life is the same Loki from Norse mythology? The god of Mischief?"

Freya nodded, then looked to her sisters. "It's hard to believe, but it appears that Loki has been helping them ever since Odin's banishment."

"He's like a brother to me," Vonni insisted.

"Loki?" Maya cried, aghast.

"Yes, Loki," Vonni defended. "He's part of my family."

Skaga gazed around at the house, barns, and outbuildings. "Right now our only concern is finding Brünnhilde. Odin is expecting her back in Asgard. She must return to keep you safe."

"We know!" Freya said in exasperation. "I told her already—she knows all about the coming war. But we don't know where she is!"

"What war?" Skaga asked.

"The war in the realms," Freya started. "There's a traitor in Asgard. They've brokered a truce between the frost and fire giants and are planning to attack. That's why Odin wants Brundi back. He is preparing for war."

Skaga and Maya were shocked into silence.

"How do you know all this? First about the Searchers and now the war?" Grul demanded.

"I promised I wouldn't say, but I swear it's true," Freya said.

Orus cawed, *"It doesn't matter how we know. What does matter is that it's coming and we must prepare!"*

While Freya and Archie filled them in as best they could, Vonni drifted away, his head lifted and his eyes closed. "Wait, Mother is near. She is . . . No!"

Vonni dashed back to Freya. "Mother's been hurt. I can feel it. You must help me get to her!"

Skaga immediately took charge. "Archie, you and Vonni ride Sylt. She knows you and will accept you. Freya, you, Maya, and I will fly." She focused on Vonni. "You will have to lead us."

"How?" Vonni asked desperately. "I can only feel her pain; it is blocking out everything else!"

Skaga spoke softly. "Listen to me. I know you're frightened

for your mother—but fear will blind you to her. You must force it down. Calm yourself and reach out with your senses. They will lead you to her."

Vonni took several shaky breaths and closed his eyes. Finally he shook his head. "I can't!"

Orus flew to his shoulder and nipped him painfully on the ear. *"Stop denying your true self. Dark Searchers are the best trackers in all the realms. No one can escape a Searcher once they are on your trail. You are a Dark Searcher. Now, use those powers of yours and find Brundi!"*

Vonni's face contorted as he struggled to call forth a part of himself he'd been denying. He calmed, and his expression was replaced with a look of great determination as he approached Sylt.

"She's that way," he pronounced.

Within moments, everyone was in the air. As Vonni led the way, Freya started to feel traces of her grandmother. She was in terrible pain.

When they crested the tallest mountain on the property, Vonni pointed. "Down there—to our old gold mine!"

Tilting their wings, they all prepared to land. Sylt was the first to touch down, followed by Freya and her two sisters. Up ahead, they saw the wooden framework at the entrance of the closed gold mine. Fresh supporting planks had been erected around the entrance, and tents were set up around it.

Brundi was lying on the ground in a heap. Her chest was covered in blood.

"Mother!" Vonni cried as he dashed forward.

Jonquil was on the ground beside her, a deep shotgun wound in her side.

"Vonni, help her!" Pym cried as he stayed with the fallen Valkyrie. *"She's been shot by intruders. They shot Jonquil, too!"*

Freya instinctively knew they weren't alone. Before she could speak, Skaga pointed to the mine and shouted, "The cowards who did this are in there. They are frightened and fleeing! I will give them something to fear!"

Skaga was the first to move, drawing her sword and charging into the old mine. Maya was directly behind her and called back to Freya, "Stay here and keep them safe. There are more men around us. Use your sword if you must, but don't touch them or reap them directly!"

"I know that!" Freya shouted back. "Just go, and be careful!"

"Gee, come here!" Archie cried. He was standing beside Vonni. "She's been hurt really bad."

As she lay cradled in Vonni's lap, Brundi's eyes flickered open. "Don't move, Mother. I'm here," Vonni said gently, stroking her furrowed brow.

Brundi coughed. "I have fought so long to keep you safe, my beautiful boy, but now I must go." Her weak eyes focused on Freya. "Take me back to Asgard. Let me die there. Odin must never know of Vonni or the children."

Fear gripped Freya's heart. "You won't die, Brundi. You're a Valkyrie; you can't die unless Odin permits it, and he won't. He loves all his Valkyries, including you."

Brundi shook her head. "I am old and have lived in Midgard far too long. My powers of healing are gone. I will not rise again. My life is finished."

"Mother, no." Vonni clutched her tightly.

"Gee," Archie whispered. "She can't die, can she?"

"I don't know. . . ." Freya rose and looked around. She could feel others approaching. Their intentions were not good.

"Vonni, stay with Brundi. I'm not going to let them get you." She looked at Archie and drew her golden sword. "Come with me—three men are heading this way."

Her senses told her the intruders were still together. They were determined to get back to the mine.

"They're terrified," Freya said. "I don't know why. They couldn't have seen us yet."

"Maybe they saw more wolves," Archie suggested as his eyes panned the area.

"No. That would be fear. This is pure terror."

Freya crept deeper into the woods. It was strangely quiet, with no sounds of wild animals. As they walked, she felt and heard movement ahead. "There." She pointed and spoke to Archie. "Can you go to them and tell me what they are doing? And remember, they can't see or hear you."

Archie nodded. "I wish I had my sword." He ran ahead. "Gee, they've all got shotguns. They're hunting something. Be careful. They look ready to shoot at anything that moves."

Freya stalked forward to where the men were clustered together. Their flashlight beams were trembling through the darkness, and Freya could see they each held a gun at the ready. She needed to know who they were and where they came from.

She was about to charge them when roars filled the air, causing the men to bolt toward the mine with their guns raised.

Four men were running from the mine, screaming, as Skaga and Maya chased them, wings open and swords held high. Directly behind the Valkyries emerged the head of a huge black dragon. With eyes blazing gold, it looked almost too big, as it wormed its large, scaled body through the opening.

Freed from the confines of the mine, the dragon rose to its full height, taller than the trees, and opened its leathery wings. Roaring, it exposed its deadly teeth as flames shot out of its nostrils.

Gunfire exploded as the men in the trees opened fire on the dragon and the Valkyries. Skaga was hit and collapsed to the ground.

"No!" Freya howled, rushing the men from behind. Her sword flashed, and the man who shot Skaga fell.

In the next moment, an Angel of Death appeared. Freya gave him a quick, respectful nod. "He's all yours!"

More angels arrived as Freya charged into the clearing. But before she could use her sword again, the dragon's fire made quick work of the other men. The fight was over in seconds. The angels moved in, collected the men, and vanished.

Freya used her sword to direct the two survivors out of the woods and forced them to the ground at the dragon's feet. When the huge monster inhaled deeply for another fire attack, she held up her hand.

"No! Leave them. We need to know why they're here." She turned to the men with barely contained fury. "Don't move a muscle or that dragon will turn you into charcoal."

She made it to Skaga just as Maya was helping her to her feet. Her sister's silver breastplate had protected her from serious injury, but not from the pain. "I should have kept my helmet on so they wouldn't see me," she complained as she brushed off dirt and leaves and settled the ruffled feathers on her wings.

Vonni was still by his mother's side. Brundi was unconscious and her breathing was labored. With one eye on the dragon, Vonni tried to soothe his mother, but as the dragon began to approach, he jumped up. "What is that thing?"

"That's enough, Loki," Skaga warned the dragon. "It's over."

"Loki?" Vonni cried.

The dragon shimmered and then shrank back into Loki's

human form. He knelt beside Brundi and took her hand. "You will be fine, dear lady," he said gently as he inspected her deep wounds. He looked at Vonni. "She's badly hurt. We must go."

Vonni knelt by his mother, unable to move as his wide eyes studied Loki.

"Von," Loki snapped. "It's me! Now, help me lift her. I'm taking her home."

"To Asgard?" Freya asked.

"Asgard is not her home," Loki said. "Valhalla Valley is." Without another comment, Loki turned back into the dragon. With Brundi supported in one huge claw, he picked up Jonquil in the other and carried them away.

"What about these two?" Archie called.

Vonni was shaking with shock and rage as he rose and stalked toward the two cowering men. He hoisted one of them up by the collar. Freya and her sisters were right behind him, with their wings open and their swords drawn and held at the ready.

The men's wild eyes were terrified as they stared at the Valkyries. "What—what are you?" they demanded. "Th-that dragon, it was real, wasn't it?"

"I'm asking the questions!" Vonni snapped. "Who are you? Why are you here?"

"Answer him or you will feel the point of my sword!" Skaga shouted harshly. "I am in no mood to play games with humans!"

Within minutes they had the whole story. A friend had told them about the old gold mine and had said that he had been sneaking onto the property at night to investigate it. They discovered that the mine still contained a fortune in gold. They were trespassing to extract as much as they could.

"You came here with weapons," Vonni charged.

"We were told you wouldn't let anyone open the mine, and you'd go after anyone who tried," one of the men said. "We need our weapons for protection. That crazy old woman keeps wolves and other predators here—but we never expected a dragon or them flying girls! What kind of insane place is this?"

"This is private property, that's what it is!" Vonni spat. "You have no right to be here!"

"There's a fortune in gold here," the other man cried. "It's not right that you get to keep it all for yourself! You gotta share it."

Vonni was shaking. "You shot my mother because of gold? My wife and daughter live here!" His hands encircled the man's neck. "I can feel your thoughts; you would have tried to kill them too if they came around here!" As rage took over, Vonni started to squeeze.

"Vonni, no!" Freya cried, catching him by the arm. "Think of Brundi. She's hurt, and we have to get back to her. . . ."

Vonni's blazing eyes fixed for a moment on Freya. Finally

he calmed and released his deadly grip on the man's throat. "Leave here—now," he rasped. "Just go. Leave Idaho. If I ever hear of either of you returning, I will feed you both to that dragon!"

Throwing them down, Vonni stormed over to Sylt. He climbed on, roared furiously, and directed the Reaping Mare into the sky.

"And he says he's not a Dark Searcher," Orus cawed to Freya. *"Who does he think he's kidding?"*

"You have made a grave mistake here, humans," Skaga warned as her wings fluttered in anger. "This property is protected by us. If you or your friends ever return here, we will show no mercy. This mine is closed and will remain that way."

"But—but you're angels. You're not supposed to kill."

"We're no angels," Skaga said. "You would do well to remember that. So stay away, do you understand me?"

The men gazed fearfully at the winged Valkyries and nodded.

"Let's go," Skaga ordered her sisters as she opened her wings and launched into the air to follow Vonni.

16

VALHALLA VALLEY WAS IN AN UPROAR BY THE TIME
the Valkyries arrived. The dragon's roaring arrival with Brundi
and Jonquil had awoken everyone. The porch lights were
blazing, and everyone was out on the lawn, staring in disbelief
at Loki and Vonni as they knelt by Brundi. The Valkyries,
landing in full view, only added to the mass confusion.

Sarah and Mims came down from the porch. Sarah stared
openmouthed at Freya and her sisters and jumped when she
saw Sylt flutter her wings. "What are you?"

"There's no time to explain," Vonni said. "We need to
help Mother."

Sarah's shaking hand held a cell phone. "I'm—I'm calling the doctor."

"Please don't!" Vonni said. "No doctors. Not for us."

Sarah shook her head. "I don't understand what's going on here, but, Von, your mother's been shot! She needs a doctor."

He put his arm around her and softened his tone. "I know. But we can't call a doctor. We've been fortunate with Mims that she's never needed one. It's just too risky. We're . . . we're not human."

Sarah's wide eyes stared up at him. "That's insane. Of course you are."

"No, we're not," Vonni said seriously.

Sarah took a fearful step back. "What are you?"

Vonni reached out and cupped her face in his hands. "I'm the man who has lived a thousand years but only now found love—in you." He kissed her tenderly and then bent down to lift his unconscious mother. "Please, Sarah, I'll tell you everything. But first, help me get Mother inside to see how bad it is."

Loki and Sarah stayed close as Vonni carried Brundi into the house.

Freya and her two sisters were left standing outside, fully exposed and facing the large group of frightened people.

"Please," Freya called gently. "Don't be frightened of us. We are family. Brundi is our grandmother and Vonni is our uncle. We mean you no harm."

Mims joined her. "It's true, they won't hurt us. I've known about Greta since she got here. You don't have to be afraid.

Yes, she's got wings, but she's still just like us." She looked back at Maya and Skaga. "I'm Mims."

"I am so happy to meet you, cousin." Maya embraced her.

"We are family—we are finally united." Skaga smiled behind them.

Tash came forward and smiled at Freya. "At least I now know why you're always wearing that stupid coat in the middle of summer."

Freya grinned. "You don't know how hot it was! But it was the only way to keep my wings hidden."

"You don't have to hide from us anymore," said George, the ranch's vet. He and John offered their hands to the Valkyries. "You may look like angels, but if you're kin to Brundi, you're kin to us."

Freya smiled warmly at the men but held up her hands. "I promise you all, we are here to help. But we must warn you. No one must ever touch our bare hands or skin. . . ."

"Or their feathers," Mims added. She stood with her cousins. "We're Valkyries. Our touch is death to you."

Beside them, Jonquil stirred and let out a pain-filled whinny. Her wing flapped as she tried to rise. Sylt and Skaga's Reaping Mare were beside her and nickered anxiously.

George's eyes were huge as he ran over to the fallen mare and looked back at Freya. "Is it safe to touch her?"

"Yes," Freya said. "It's only us you can't touch."

He looked at the others, suddenly becoming all business.

"Everyone, snap out of it! John, go get my medical kit. Ben, you and Tash get a large bucket of warm water. And I'll need more lights. If this is Brundi's mare, we want her up and moving by the time Brundi wakes."

With the Reaping Mares being cared for, the Valkyries arrived at Brundi's bedroom just as Sarah was coming out. She was carrying a bowl of bright-red water and soiled cloths. Her eyes were sunken and she looked exhausted.

"Sarah, you must stop," Freya said gently. "You must think of the baby. Please go and rest. We're here—let us help Brundi."

Sarah shook her head. "I don't care if she's human or not. Brundi has been as much a mother to me as she is to Vonni. You won't tear me away from her." Her eyes grew hard as she faced Freya. "Everything was perfect until you came. Why did you have to ruin everything?"

Sarah's pain and fear were obvious. Her simple life had been destroyed, and she was angry. Freya responded as kindly as she could. "We came to protect you. There is more going on here than you know. But I promise you, hurting this family is the last thing I wanted."

"Mom, don't blame Greta," Mims said. "She's telling the truth. She came to help us."

Sarah sighed and lowered her head. "I'm sorry. I didn't mean that. I'm just tired and worried."

The Valkyries entered the room. Vonni was beside the

bed, bandaging his mother's wounds. Loki was handing him tape for the bandages.

"How is she?" Skaga asked, approaching the bed.

"Not good," Vonni said. "She's lost a lot of blood. We've been so careful for so long. In all our centuries, we've never really been hurt. But here, on our own ranch, men came and shot my mother. I won't stand for it."

Loki rose. "Brundi woke briefly. She's asked us to take her back to Asgard. She insists it's the only way to protect the family."

Freya looked over at the pale face of her grandmother. "If there were any other way . . ."

"I know," Vonni agreed sadly. "But if there's any hope of saving her, it will be there, not here. We should wait a bit before we move her. The bleeding is just slowing down. I don't want her wounds to open again."

When Sarah returned, Vonni invited her to sit. As they waited for Brundi to stabilize before they moved her, he asked the Valkyries to stay as he started to explain his life.

Freya and Archie were fascinated to learn all the things that Vonni and Brundi had lived through and the many wars Vonni had fought in.

"I have seen the Valkyries before, you know," he said. "It was in France, hundreds of years ago." Vonni's eyes became distant. "A good friend of mine had been wounded. There were dead all around us. I remember picking up Olivier when I heard the call of the Valkyries. I didn't realize what they were at the time. But then I felt something strange. I turned and saw this beautiful winged woman. I thought she was an angel. She was staring at me, and somehow—I don't know how—I knew her. But when I called to her and tried to approach, she told me to go."

"That was our mother," Maya said. "She just told us this story. That was when she realized you were her twin brother."

"If she knew I was her brother, why did she fly away from me?"

"She had to, to protect you," Maya said. "She couldn't let Odin know about you. But she says she's felt you all this time."

"And I've felt her," Vonni said. "I have searched for her my whole life and I've felt her often. But I never saw her again."

Loki nodded. "There is a powerful bond between siblings." His eyes settled on Freya with extra intensity as he tilted his head to the side. "Especially between twins. I've heard it said many times that when they are separated, twins can still feel each other, even if they've never met." He looked back at Vonni. "Just like you felt Eir, and she felt you."

Freya inhaled sharply as realization blazed within her. Her head started to spin and the room was too hot and stuffy. She staggered on her feet. *"Twins feel each other, even if they've never met. . . ."*

Her mother had a twin brother she'd always felt. Suddenly Freya understood what Loki meant about her knowing the answer. Her mother wasn't the only twin. The white-winged Dark Searcher . . . They had touched on the battle-field, and in that moment, Freya knew it as clearly as she knew her own name.

He was her twin brother!

"Are you okay, Gee?" Archie asked. "You look like you've just seen a ghost. . . ." He corrected himself. "I mean another ghost, not me."

"I—I'm fine," Freya stuttered. "It's just very hot in here."

Loki studied her closely. When she caught him watching her, he nodded slightly, confirming her thoughts.

A world of understanding exploded in Freya's mind. The feelings of loneliness she'd carried all her life, the sense that part of her was missing, her restlessness. It was all right there. Suddenly she yearned to speak to Loki—to ask him a million questions about her brother. She needed to know why, if he'd known about her brother, he hadn't said anything sooner.

"This is so sad," Sarah was saying. "You both knew of each other but could never meet."

Mims approached Loki. "Where have you and Gran been? What were you doing at the mine?"

Loki gazed down at Brundi again, and there was genuine pain in his eyes. "She knew she had to return to Asgard. Before she left, she needed to make sure there was a safe hid-ing place for the family. Gold has shielding power. Brundi believed, with all the gold still in the mine, that no one from the other realms would feel Vonni or Mims in there."

"It worked," Vonni said. "I kept feeling Mother, but then she would disappear. It must have been when she was deep in the mine." He shook his head. "But we can't hide in there. That cursed mine is unsafe. It's a tomb that has taken too many lives already."

Vonni sighed heavily, gazing at Sarah. "That mine is where this family made its fortune. It's filled with gold and other precious minerals. It paid for the property and helped us build Valhalla Valley into the sanctuary that it is. But there was a big collapse almost a hundred years ago. So many men who worked for me died there. That's why we closed it and swore it would never be opened again."

"Brundi knew that's how you felt, but it's the only safe place for you," Loki insisted. "You must rebuild the supports and make a home for yourselves in there."

"What are you talking about?" Sarah demanded. "Why does Von have to hide?"

"It's not just me," Vonni corrected her. "It's all of us. We must hide." He took his wife's hand and started to explain about Odin, Brundi's deception, and finally about the impending war in the realms.

Sarah shook her head and wiped away tears. "I don't want to believe that my husband has lived thousands of years, or that my own daughter is a Valkyrie—I want to run away screaming, but I can't." Her eyes landed on Freya and her sisters. "I look at you and see it's true. Why didn't Brundi tell us who she really was?"

"Her old life was over," Loki explained. "Brundi wanted nothing more to do with Odin or Asgard—she wanted to keep her past as far away from Vonni as possible. She succeeded all this time. Were it not for this unfortunate situation between the giants and Odin, none of this would have happened. But it has. And to keep everyone safe, we must move you into that mine just in case the tension between Odin and the other realms escalates into war. If the frost or fire giants ever invaded Midgard, they would sense you and take you as hostages against Odin."

"What about the men who shot Brundi?" Maya asked. "We left two of them alive. We warned them not to return, but what if they come back with more men?"

"Let's try it the human way first. I'll go into town and talk to the police," Vonni said. "I'm Vonni Angelo, the famous singer. Maybe that can get us more protection."

"And if that fails?" Skaga asked.

Vonni's expression darkened. "If that fails and if they dare come back, then I shall make them regret the day they crossed a Dark Searcher."

17

JUST BEFORE NOON BRUNDI WAS PREPARED TO RETURN
to Asgard. Cradled in Vonni's arms, she remained unconscious. With a heavy heart, he carried her out of the house.

"Will you come back and tell us what happened?" Mims
begged.

Freya felt very sorry to be saying good-bye to her cousin.
It was as if she were leaving a sister behind. "I will try. Jonquil
must remain here to heal. I'll ask Odin's permission to bring
back a healing potion for her."

"It's time," Maya said softly as she caught hold of Freya's
arm. "We must get Brundi back."

Freya and Maya helped Vonni lift Brundi up into Skaga's
arms. Pym flew up to Freya and landed on her shoulder, beside
Orus. The raven was inconsolable with fear and grief for Brundi.

"I will stay with her until I know she is safe," Loki reassured Vonni. "Then I will return. You must prepare that mine as quickly as possible. You may have to stay there for some time."

"I understand," Vonni said. "We'll start today."

Loki turned to Sarah. "And you take good care of that godson for me."

Sarah sniffed and nodded as Loki turned himself into a fly and flew up and landed on Brundi's hand.

Freya looked at the large gathering of people who had opened their home and hearts to them. She would miss them all. "Remember what I told you," she warned Mims. "You are a Valkyrie. You can't change that. You must always be careful."

Tears trailed down Mims's cheeks as she stood with her father. "I'll remember."

The journey wasn't long. As the shimmering colors of the Rainbow Bridge glowed to meet them, sadness tugged at Freya. The family seemed so vulnerable on Midgard. There was no one to protect them if the war came.

"They'll be fine," Archie said, as if reading her mind. "Vonni is there, and he won't let anything happen to them. Just focus on Brundi."

Crossing Bifröst, Freya and her sisters were surprised to see their mother standing with Heimdall at the entrance.

Her arms were crossed, and the expression on her face gave away all her emotions. She was desperate to meet her mother.

"Greetings, Heimdall," Skaga said formally, leading her Reaping Mare off the shimmering bridge.

"Greetings, Valkyrie," the Watchman responded. "I hope you journeyed well." His eyes landed on Brundi in Skaga's arms. "What's happened?"

"Mother?" Eir cried as she ran forward.

"She was shot," Freya explained as she climbed down from Sylt. "It was terrible. Mother, we must get Brundi to the healers, and then I must ask Odin for permission to return to Midgard."

"I'm coming back with you," Maya said.

"And me," Archie agreed.

"We must all go back," Skaga announced. "Once Brünnhilde is healed, we will avenge this violence done against her."

Eir gently lifted Brundi down from Skaga's arms. Without waiting for her daughters, she launched into the air, carrying her wounded mother in the direction of the healers' hut.

"Go on," Heimdall said to the Valkyries. "I'll take care of your Reaping Mares. Follow your mother."

Freya carried Archie as she and her sisters tried to keep up with their mother. Freya had never known her to fly so fast. When they landed at the healers' hut, Eir kicked open the door. "I need help here!"

The same healer who had treated Freya at the Ten Realms Challenge appeared. "Who just kicked in my door?"

"I did," Eir said. "Please, Healer, this is Brünnhilde—my mother. She was shot in Midgard."

The tiny woman easily lifted Brundi from Eir's arms. "She is Valkyrie?"

Eir nodded. "She was known as Frigha."

The healer inhaled sharply. "The runaway Valkyrie? Does Odin know she is returned?"

"He is the one who sent for her. But she was shot by a human. With no armor for protection, she was badly wounded," Freya explained.

The healer placed Brundi down on a cot. Pym flew from Freya and landed on Brundi's leg. When the healer tried to shoo him away, the raven refused to go.

"Stupid bird," the healer spat.

She turned back to the Valkyries. "Leave her with me. I will do all I can to save her, but she has been away from Asgard too long. Her life force is weak." She shoved Freya and her sisters toward the door, but their mother refused to budge.

"You too, Eir," she ordered. "Out!"

"I must stay," Eir insisted. "This is the first I've seen of my mother—I will not leave her."

"You will go!" the healer cried. "Do not force my hand, Eir. You know what I can do. Go. I will take good care of your mother."

Eir stood tall, challenging the healer.

"Mother, please," Freya begged. "Let her work. There is so much we must tell you about the others we met in Midgard."

That stopped her. Eir nodded to the healer and left with her daughters.

"Vonni," Eir repeated as she sat with her daughters in the living area of their private palace. Freya told her mother everything they'd done since she and Archie left Asgard, and also filled her in on the details of the possible war.

"Brundi thinks they'll be safe if they hide in the gold mine," Archie added.

"Gold has powerful properties," Eir agreed. "It is the best possible solution. But please, tell me more about my brother. He's a singer?"

Freya nodded. "He's famous in Midgard. He has the most beautiful voice I've ever heard. Now I understand what it's like for humans when they hear us. He was enchanting. When he sang, I couldn't do anything—all I wanted was to listen to him forever."

"*It was sickening,*" Orus cawed. "*Freya mooning over her uncle like that.*"

"My brother," Eir said wistfully. A shadow crossed her face. "I envy you. You have spent time with him. I would pay almost any price for that."

"And there's Mims," Freya added. "She's a wingless Valkyrie. Her powers are developing and she's very frightened. I wish I could be there for her, to teach her what she needs to learn."

"Mother," Skaga said. "If the war is coming, they are very vulnerable on the ranch. Vonni said he was going to work on the mine, but it is dangerous and they may not have time to make it safe. They need our help."

Eir rose. "With tension so high, I doubt Odin will allow us to return without good reason. We must convince him to let us go without giving away our true intentions. I have lost enough of my family; I will not surrender more."

That one comment stuck in Freya's mind. Her mother had lost enough family? Was she talking about surrendering her son? Despite all the talk of saving Vonni and Mims, her mind kept going back to the missing part of her life. Her twin brother.

"But others are trespassing and trying to steal the gold for themselves," Maya added. "They are prepared to kill to take it."

Gwyn said, "I will not tolerate humans endangering our family. We must go back to protect them."

"Family?" Odin's deep voice sounded. He had entered the home without knocking. "Family?" he repeated. "What family? Who are humans endangering?"

Loki was beside him. His eyes fell on Freya and held a

secret warning that sent a chill down her spine. Had Odin overheard more of the conversation than was safe?

Freya nodded subtly to him and then hoped she would be able to speak privately with him. He knew more about her brother. She couldn't ignore that. She had to speak with him as soon as possible.

"Great Odin," Eir said. "Be welcome in our home. I trust you have heard about my mother?"

"That Brünnhilde is back, yes," he said. "Loki has informed me. I am also told she has been gravely wounded and is with the healers."

"Yes," Eir said. "She was shot by a human."

He looked at everyone in the room. "And you are talking of going back and avenging her."

Eir approached and knelt before him. "Great Odin, you know I have served you loyally my whole life. Now I ask your permission to defend my family. We are your Battle-Maidens. We have never shied from a fight or showed fear in conflict. But an attack has been waged against us. We must not ignore this challenge."

Eir rose but kept her head lowered in respect. "It is true that Brünnhilde broke your rules, but she is still one of your Valkyries. She has done you proud. She's created a sanctuary in Midgard for animals, especially wolves. To honor you, she has called this sanctuary Valhalla Valley. But others are trying to take it from her—which is why they hurt her. The humans who serve her have become her family and sheltered her. But now they are in danger. I beg you, when she is healed, please allow us to return and do what is our right."

Odin shook his head. "This is not the time to be venturing away from Asgard. Brünnhilde is home; that is all that matters. Valhalla Valley will have to fend for itself for the time being."

Freya could feel tension in Odin. He was trying to hide it, but it was there. Was the war drawing near?

"What about Jonquil?" Orus cawed. *"We have left her behind."*

"You did what?" Odin demanded.

"We had to," Freya insisted. "She was shot by the same men who hurt Brünnhilde. She was badly wounded and we could not move her. The people on the ranch are caring for her, but she is a Reaping Mare; she doesn't belong in Midgard."

Odin rubbed his beard. "Indeed. No one must be left behind. . . ."

"Please, Great Odin," Eir begged. "You know how important Reaping Mares are to their riders. My mother will not rest knowing Jonquil is still there."

His gaze passed to the other Valkyries in the room. "You all want this?"

The Valkyries and their ravens all nodded.

Odin considered this for several heartbeats and then spoke. "Over the years that Jonquil lived at my palace, Frigg developed deep feelings for her. It will distress her greatly to hear of Jonquil's wounds." He focused on Eir. "I will grant your request, my most favored. You may return to Midgard to collect the Reaping Mare, but you must not linger. I give you one day—no more. That should be ample time to rescue Jonquil and bring her home."

18

"I MUST RETURN WITH YOU!" BRUNDI INSISTED.

Eir shook her head. "I'm sorry, Mother, but you are not well enough to travel. You have only just been released by the healer. She says you must rest."

"I'm fine," Brundi insisted. "The healer's potions worked perfectly. I am strong and prepared to fight."

"You are not fine," Eir insisted. "The potions worked, but you are not completely recovered. I can feel your pain. You can't hide it from me."

"You're wrong," Brundi said.

"Mother, you nearly died from your wounds. You need time to finish healing and grow strong again. Odin has only granted us one day to collect Jonquil. That is but a couple of weeks in Midgard. We will need every moment of that time to help Vonni. We won't be able to focus on that if we're worried about you."

Freya stood back with Archie and her sisters as her mother and grandmother argued. Eir was strong-minded and determined, but Brundi was even more stubborn.

As the argument heated up, Eir looked back to her daughters. "Don't you all have other work to do? Go on. Get to it!"

Not needing to be told twice, Freya and Archie left the room. Since Brundi's return to Asgard, to help pass the time they had returned to their duties in the stables of the Reaping Mares. Because she had completed her mission to return Brünnhilde to Asgard, Freya's probation had ended and she was restored to the rank of full Valkyrie. But due to Brünnhilde's injuries, she and her family were excused from reapings.

"Gee, what's wrong?" Archie pressed as he cleaned the final stall. "You're as anxious as a cat in a room full of rocking chairs. You've been that way since we got back here. Don't worry about your mom and Brundi. They'll work it out."

Freya still hadn't told Archie about her brother. But she couldn't keep it in anymore. "It's not them I'm worried about. Loki's gone and I can't find him."

"Loki? Why would you care about him?"

Freya shook her head. "Normally I wouldn't, but now I need to talk to him."

"*He's probably gone back to Midgard to help with the mine,*" Orus offered. "*That, or he's causing mischief again. Whatever it is, we're better off without him.*"

Freya threw down her pitchfork and started to kick at the straw. "The one time I really need him and he's gone!" She turned sharply on Archie. "I bet he's doing this on purpose. He knows I need him so he's staying away!"

"Gee, stop it!" Archie cried. "Talk to me. What's wrong? What has Loki done?"

Freya sighed heavily and sat down on a bale of hay. "He hasn't done anything. He knows I know something and now he's hiding so I won't ask him about it. Probably to torture me."

"*Freya, you're talking in riddles,*" Orus cawed.

Freya lifted sad eyes to Archie. "Do you remember the Ten Realms Challenge and that small Dark Searcher?"

"The one with white wings?" Archie asked. "You asked Loki about him."

"He's my brother," Freya said flatly.

"*What?*" Orus cried.

Freya nodded. "When we were on the battlefield during the Challenge, we bumped into each other. As soon as we touched, I knew. Just like Mother when she first saw Vonni."

"So now you think that Dark Searcher is your brother?"

"I *know* he's my twin."

"*How?*" Orus cawed.

"Because I feel him!" Freya faced her raven. "Orus, my

whole life, I've felt like something was missing. You always said I was restless. But it was more than that. It's like a part of me had been cut off." Her pain-filled eyes turned to Archie. "Finding you has eased a lot of it. But even so, I can still feel the pull of something else. Something unknown. But when I touched him, I knew. And I know he felt the same from me."

"Gee, this is insane! Your mother would have told you."

"*No, she wouldn't,*" Orus mused darkly. "*Not if she was grieving over him.*" Comprehension shone in the raven's eyes. "*Azrael told us that male babies were taken from their mothers and given to the Dark Searchers. Eir said she'd lost enough family—but she's only just found her brother. She must have been talking about her son. Loki has been hinting at it since the Ten Realms Challenge.*" Orus flew to Freya's shoulder. "*You must be right.*"

"I know I'm right. And I've got to find him."

"*Freya, no!*" Orus cawed.

"I must," Freya insisted. "I can't bear the thought of him in Utgard and being turned into a Searcher. We must go there to rescue him."

"Utgard?" Archie cried. "Don't the frost giants live in Utgard? And aren't the frost giants plotting to attack Asgard?"

"So?" Freya asked.

"So?" Archie cried. "Gee, it's too risky. You can't go. Especially now, with the war coming. Besides, if he felt it too, why isn't he trying to find you?"

"Maybe he is."

"And maybe he doesn't care! He's a Dark Searcher, Gee."

"I have to," Freya insisted.

"*Are you insane?*" Orus cawed. "*Have you forgotten about Dirian? He killed you. He was de-winged, demoted, and banished. He's there. If he discovers you, he'll take his revenge. They all will. I know you want to find your brother, but in Utgard all you will find is death, or worse!*"

"What's worse than death?" Archie asked.

"*A lot!*" Orus cawed. "*I don't want to see anything happen to either of you.*"

"I'm sorry, Orus. But you can't stop me," Freya insisted. "My brother is out there somewhere. And just as soon as I find Loki, he's going to tell me how to find him. I'm going to Utgard with or without your help!"

19

GROWING TENSION FILLED THE AIR OF ASGARD, AND
Freya felt it everywhere. Rumors of traitors and spies were
whispered throughout the city, and trust was at a premium.
Citizens looked at each other suspiciously, wondering who
could have betrayed Odin.

Dark Elves and dwarfs slipped away silently and returned
to their own realms while Light Elves poured into Asgard,
offering their support.

The dead warriors of Valhalla intensified their battle
preparations and worked with Thor on strategies. Armorers
toiled day and night, creating weapons to outfit those preparing to fight for Asgard. All nonessential travel was canceled.
It was rumored that soon Odin would close Bifröst.

The secret was out, and everyone was preparing for war.

As Freya's family settled down to their evening meal, Eir announced, "I heard from a friend today that some Light Elves are going to Valhalla to visit Odin. Word is that they've heard of more secret meetings between the kings of the frost giants and fire giants, brokered by an unknown person."

"The traitor," Brundi mused. "But peace between the giants should be impossible. They've been enemies forever. Unless that's changed since I left."

"No, they are old enemies," Eir agreed.

Skaga nodded. "I heard that Thor and Balder are going to Utgard to visit the Keep of the Dark Searchers. I bet it's to prepare them for battle."

"This is not good," Eir said. "If Thor is going to Utgard, it can only mean one thing—war."

"We must warn Vonni," Brundi said.

A large eagle screeched and flew in the window. It landed beside the dining table and shimmered into Loki. He ran over to Brundi. "There is no time to waste. You must come back to Midgard now. Sarah is having the baby, but there is a problem. They need help now or both of them could die."

Brundi rose slowly. "I must go to her."

"Mother, we agreed to give it another day. You are not well enough to travel. We'll go and you can follow us tomorrow."

"No," Brundi insisted. "I am going with you now. Go to Odin. Tell him that we are heading back to Midgard to collect Jonquil. Let him know you've heard some of the rumors and think it is best not to delay."

When Eir hesitated, Brundi snapped, "I will walk there if I must, but I am going back. Now, stop wasting precious time and go to Odin!"

Eir nodded. "Skaga, fly to the healer and explain the situation, but don't mention Vonni. Ask if there is any potion she can give us to protect Sarah and the child—but make sure you don't tell her that the baby will be a Dark Searcher. The rest of you—put on your armor. We'll meet at Bifröst!"

"Brundi, are you sure you're up to this?" Orus asked. "We can go. You are still recovering."

"Of course she is," Pym shot back at him from Brundi's shoulder. "Brundi is stronger than all of you put together."

Brundi's eyes filled with fire as she walked carefully out onto the flight balcony. "Nothing is going to keep me away. Now, who is going to carry me to Bifröst?"

"Archie and I will," Freya offered. She called to Maya, "Would you bring my armor with you? We'll meet up at the bridge."

Within a short time, the Asgard members of Brundi's family were gathered at the Rainbow Bridge, looking ready for war in their battle armor, winged helmets, daggers, and swords.

"Greeting, Heimdall. We have been given leave to return to Midgard," Eir explained.

"I have been informed," Heimdall responded, dropping

all formalities. "I beg you to hurry. I fear I may be ordered to close Bifröst at any moment. You must be back before then."

"We will," Brundi assured.

"Stay safe and travel well, Valkyries," the Watchman said as he bowed and invited them onto the bridge.

They arrived at Valhalla Valley late in the evening with the vial of potion that would help Sarah. Vonni had refused to call a doctor and was more than relieved to see the arrival of his mother and her Valkyrie entourage.

Brundi, Eir, and Loki went upstairs to Sarah, carrying the healer's potion, while Freya and her sisters were ordered to stay with the others.

As they waited, the residents of Valhalla Valley told the Valkyries what had been happening in the time they had been away from Earth.

"How long have we been gone?" Freya asked. She and her sisters were standing at the back of the dining room, pressed against the wall. With so many people gathered in the room, it would be easy to make a mistake and touch someone.

"Just over a month," Tash answered. She was seated near Freya, and her curious eyes lingered on all the Valkyries. "We've been working on the mine since you left. But we've still got big trouble with hunters. They're killing wolves, bears, and anything that moves. Vonni tries to drive them away, but there are so many. He says they aren't really hunters. They want the gold in the mine."

"What did the police say?" Freya asked.

"Nothing," George, the vet, said. "We think they must be working with the hunters."

"Hunters are bad," Gage said.

George nodded. "Seems they've been trespassing and taking gold from that mine for a while now. They won't give it up without a fight."

"They'd better," Skaga said. She spoke to the large gathering. "Brundi is our grandmother. That makes this our property too. No human on this Earth will ever drive us away. We need that mine to shelter you, and we'll fight to protect it if we must."

A healthy, welcome cry sounded from upstairs. It was the breathy, strong cry of a newborn baby.

"He's here?" Freya exclaimed. She opened her senses fully and could feel Sarah's presence. It was growing stronger. "Sarah is alive. She is recovering!"

Freya threw her arms around Archie as cheers erupted and relieved celebrations began around them.

Before long Vonni entered the dining room, carrying the baby wrapped in a blue blanket. His face was flushed with emotion. Loki stood directly behind him, beaming with pride.

"Everyone, I would like to present Michael Loki Angelo . . ." Vonni's voice broke. "My beautiful son."

"*Mims*," Orus cawed as he flew from Freya's shoulder. He

landed on Mims's arm and cawed excitedly, *"You have a new brother!"*

Everyone in the room came forward to greet the new arrival. Vonni's eyes found the Valkyries as they stood back, away from the people. He carefully handed the baby to Mims and crossed the room to them.

"Thank you!" he cried as he wrapped his arms around Freya.

Freya held her uncle tightly. "I didn't do anything."

He released her and kissed her forehead. "You did everything." He looked at her sisters and embraced each of them in turn. "For so long it was just Mother and me. Now I have a wife and children, a twin sister, five beautiful nieces, and a ghost nephew! I am truly blessed."

"Vonni," Archie asked, "does he really have wings?"

Vonni nodded. "The most adorable wings I've ever seen. They have the softest downy black feathers. He's even flapped them already. Sarah and I are thrilled."

"She isn't frightened?"

"No. My Sarah is an exceptional woman. She's excited to be part of such a . . . unique family."

"Will you let him keep his wings?" Maya asked.

Vonni nodded. "I understand why Mother had to remove mine. She was blind and alone, and she feared for my safety in the human world. But no one is going to touch a feather on my son."

When Eir returned, she stood beside her brother, holding

his arm and never looking so radiant. They were almost the same height, with very similar features. As they stood next to each other, it was obvious that they were twins.

Loki crept up behind Freya and tapped her lightly on the shoulder. "Isn't this a touching reunion?" he said, gazing around the room. "Look at all those happy faces."

"Loki!" Freya cried. "Please, I need to speak with you."

"Could this be about a certain Dark Searcher called Kai?" he whispered.

"Kai?" Freya asked.

Loki nodded. "That's his name, you know."

"My brother is called Kai?"

"Ah—now you understand."

"Why didn't you tell her about this before?" Archie challenged.

Loki's expression darkened. "I've warned you about that tone, ghost. One more word from you, and I won't help Freya get to her brother before the war begins."

Before Freya could say another word, Loki walked over to Vonni. "It's my turn to hold my godson."

"He's lying," Archie said. "He'd never help you find your brother."

"*Of course he's lying,*" Orus agreed. "*Freya, he's doing this to trick you. I know you are desperate to find Kai. But if Thor has gone to Utgard, it can only mean the fighting is about to start. It would be too dangerous for you to go.*"

Freya watched Loki moving through the room. He stole a look back at her and winked playfully. Then he nodded his head and mouthed the word "Kai."

The next morning Freya was invited to visit Sarah. The baby was cradled in her arms. His deep-blue eyes were open and taking in his surroundings.

Sarah pulled the blanket away to reveal the baby's tiny wings, neatly folded on his smooth back. Just like Vonni had said, they were covered in soft, black downy feathers.

"They are so cute!" Mims cooed as she gently petted her brother's little wings. "And they're just like yours, Greta. They're as black as night."

"He's lovely," Freya agreed.

"He's my perfect boy." Sarah blushed. "I mean, I know all mothers say that. But he really is so very beautiful."

"He sure is," Freya agreed when Sarah handed the baby to her.

Freya cradled her small cousin carefully, and smiled when he caught hold of her finger in his tiny hand. The grip already promised the great strength he would grow into. "Hello, Michael. Welcome to the world." She gazed at Sarah and felt the woman held no fear at her son's wings. Her mother's love was perfect.

After the visit, Freya was more determined than ever to find Loki and ask him to take her to her brother. But once again, he was frustratingly absent. However, after a few inquiries, she learned that Loki was with her mother and Vonni at the mine.

"Gee, I know you are anxious to find your brother, but look around you—we're really needed here. We only have one Asgard day to prepare the mine. We can't waste a moment of it," Archie reminded her.

"I understand," Freya agreed. "But I must go. I can't explain it, and I realize it makes no sense. But I can't leave Kai there."

"What choice is there?" Archie asked. "Gee, think. Let's say you find him. What are you going to do?"

"I don't know. Try to get him away from them somehow. Show him that there is another life he could have."

"Where?" Orus cawed. *"Odin would never allow him to remain with you in Asgard. He would send him back to the Searchers."*

Freya hadn't thought that far ahead. What was she supposed to do with a fourteen-year-old Dark Searcher? Then it struck her. Brundi said that Valhalla Valley was a sanctuary for all. "We'll bring him here," she offered. "Vonni can show him that he has choices. He doesn't have to be a Dark Searcher."

"I don't know about this. What if he's already a fully trained Searcher? He may be dangerous."

Freya turned to Archie. "Please, Archie, I've never asked

you for anything before. But I am now. Will you help me find my brother? If he's dangerous, I'll leave him. But if there is any hope for him, I've got to try."

Archie grinned. "You don't have to ask me. You know I would go with you anywhere."

"Me too," Orus cawed. *"Even if it means we'll all face certain death. At least we'll be together."*

Breaking the tension, Archie laughed. "Well, at least I don't have to worry about that. I'm already dead."

Freya, Archie, and Mims joined the other Valkyries inspecting the new work on the mine. The area around it still bore the scorch marks from Dragon Loki's flames, but lots of progress had been made to secure the mine since the night Brundi had been shot.

The exterior now had a heavy locked door, while inside the mine itself there were more support beams and the rough dirt walls had been brick-lined and plastered. But despite all the work done, it was a far from comfortable, or even livable, place.

"It's moving too slowly," Vonni complained. "We get one area supported and then another part collapses deeper inside. I can't see how we can get water or heating in here." He shook his head. "I can't bring the others in here. It's a death trap."

"You don't have much choice," Eir said as she inspected

a support beam. "The gold in this mine will shield you from others. You must stay safe. I have lived an eternity without you—I won't see you endangered now."

Vonni sighed heavily and caught his sister by the arm. "Eir, I've been thinking about this a lot. I want you to bring us back to Asgard with you. I would much rather face Odin and beg him to let us stay than risk my family in here. I will offer to fight for him, do whatever he asks of me. I'm strong—you know I am—and I've fought in many wars. But this mine is just too dangerous for any of us."

"Vonni, you can't!" Freya cried. "Why would you want to go to the one place about to be attacked by frost and fire giants, when they may never come to Midgard?"

"Freya is correct," Eir said. "But more than that, I doubt you would leave Sarah behind."

"Of course not. She would come with us."

Eir shook her head. "She cannot. There are no living humans in Asgard, for a very good reason. They can't survive there. It's another realm. The only way Sarah could join us is if I gave her my name and then reaped her. Only in death could she remain with you in Asgard."

Vonni's eyes widened. "Never! Sarah is my life. But surely there must be another way?"

"No, there is none. That is why we are desperate to secure this mine. When the war comes, you must be as deep in here as you can go. We are here for several days and we are strong. We don't need to sleep, and can work steadily until we return to Asgard."

"But—" Vonni said.

"No buts," Eir insisted. "If you are to survive the war, this is the only place for you."

20

THE VALKYRIES JOINED THE OTHERS FROM THE RANCH, working in the mine to make it safe. The shifts were long and hard and the work dirty, but after only one day with the powerful Valkyries helping, they were making progress.

As day turned into night, while the human members of Brundi's extended family retired to bed, exhausted, the Valkyries and Vonni headed back to the mine to continue work.

Freya finally managed to convince Loki to lead her to Utgard. But he made her swear that she would do absolutely everything he told her. She agreed, and they arranged to meet at the lake during her patrol shift.

"Are you sure you want to leave here now?" Orus asked as they made their way through the woods to the lake. *"There is a lot going on at the ranch. We are needed here."*

"I know, but the others are at the mine. Our job is only to patrol for hunters. We've searched the property twice, and there's no one here. If we don't go now, we may never get another chance."

"I'm just worried it's another of Loki's tricks," Archie said.

"Look, I'm sick of you two trying to stop me. It's not a trick," Freya insisted. "He promised. He told us to wait here, and that's what we're going to do. If you don't want to come, that's fine. Stay here. But I'm going!"

"All right, all right," Archie soothed. "We're one hundred percent behind you, okay?"

"*Even if it's a crazy idea*," Orus cawed.

"What are you up to, Freya?" Maya's voice broke through the tension as she emerged from the trees. "And don't lie to me. I know something is wrong. I've felt it from you all day. What's going on?"

Grul cawed, "*What has Orus talked you into?*"

Freya glared at her sister's raven. "Orus hasn't done anything."

"*Ha!*" Grul cawed. "*Don't make me laugh! Orus is always talking you into doing stupid things.*"

Orus cawed back, "*Don't start with me, feather face!*"

"Enough!" Freya cried.

"Tell her," Archie said. "She deserves to know."

"Know what?"

Freya caught hold of her sister's hands. "Maya, we have a brother. He's my twin."

"A brother?" Maya cried.

Freya nodded and explained to her sister what she knew. "I know it's true," she insisted. "It's just like Mother with Vonni. So please don't try to tell me it's not."

Maya walked over to the edge of the lake and dipped her boot in the cold water. "You're right, it is true. I was very young, but I remember the day you were born. Everyone was so happy when they carried you out of Mother's room. But then someone dressed in black came and took a bundle away. I remember Mother crying and begging them to stop. She cried for days and days but wouldn't tell us why."

"They took away her son," Archie said.

Maya nodded. "After that, Mother changed. She became harder. She said she would never have another child and told us we were not to discuss your birthday—ever! I'd completely forgotten about it."

"His name is Kai," Freya said softly. "We're going to Utgard to find him."

"What? Freya, you can't!" Maya cried. "You know what's happening! If the frost giants don't kill you, the Dark Searchers will. And have you even thought about Thor and Balder? What if you encounter them?"

"It's a huge risk, I know, but I have to go," Freya said. "I can't explain it, but all my life something has been missing.

That's Kai. I must find him before the war starts."

"What happens then? What will you do?"

"We're going to bring him here," Archie offered. "He'll be safe, away from Utgard and the war."

Maya shook her head. "This is madness. You can't bring him here. The others will follow. You'll expose the family."

"Not if we're careful," Freya argued.

"What if he doesn't want to leave Utgard?" Maya asked.

"Then we'll come back without him. But at least I'll know."

Maya shook her head. "Freya, listen to me. I know you've been missing him for a long time. You've been restless and unhappy. But this is just too dangerous. I don't know what I'd do if anything were to happen to you. You're my little sister and I love you more than anything. Please, don't go. Not now."

"I have to, please try to understand that."

"Is there nothing I can do to stop you?"

"Don't bother trying," Orus cawed. *"Nothing can stop her. I've tried."*

"I must do this," Freya insisted. "Please don't tell Mother where we've gone. She has enough to worry about here. With luck, we'll be back very soon."

"Freya, don't go," Maya begged. "They'll hurt you."

Loki emerged from the woods. "No one can stop Freya when she sets her mind on something."

Maya's eyes narrowed as she turned on Loki and jabbed him in the chest with an accusing finger. "You did this, didn't you? You filled Freya's head with ideas of how she can rescue Kai. You're leading her right into the Dark Searchers' hands."

Loki caught hold of her hand. "Your sister is quite capable of thinking for herself. I simply offered to guide her. If you prefer, I won't go. There's plenty for me to do here." Loki started to walk away.

"No!" Freya ran after him. "I know you're not doing this to hand me over to the Searchers. Loki, you promised you'd take me to my brother. Please . . ."

"Yes, I can lead you there." He indicated Maya, Archie, and Orus. "But none of them want me to help you."

"But I do!" Freya begged. She turned to Maya and Archie. "You can't understand how it feels to have part of yourself missing. I don't have a choice. I must go to him."

Loki stood for a long moment as his eyes moved from Maya to Archie and finally to Orus.

"Please," Freya begged.

Loki finally gave in. "All right, I will lead you. But you are warned. This is very dangerous. With tensions so high, one little mistake could be all it takes to start the war. Are you prepared for that?"

Freya didn't waver or hesitate. "Yes."

21

UNDER THE COVER OF NIGHT, FREYA CARRIED ARCHIE up into the darkened sky as they followed Loki, now an eagle, toward the Rainbow Bridge. As a very young child, she had gone to Utgard when they had hosted a Nine Realms Challenge. She had not been back since.

They entered the shimmering bridge and traveled halfway across when Loki stopped and called out: "Bifröst, lead me to Utgard!"

They waited for something to happen, but the bridge remained unchanged.

"It didn't work," Archie said.

"Foolish ghost," Loki called. "Follow me."

They continued to travel along Bifröst in the same direction they would normally take to reach Asgard, but soon emerged into a world vastly different from either Asgard or Midgard. This was Jotunheim—home to Utgard and land of the frost giants, the trolls, and the Keep of the Dark Searchers.

"How is this possible?" Archie asked. "We didn't change direction—how can we be in Jotunheim?"

"We don't change direction," screeched the eagle Loki. "Bifröst moves for us. Now, take care and be silent; remember where you are!"

The first difference was the temperature. It was freezing. Even though Valkyries never felt the cold, there was something about the air around them that chilled Freya to the bone.

They soared across the open sky. Finally the eagle touched down on the frozen, snow-covered ground.

Archie crossed his arms over his chest and jumped up and down to keep warm. "Whoa, it's freezing here! Are you sure I'm dead? I sure don't feel like it."

"I'm sure," Freya said, as her teeth started to chatter. "But I told you. Here and in Asgard, you have a body."

"Then you should have warned me to wear more layers!"

Orus settled on Freya's shoulder and puffed up his feathers. He huddled close to her for warmth. *"I don't think I've ever been so cold!"*

"Now I know why they call them the frost giants," Archie said. "Does this place ever warm up?"

Freya shook her head. "I don't think so. I've heard it's the coldest place in all the realms."

"Would you stop complaining and be silent!" Loki ordered. He turned back into his man shape. "Freya, use your senses. Is anyone near us? We can't risk being seen."

The sky above them was brilliant blue and filled with fluffy white clouds. Snow-capped mountains rose high in the distance. As far as they could see, the landscape around them was frozen and covered in a thick layer of snow.

Freya turned and looked behind them. Dark clouds were gathering in the distance. "We are alone. But I think a storm is moving in; we'd better get going."

"Where?" Archie asked.

Freya pointed. "If I remember correctly, on the other side of those mountains is Utgard."

"Very good," Loki said. "Now, are we going to stand here all day talking about it, or are we going to get to your brother before sunset, when the temperature really drops?"

"It gets colder?" Archie cried.

"Much," Loki said. He paused, and a trace of mischief came into his eyes. "Oh, and did I mention that, due to the threat of war, Kai's Searcher Ceremony has been moved forward?"

"What Searcher Ceremony?"

Loki shrugged and inspected his fingernails. "It's not too unlike your First Day Ceremony, when you swore your oath to Odin and became a full Valkyrie. Normally it would happen when Kai becomes a full Searcher. But under the present circumstances, they are holding it on the next full moon—which, by the way, is tonight. Kai will swear his oath of allegiance and drink the potion that will destroy his voice—forever."

Freya's expression dropped.

"You didn't know about that?" Loki asked. "Haven't you ever noticed how silent Dark Searchers are? Their voices are destroyed at the Searcher Ceremony. They can speak, but only in a harsh, guttural growl."

"Why?" Archie asked.

"Odin knows the power they hold in their voices," Loki explained. "They can enchant Valkyries, just like Vonni's voice enchanted Freya. Knowing what could happen, Odin ordered the Searchers to swear an oath of loyalty and to drink a potion that damages their vocal cords. I don't want to see that happen to Kai."

"Why do you care so much?" Archie challenged. "It's not like you to think of anyone but yourself."

"You really do want me to kill you, don't you, ghost?" Loki stalked Archie and drew a hidden dagger from his shirt. "So be it."

"Loki, no." Freya flew between the two. "I'd like to know also. Why do you care what happens to Kai?"

Loki hesitated, holding the dagger. He sighed and put

it away. Crossing his arms in front of his chest, he glared at Archie before turning to Freya. "If you must know, it's because of Vonni. Until I heard him sing, I never realized how beautiful Dark Searchers' voices truly are. Just as you are the youngest Valkyrie, Kai is the youngest Dark Searcher. I doubt there will be more after him for some time. It would be a tragedy to lose his voice."

"So you were manipulating us," Archie challenged. "You teased Freya about her brother just so we'd help you get him away from the Searchers before they ruined his voice."

"*Freya, you can't trust him!* Orus cawed. *"He lied to us about this and he'll hand us over to the Searchers or tell Odin. Odin won't forgive us a second time."*

Loki nodded his head. "All right, all right, it's true. I did want your help to free Kai from his fate. And yes, from time to time I can be a little mischievous, but not about this. I've heard Kai sing when he's alone. That voice is too precious to destroy." Loki stepped up to Freya. "I swear he is your twin brother. Do you really want him to surrender his voice and any chance of freedom he may have? Do you want him to become a full Dark Searcher?"

Freya already knew it was true about Kai being her twin. But Loki had used her. What other tricks did he have up his sleeve? "How can we trust you?"

"You can," Loki insisted. "You have my word. I will lead you to your brother and help get him away from the keep."

"Gee, we can't trust him; he's just a filthy liar." Archie warned. "He'll lead us in, and then abandon us to the Searchers."

Loki advanced on him and leaned close to his face. "If Freya weren't here, I would make you pay for that remark, ghost!"

"Try it!" Archie cried, tensing for a fight. "I'm ready for you."

"Stop it, both of you!" Freya snapped. "This is too important. Loki, look at me."

Loki was staring down Archie but broke off to turn to Freya. "Go on, Valkyrie, use your powers on me. See that I am telling you the truth. I am here to help Kai."

He remained still as Freya gazed into his dark eyes. She nodded. "He's telling the truth. He wants to help us get Kai away from here before the war."

"Now, may we go, or shall we let the ghost waste more precious time?" Loki asked angrily. He leaped into the air and turned back into the large eagle.

Before Archie could form a biting response, Freya grabbed him and leaped into the air to follow.

They flew over the snow-covered landscape and climbed higher in the sky to soar over a tall mountain range. Sharp peaks rose up to meet them, but with each flap of her black wings, Freya flew easily over the tops.

After they had cleared the large range, the ground beneath them evened out. A lush forest of tall, snow-covered pines spread out before them. Farther in the distance, dark spires rose high into the sky.

"That's Utgard," Freya said to Archie. "It's bigger than Asgard and surrounded by even higher walls. There is only one way in, but it's heavily guarded."

"Can't we fly over the walls?" Archie asked.

"No," Loki called. "Powerful magic protects Utgard. If you tried to fly over the walls, you would smash into an invisible barrier that climbs far into space. You would never find the top of it."

"Then how do we get in?"

"We take the main gate," Loki said.

"That won't be easy," Orus cawed. "I've heard there's a nasty troll who guards the gates, and frost giants defend it. They don't like the Valkyries and won't let us pass—especially now."

"I have already considered that," Loki called. "Land here. I have something for you."

They followed Loki down into the thick pine forest, where the trees opened up into a small clearing. Back on the ground, Loki returned to his usual form.

"This way," he called, leading them forward. "I have a plan."

They walked through the tall pines until they came upon an immense tree with a natural hole in its trunk. Loki reached inside and pulled out a large chest.

Inside were cloaks, masks, and costumes. Loki removed

two cloaks, a mask, and a visored helmet. "As you know, Valkyries are not allowed in Utgard without the king of the frost giants' permission. With tensions so high, you'll never gain that permission. However, Dark Searchers and elves can come and go as they please." He handed Searcher clothes, a cloak, and a helmet to Freya, and a Dark Elf outfit to Archie. "Here, put these on."

"Why do you have all of this?" Freya asked as she started to change.

"You never know when you might need a disguise," Loki said.

"What about Orus?"

"He will have to hide under your cloak."

"*Oh no, not again,*" Orus moaned.

Freya put on the black, leatherlike trousers and top of the Dark Searchers. They had been designed to accommodate large wings, and they fit her comfortably. Loki helped her pull on the long black cloak and settled it around her exposed wings.

"Where did you get these?" Freya asked.

"I know the dwarfs who make the uniform for the Searchers. They owed me a favor and I collected on it." He stood back and scrutinized Freya. "It's a good thing you've got black feathers. You'll blend right in. Of course, you are much shorter than other Searchers, so you will have to walk with their attitude."

"I'll try," Freya said. She pulled on the Searchers' black gloves and visored helmet. The world around her turned dark. "How do they see in these things?"

"They use their senses more than their eyes," Loki said. "Now remember, do not speak to anyone. If anyone tries to talk to you, growl at them. I'll be there to cover you."

"What about you?" Archie asked as he pulled on the dark-green elf cloak. "Won't you get into trouble being here?"

Loki gave him a dismissive look. "Freya, didn't you tell your dead friend about me?"

Freya shrugged and faced Archie. "Loki is part frost giant. He's allowed here. He has a frost giantess wife."

"We have a home deep in Utgard," Loki added. "We spend as much time here as we do in Asgard. Now, let's get moving. The sun will be setting soon."

They trekked through the deep snow and finally made it to the edge of the forest. Utgard loomed directly ahead of them. The closer they got to the gates, the higher the walls and tall gates climbed into the sky. Near the ground was another set of gates, built right into the larger set.

Orus was hidden under Freya's cloak. *Just don't forget about me in here.*

A troll sat in a guardhouse and followed their approach with mild interest.

Loki nodded curtly. "Let us in, Frogg. The sun is setting

and the temperature is dropping. My wife is expecting me for dinner."

The heavyset troll rose from his chair. He sniffed the air and looked at the two cloaked figures suspiciously. "Who is this?" he growled.

"I met them on the trail. We have journeyed from Svartalfheim together to watch the Searcher Ceremony this night."

Frogg leaned closer to Freya and studied her intently. His black eyes searched every inch of her and he made strange, guttural noises.

Freya could feel his mistrust. This wasn't going to work.

"Well?" Loki challenged. "Are you going to let us in or not?"

"Not," said Frogg as he sat again.

Freya wasn't about to be stopped at the first hurdle. She moved as if to go for her sword and growled with as deep a voice as she could manage.

"I'd let us in if I were you," Loki warned the troll. "If he loses his temper, there's no telling what will happen. Especially with the Searcher Ceremony tonight. Have you considered what the others will do if they learn of your behavior toward one of their own?"

The troll muttered angrily to himself, but he walked out of the guardhouse and over to the smaller gate. He opened it and spat at Archie and Freya as they passed through.

"He just spat at us," Archie cried in disgust, once they were inside.

"Shhhh! Do you want to get us killed?" Loki warned. "And stop staring at everything. You're supposed to live here!"

Freya had forgotten just how huge everything was in Utgard. It was built for the frost giants. The others who lived here did so at their own peril and had to build around the giants' homes and streets, which were many times the size of their own.

Dark Elves had built their little houses on the front steps of frost giants' massive homes. The streets built for giants' feet had small trails running alongside them for the non-giant population.

Loki pulled Freya and Archie out of the way just as a huge foot came down on the ground. The frost giant kept walking without pausing to see if he had stepped on them.

"You two wouldn't last a minute here without me!" he muttered. "You must watch where you are going—always. Frost giants don't care if they tread on you and squash you into nothingness. Just stay close to me and you might survive."

"This place is insane," Archie whispered to Freya as they followed Loki onto the Dark Elves' trail.

Not far ahead, two drunken frost giants were lying in the road, wrestling over a large keg of mead. Their slurred voices boomed so unbearably loud, Freya and Archie were forced to cover their ears. As the giants exchanged punches, the open barrel they were fighting over slipped from their hands and started to roll. Mead began to pour out as the barrel rolled away from the giants . . . and toward Freya, Archie, and Loki.

"Fly!" Loki shouted as he turned into the eagle and took off.

Freya grabbed Archie and launched into the air just in time to avoid the racing river of mead that rushed past the place where they had been standing. Freya looked back and saw several trolls being washed away.

"This way," Loki screeched, keeping to the air.

Holding Archie close, Freya followed Loki through the complicated design of Utgard. Beneath them, none of the streets followed a straight line and they seemed to constantly wind and twist into each other. It seemed as though buildings had been stacked recklessly on top of one another and looked ready to topple over in the slightest breeze.

This was nothing like the ordered design of Asgard. It was confusing, deceptive, and impossible to navigate, unless you'd been raised here.

The sky was full of flying Dark Searchers. Fear knotted in Freya's stomach. Utgard was their territory; she was the invader. One mistake and it would be over. She realized this may not have been one of her best ideas. They were badly outnumbered, and she was on the Dark Searchers' most wanted list.

But the Dark Searchers weren't the only danger here.

As they followed Loki over the city, Freya sensed the tension from the population even more acutely than in Asgard. There was anger in the air and more than a trace of excited anticipation. There was no doubt about it—war was on their minds, and with disgust Freya realized that they were looking forward to it.

They flew away from the congested city and into a sparse area where the structures became notably smaller and more proportioned to their size. Freya spied Dark Elves on the roads and a market filled with elf traders, trolls, and dwarf shoppers.

Farther ahead were rolling snow-covered hills and open land that gave way to another forest.

"Are we still in Utgard?" Archie asked.

Freya nodded. "It is walled, just like Asgard. And like there, you can't see from one wall to the other."

On and on they flew. As the skies above them became darker with the approaching storm, the land beneath looked more threatening and sparse.

"There it is," Loki called. "The Keep of the Dark Searchers."

The immense keep rose in the distance. It was made of huge rough-cut rock, as black as the Searchers themselves. Four tall spires marked each corner—at the top of each tower flew the flag of the Dark Searchers. There were very few windows, and those that were there held no glass to keep out the intense cold. The thick, heavy doors at the entrance looked as old as time itself and completely impenetrable.

Along the top of the outer walls were heavy wrought-iron balustrades so the Dark Searchers could move along the wall-walk with little risk of falling off. No trees grew around the keep, and not even snow rested on the dead, black ground.

Freya tried to take it all in. Her brother was somewhere in that vast, ugly structure. But so were all the other Dark Searchers—including Dirian, the one who had sworn vengeance against her.

As they approached, Freya spotted Dark Searchers building a large seating area around a tall scaffold and platform. They wore their visored helmets and double swords at their waists, but they were without armor.

"That is for Kai," Loki explained. "He will swear his oath and destroy his voice on that tall platform."

"How do we find him in there?" Freya called.

"That's up to you. He's your brother—use your senses."

Freya tilted her wings and veered away from the keep. She landed on the ground and released Archie.

Loki landed beside her and turned back into himself. "Well? Are you planning to stop for a picnic?"

"No," Freya snapped. "I need a moment to focus and not be distracted by all those Searchers working over there."

"Go on, then," Loki ordered. "We don't have all day."

Freya ignored him and closed her eyes. She focused on

overcoming her fear of the Dark Searchers and concentrated fully on the keep. She could sense the layout and feel the Searchers moving around inside. "Where are you . . . ?" she muttered softly.

Suddenly she felt a strange, familiar sense—the same one she'd had on the battlefield at the Ten Realms Challenge. "There!"

"*Where is he?*" Orus cawed.

Freya opened her eyes. "He's not in the keep."

"Not there?" Archie cried. "Where is he?"

"He's beneath it."

"Ah, yes," Loki agreed. "Tunnels run beneath the keep. The acoustics are amazing for someone with an intact voice."

"He goes down there to sing?" Archie asked.

"What would you do if everyone else around you had no voice, while you had a voice that could charm the stars from the heavens?"

"You would hide it so you don't remind the others of what they've lost," Freya answered.

"Exactly," Loki finished. He turned back into the eagle. "I know a secret way in. Hurry, before anyone sees us."

They traveled back over the forest, and Loki led them to a small area that had been cleared. He returned to his natural form.

"This way," he ordered, entering the trees. He stopped in

front of a pine tree that was distinguishable from the rest by its thicker trunk and pale, soft needles.

They watched as Loki pressed five spots around the trunk. There was a strange hissing sound, and with a click, a small door appeared. It moved back, deeper into the trunk of the tree, and revealed an opening. Loki turned back to Freya and held up a warning finger. "You will tell no one of this entrance. Is that understood?"

Freya nodded.

"Does Odin know about it?" Archie asked.

Loki frowned. "Why do you want to know?"

Archie shrugged. "Just curious."

"Curiosity will get you killed—again!"

Loki passed through the hidden entrance, with Freya and Archie following close behind. It slanted down into a narrow tunnel that cut deep into the earth. There were no support beams, and the thick roots of the trees high above them hung down from the dirt ceiling and caught in their clothes. Freya had to remove her helmet, as she could hardly see a thing.

Loki turned to her. "You will put that back on when I tell you to. Now, open your wings fully."

"Why?"

"Must you question everything I say? Just do it," Loki said tiredly.

Freya opened her wings—they just about fit, but the

long feathers on either end grazed the dirt walls.

"Do you think you could fly through here if you had to?"

"I think so," Freya said. "But it might damage my feathers."

Loki nodded. "Better a few damaged feathers than letting the Dark Searchers get ahold of you. Their wings are too large for this tunnel and they would have to run. Just be prepared—we may need to make a hasty retreat, and I need to know if you can keep up with me."

"Don't worry about us," Archie said. "You just lead us to Kai."

"You," Loki said, poking Archie in the chest, "you, I would gladly leave behind for the Searchers." He stormed into the darkened tunnel.

The tunnel seemed never-ending. But they knew they were getting closer when they heard faint notes echoing softly toward them. Someone was singing. Freya paused to listen. The sound was beautiful. More amazing than anything she'd ever heard before. Vonni's voice had enchanted her, but this sound captured her heart. She soared with each note, carried along a wondrous path to an unknown land. . . .

A sharp slap across her face woke her up.

Loki's piercing eyes loomed in front of her. "Freya, snap out of it!"

Freya shook her head. "What happened?"

"Your brother—that's what happened."

"Kai?" Freya asked. "Is that him singing?"

Loki nodded. "This was where I first heard him. He spends a lot of time in these tunnels, singing to himself. The Searchers won't let him sing aboveground. Unless we get there quickly, that voice will be lost forever."

He pulled a tissue from his pocket and tore pieces off it. "Here, shove these in your ears and put on your helmet."

"Why?"

"Again with the questions? Do it because you are no good to anyone when you hear him sing."

"He's right," Archie agreed. "You went all dreamy and stopped. You didn't even hear me."

"*Or me,*" Orus called from beneath the cloak.

Freya plugged her ears with the tissue and pulled on the Dark Searcher helmet. She could still hear faint sounds, but not enough to capture her again.

"This way." Loki motioned to the left as they came to a crossroads.

They saw the flickering of a torch. Now Freya could feel the presence of her brother. Kai was just ahead. She started to run, but Loki caught hold of her wings and wrenched her back.

"Are you mad as well as stupid?" he whispered sharply. "You're supposed to be a Dark Searcher. They walk, not run!"

Loki was right. Kai was her brother, but they had no idea how he would react to her. After all, he was a Dark

Searcher. She folded her wings again and walked toward the flickering light.

As they rounded a bend, she saw him.

Alone in the dark tunnel, he poured his heart out in every note of his secret song. His Dark Searcher helmet lay on the ground beside him. He looked taller than Freya, and long black hair fell down his back and cascaded between his half-opened wings. But his most striking feature were his amazing white feathers.

Sensing their presence, Kai turned sharply. His hands instinctively went to the double swords he wore on his belt.

"Kai, it's me!" Loki called.

"Loki?" Kai asked. He relaxed when he saw it was him. "What are you doing here with this Dark Elf and . . . ?"

Freya could feel Kai's powers reaching into her, sensing her.

"Who is this?" His dark brows knitted together as he advanced on her. "You're not a Searcher. Who are you?"

Loki stepped toward him. "Kai, this is someone I thought you might like to meet."

Freya stared at her brother in wonder. Kai looked so much like her! As she stepped closer, she noticed his eyes. They were as unexpected as his wings. They weren't the dark sapphire blue of Vonni's eyes and her own, but were as pale as Maya's. Somehow, she and her twin brother had switched features.

She pulled off her helmet and removed the plugs from

her ears. She could barely contain her excitement. "Kai, I'm Freya. I'm your twin sister!"

Kai's eyes widened at the sight of her. He inhaled sharply. "You! You're the one who caused Dirian to be de-winged and disgraced!" He howled at the top of his lungs, "Guards, sound the alarm! There's a Valkyrie in our keep!"

He drew his two black swords and launched his attack.

22

MAYA WAS CONFLICTED. SHE SOARED OVER THE TREES, patrolling in Freya's absence when she knew she was needed at the ranch, helping everyone work in the mine. But she was frantic about Freya and Archie and desperate to go after them.

"I should have stopped them," she said to Grul as he flew in the sky beside her.

"*You couldn't have,*" Grul shot back. "*Freya is too strong-willed for her own good. If the Dark Searchers catch her, there is no telling what will happen.*"

"Which is why we should have gone with them," Maya said.

"*Then you would risk capture as well.*"

"It's better than not knowing." Finally she changed direction in the sky. "If we fly fast enough, we might just catch them."

"Maya, you can't!" Grul cawed.

"I must!"

But just as she climbed higher to find Bifröst, Maya's senses picked up unfamiliar movement in the trees beneath them. She cursed.

"Grul, we're not alone. Hunters are at the lake."

She turned and flew back in the direction of the intruders. Flying low, she glided over the surface of the water. Men were gathering on the opposite shore. Her senses immediately picked up danger. With her helmet on, she knew they wouldn't see her as she moved silently toward them.

She landed several feet away and counted eight men moving around the lake. They all carried packs on their back and had weapons in their hands. She could feel that they weren't here to hunt animals. Their target was the main house. But there was more than that. They were planning something big. Maya crept closer to find out what. And then it hit her. They were going to burn down the house to drive everyone away, sure that it would leave the gold mine unprotected for them to take.

Maya gasped. Their greed had made them willing to kill anyone who stood in their way. Now she was even more torn. Should she continue to stalk the men, or go back to the mine to get her mother and sisters?

Before she could decide, the choice was made for her. The men picked up their pace. Moving swiftly through the undergrowth, they headed straight toward the house.

"They'll make it to the house before we reach the mine to get Mother and the others," she whispered to Grul. "We're going to have to stop them ourselves."

"*How?*" Grul asked. "*There are too many for you to fight alone.*"

"I don't want to fight if we can avoid it. Maybe we can scare them away. I've got an idea."

Maya charged forward and ran straight at the first man. Still invisible, she kicked his legs out from under him and howled her loudest Valkyrie cry. He went down like a sack of wet sand. She attacked the next man. Careful not to touch him with her bare hands, she kicked him back into the trees.

The remaining men fell to the ground, pulled on heat seeking goggles and raised their weapons. She sensed no fear from them. Maya realized too late that they were ready for otherworldly beings and had also come prepared to fight the Valkyries. With their specialized equipment, she also realized that they could now see her.

Before she could get away, they opened fire.

Bullets pinged off Maya's armor, her helmet, and cut into her exposed wings. Despite being raised on Earth's battlefields, she had never been the target of war before. If a Valkyrie was hit by a stray bullet, it was an accident and usually caused no harm. This was no accident. These men came specifically to hunt the Valkyries with powerful weapons.

"*Maya, it's a trap, fly!*" Grul called.

Maya opened her wings, but bullets continued to hound her. They tore through her wings and chopped at her feathers. She had no choice. She howled again to call her mother and sisters to the lake. They had to be warned of the attack.

Beside her, Grul was hit. He let out a strangled caw and fell to the ground.

"*Grul!*" Maya shouted. As she reached down for him, more bullets found their target.

Clutching Grul, Maya tried to run, but her legs were being shot out from under her. More men soon emerged from the trees. Wearing their heat-seeking equipment, they pointed their weapons at Maya and opened fire.

23

KAI DIDN'T HESITATE AS HE CHARGED FREYA. HIS FIRST cut went across her upper arm while she reached for her flaming sword.

The blow was intended to do as much damage as possible. "Kai, stop!" Freya cried. "I'm your sister!" Freya drew her sword and defended herself against Kai's second slash.

"I don't have a sister!" Kai cried. He charged again, and his two swords flashed against Freya's one. "No Searcher does!"

"That's a lie. Look at me, Kai. You can feel it. We're twins!"

"No!"

"Kai, stop!" Loki demanded. "You'll call the others!"

"Guards!" Kai shouted. "Guards—come quickly! Valkyries!"

Freya was trying to defend herself. But she refused to strike her brother with her sword. She could sense others entering the tunnels. It wouldn't be long before more Searchers arrived.

"Kai, please," she begged. "Just give me a moment to explain. . . ."

"Never trust a Valkyrie!" Kai shouted, pressing his attack.

A second cut slashed across her abdomen and sliced through her black leather outfit, grazing her skin.

"No!" Archie charged at Kai from behind. He wrapped his arms around Kai and knocked him down. "Stop it!" he shouted, pinning him down. "She's your sister!"

But Kai had all the strength and training of a Dark Searcher. He spun out from beneath Archie and tossed him aside as if he were a feather. Archie struck the wall and fell to the ground.

Kai gained his feet and charged at Freya again.

"Freya, get out of here!" Loki cried. "Fly!"

"I won't leave Archie or Kai!"

"Go," Archie called as he ran at Kai again. "I'll be right behind you!"

"Go!" Loki commanded.

In the tight confines of the tunnel, it was impossible to reason with her brother. She could feel his intense desire to capture her, perhaps even kill her. It was then that Freya had an idea.

"Kai, if you want me," she shouted at him, "you're going to have to catch me!"

Freya turned, opened her wings and launched into flight. But the tunnel walls weren't even. She had to tuck in her wings to avoid the parts of the walls that jutted out.

"Stop!" Kai shouted as he chased her through the tunnel. "Stop, Valkyrie!"

"I'm Freya!" she shouted. "Your sister Freya!"

Freya was grateful to be the fastest flyer in Asgard. Despite the tight confines of the tunnel, she was broadening the distance between them. But as she reached the crossroads and tilted her wings to turn into the exit tunnel, she smashed headlong into two Dark Searchers.

They tumbled to the ground.

Freya fought to gain her feet first, but powerful hands caught hold of her wings. Another hand wrapped around her neck. Seconds later Kai landed beside her and caught hold of her hair. She was dragged to her feet.

Freya looked for a way out, but she was well and truly trapped. The Dark Searchers held her tight in their firm grip. There was no escape.

Her mind raced with all the horrors about to come. A single Valkyrie, trapped in the Keep of the Dark Searchers. She feared they wouldn't tell Odin and would simply hand her over to Dirian, who would make her disappear forever. . . .

"Let me go!"

"What is this?" rasped a Searcher, more a growl than a voice. "A Valkyrie in our keep?"

"She claims to be my sister," Kai spat. "She says we're twins."

"We *are* twins!" Freya shouted as she fought to break free. "Look at your wings. They're white. Look at mine, they're black! Your eyes are pale; mine are dark. Something has switched. We have the same mother. We were born at the same time. Kai, we are twins!"

"Lies!" Kai cried, wrenching her hair back. "I have no sister!"

"Actually, you have five!" Loki appeared out of nowhere, in true Loki style. He faced the Searchers holding Freya. "Would you please release that Valkyrie? I am in need of her."

The two Dark Searchers rumbled annoyance. The larger one rasped, "Do not interfere, Loki. She has broken our laws and invaded our keep. She comes with us and will be punished."

"I don't think so," Loki said.

Freya struggled to turn back to the Searchers holding her. "Please, I beg you, listen to me. We are the same. Dark Searchers are the sons born to Valkyries. We are not different. There is no need to fight!"

"Stop lying," Kai cried.

"Use your powers!" Freya implored the two senior Searchers. "You have the same senses as me. Use them. Know that

I am telling you the truth. Valkyries and Dark Searchers are the same race!"

The two Searchers said nothing, but Freya could feel their growing hesitation as their grip loosened. They were scanning her mind for betrayal.

"It's true," Archie added. "We have seen that a Searcher can have a wife, children, and a home. You don't have to live like this. You can be free!"

"I don't believe you!" Kai cried.

There was fury in his voice, but also a trace of doubt that Freya picked up on. "You can feel our connection, Kai. Admit it. You felt it during the Challenge, and you feel it now. Why do you deny me?"

"I am proud to be a Searcher—it is my duty; there is nothing else."

"You should be proud," Freya insisted. "You have served Odin loyally. But you are also my brother."

"Enough," one of the senior Searchers ordered. He tightened his grip on her neck again. "You will answer for your presence here."

"Kai, you know who I am. Help me!" Freya begged.

"No!" Kai cried. "It's a trick!" He turned from Freya and ran down the tunnel. Leaping into the air, he flew out of sight.

"I swear it's true," Freya cried to her captors. "You can be free. I've seen it for myself. You can have full lives and families if you want them."

The viselike hand around her throat tightened. Freya was lifted off the ground and held at face level as the Dark Searcher scanned her eyes for deceit. She started to cough and gasp for air but kept her hands at her sides.

"*No!*" Orus cawed from under the cloak. "*Let her go!*"

Archie charged forward. "You heard him. Let her go!"

The second Dark Searcher dropped his grip on Freya's wings, drew his two swords, and advanced on Archie.

"Oh, that's brave," Archie challenged. "Two swords against me—I thought Searchers were supposed to fight fair."

"That is enough!" Loki shouted. "Release her now!"

In the tight confines of the tunnel, Loki started to shimmer and change. In moments he turned into a smaller version of his black dragon. Though not as large, this one was just as deadly, with flames sparking from his nostrils and claws longer and sharper. The dragon inhaled deeply to let go of a blast of flames.

The Searcher holding Freya dropped her and reached for his swords. "Foolish little dragon," he growled.

"Go!" Loki roared as he pressed forward and knocked Freya away from the Searchers with the back of his sharp claws. "Find Kai!"

Archie ran over to Freya and helped her up. "C'mon. It's going to get hot in here!"

They stumbled away from the scene as the two Dark Searchers raised their swords and charged at Loki. Freya carried Archie and flew as fast as she could through the tunnels, cringing at the sounds of the dragon's roars behind them. They exited through the large pine tree. There were fresh footprints in the snow that didn't belong to them. The footprints stopped abruptly.

"He must have come through here," Freya said. She closed her eyes and felt Kai flying away from the keep.

They launched back into the air. "We have to find him. The sun will be setting soon."

Freya could sense that her brother was directly ahead and moving fast. But even carrying Archie, Freya was faster. She beat her wings as hard as she could, and before long a dark shape came into view in the distance.

"That's him!" Archie cried.

"Kai!" Freya shouted. "Kai, please land!"

Putting on more speed, Freya gained on her brother. They were now flying over snow-covered mountaintops. Freya stole a glance backward. There were no other Searchers flying after them.

"Please, Kai!"

Ahead of them, Kai pulled his two swords from their sheaths. The black blades glinted in the gray light. "Stay back or I'll kill you!"

"Gee, put me down," Archie called. "You can't carry me and fight your brother. You can come back for me."

"It's too dangerous. I won't leave you behind!"

"Do it!" Orus cawed from her cloak. *"You will be safer with both of us off you. We can look after ourselves."*

Reluctantly, Freya swooped down to a mountain peak. She released Archie and freed Orus from her cloak, and then, without missing a wing beat, she took off again. "Stay right here. I'll be back!"

Freya focused fully on her brother. He had changed direction. She tilted her wings and swerved to find him until she had him in her sights. In no time she was flying directly behind him.

"Stay back!" Kai warned. "I don't want to fight you, but I will."

"Land and we can talk about it."

He was deeply conflicted. Freya was hit with fear, confusion, anger, and desperation as his swords flashed and he swooped closer to her. "Leave or I'll kill you."

"Then you're going to have to kill me, because I'm not going anywhere!" Freya drew her sword and prepared to defend herself.

Sparks flew as the swords clashed high in the sky. It was two swords against one. But as Kai maneuvered for another pass, Freya could sense his heart wasn't completely in it.

"You don't have to do this!" She flew closer. "You don't have to swear the oath and ruin your voice. You can come with me and be free."

"I'm a Dark Searcher," Kai cried as his swords flashed again. "It is my honor and my duty!"

"And I'm a Valkyrie with my own duties!" Freya cried. "But we are family. That comes first!"

"Your words mean nothing to me!"

"That's not true. I can feel your doubt."

Kai suddenly changed direction again. He glided low and landed on a cliff top. Folding his white wings tightly, he raised his weapons and slashed at her in the air. "Go back to Asgard, Valkyrie. My duty is here!"

"War is coming; you're not safe here!" Freya tucked in her wings and dove at her brother at full speed. She struck him hard and knocked him backward into a snow drift. He made a grab for her and took her down with him. They immediately started to wrestle. Freya tried to pin him down. She had to make him understand. But their strength was equal; neither one was able to gain the upper hand. . . .

"Listen to me, Kai—"

Suddenly the ice beneath them let out a loud, cracking boom. It gave way and they fell into a deep crevasse.

They screamed as one as they tumbled down the deep hole.

Together, they crashed to the bottom.

24

FREYA WAS THE FIRST TO REGAIN CONSCIOUSNESS.
She coughed and choked as she tried to sit up. Weak light
filtered down from high above, though they were so deep she
couldn't see the sky. They must have fallen at least half the
depth of the mountain. They were lying on a hard ice shelf
in a cavern, no more than a couple of meters wide, lined with
thick ice.

A soft moan shattered the stillness as Kai stirred.

"Kai." Freya leaned closer and checked to see if he was
all right.

He moaned again.

Freya pulled her brother onto his side, removing his
weight from his wings. "Kai, wake up!"

Looking around at the tight confines of the pit, Freya

knew that getting out would not be easy, especially if her brother didn't wake up.

"Kai, please," she urged gently.

Her brother moaned again and opened his eyes slowly. Seeing her leaning over him, he sat up quickly. As he reached for his swords, he cried out in pain.

"Is it your wings?" Freya asked in alarm.

He looked at her. "No. It's my elbow. I landed on my arm."

"Then it looks like the fight is over," Freya said. "Now will you listen to me?"

"Listen to more lies?" he said bitterly.

"Why won't you believe me? Surely your senses are telling you the truth. I am your sister."

He was fighting himself as much as her. "Searchers have no family other than the brotherhood."

Kai climbed painfully to his feet and gazed around. He touched the wall. Then he opened his wings to discover that they were wider than the hole they were in. He reached for one of his swords.

Freya also reached for her sword and climbed stiffly to her feet. "So is this it? We're going to fight in this pit until one of us is dead?"

Kai shook his head. "No. I was going to use my blades to climb out of here. The tunnel is too small for either of us to fly through."

Freya looked up and realized he was right. The only way out was to climb. "Oh." She watched him reach for his other blade. "So, do you believe me?"

He paused and looked at her. "I don't know what to believe anymore. My life was so simple. I had my duty and my Searcher Ceremony tonight. After all the years of being treated as an outcast because I was different, I was finally going to be accepted into the brotherhood. Now you come and ruin everything."

"I don't want to ruin anything. But I couldn't leave here without you knowing you have a choice."

"A Searcher has no choice."

"But you do," Freya insisted.

She extended her wings. "Look at me. Can't you see how alike we are? My wings are black; yours are white. I'm different from all the other Valkyries, just like you are from the Searchers. I've always felt like an outsider and have never really been trusted because I'm different. Now you tell me it's the same for you."

Kai looked down, and Freya felt a quiver of recognition at her words. Encouraged, she moved toward him.

"Kai, you don't have to stay here. You have a choice. You can come with me and be free. We have an uncle. He was born a Searcher but was raised in Midgard. He's as powerful as all the others, but he has a family who loves him. You can stay with him."

"Utgard is my home. . . ." He paused. "Was my home."

"What do you mean—was?"

"The Dark Searchers are going to abandon the keep."

"What?"

Kai nodded. "Thor and Balder are here. They came under the guise of attending my Searcher Ceremony, but the truth is they are calling us all to Asgard."

Freya walked to the icy wall and gazed up. "The war."

Kai caught her arm. "What do you know of the war?"

"Only that it's coming. That's why I came here. I want to take you to a safe place before it starts."

"Odin has ordered the Searchers to Asgard to fight for him. I must leave with my brothers."

"Will you fight?"

Kai nodded. "So will you. You are Valkyrie—one of Odin's Battle-Maidens. You will be called to defend Asgard, as will we. Will you do it?"

Freya felt her heart skip a beat. She hadn't thought about that. She'd been so concerned about finding him and protecting Vonni and the family that she hadn't realized that she too would have a part to play in the war.

"I'm not so different from you, Kai," Freya finally said. "If Odin commands me to fight, I will fight."

"You will fight, but you expect me to hide from the war in Midgard?"

"I don't know what I expected," Freya said desperately.

"All I know is that you are my brother. I needed to find you.
I never thought beyond that."

"Or that I might choose to stay with my brothers?"

"Yes," Freya admitted.

Kai leaned against the ice wall, staring at her. His emotions were locked beyond her reach, and Freya had no idea
what he was thinking.

"Say something," she said, feeling uncomfortable under
his intense gaze.

"You came all this way, risking your life, just to see me?"

"Yes."

"I don't understand why," Kai said. "You are a Valkyrie;
I am a Dark Searcher—we are natural enemies. Why would
you do this?"

"You know why," Freya challenged.

"Because you claim I am your brother."

After all she'd been through, he still didn't believe her.
"You *are* my brother! And whether you want to admit it or
not, you know it's true!"

Kai sighed. "I told you, I'm not sure what I believe anymore."

"So, will you hand me over to Dirian?"

Kai paused, and Freya was certain he would say yes. But
he shook his head.

"I'm not saying I believe you, but I would never turn anyone over to him. When we get out of this pit, I'll help you get

out of Utgard. But no more than that. I am a Dark Searcher and always will be. I will stay with my brothers and fight. Whatever happens, this will be the last time we ever speak."

Freya nodded. "I understand. Just know this, Kai. Whatever path you choose, I will always be your sister."

For the first time, Kai smiled, and it lit up his whole face. "You just don't give up, do you?"

Freya smiled back at him. "Nope."

Kai turned and drove the tip of his sword into the rocky wall. He stepped up onto the blade. Then he drove his second blade higher up and climbed onto it. He reached down and, retrieving his first blade, drove it in the wall even higher.

Before he climbed out of her sight, Kai reached his hand down to her. "Well, sister, are you coming?"

Freya grinned and took her brother's hand.

The climb was long and hard. Freya had to give Kai her flaming sword to help get them out of the crevasse. With each step came more mixed emotions. She had found her brother and he had acknowledged her as his sister. But now she was about to lose him again as he joined the Searchers heading to Asgard to fight in the war.

As she gazed up to the entrance, she could see the light fading. Night was rising. Knowing everything he now knew, how could Kai still surrender his voice in the service of his duties as a Dark Searcher? As her mind played out all the different scenarios, Kai crested the top of the crevasse and climbed out, disappearing from view.

Freya heard a muffled cry. "Kai?" she called.

When he didn't reply, Freya's heart pounded. Climbing faster, she reached the top. And what she saw there made her blood run cold.

The entrance was surrounded by Dark Searchers. One of them held Kai, his hand pressed firmly over her brother's mouth. The others were waiting for her.

Swords lifted, they moved forward.

25

MAYA WOKE. SHE WAS LYING ON HER SIDE IN A SOFT BED.
Her wings ached and her legs stung. She felt a hand
stroking her cheek and lifted her head to see her mother by
her side. Her three sisters were standing back, looking concerned, and Vonni and Sarah were at the end of her bed.
"You're safe. Just stay still. George is changing the bandages
on your wings."

Maya winced. She looked back to see George lifting her
wing as he wrapped gauze around it. He was wearing heavy
leather gloves and wore extra protective clothes and a mask
on his face. To her shock, her wings were in tatters—only a
few broken feathers still clung to them.

"What happened?"

"We heard your calls," her mother said. "By the time we

reached the lake, you were on the ground and surrounded. We fought the hunters and brought you back to the house."

George spoke. "Those men sure shot you to pieces. It looks like your wings took the worst of it."

"Mia?" her mother asked, drawing her attention back. "We can't find Greta or Archie. Were they with you? Did other men capture her and take them away? I can't feel them anywhere."

"Greta?" Maya repeated. "No, it was just Grul and me...." She suddenly remembered. Freya and Archie had gone to Utgard. She had promised Freya not to tell her mother. "No. Greta was patrolling the mountains."

She looked back to George again as he finished securing the bandage. "All done," he said, removing his mask.

"Just how bad is it?" Maya asked.

"Well, it ain't good. Your right wing is broken clean through. Your left ain't much better. They've been cut to pieces. I'm afraid you're gonna be grounded for some time while those bones knit together again. Sorry about the feathers. There was nothing I could do to save them."

Maya smiled gently at him. "I understand. Thank you for your kind care."

George's face turned bright red under her radiant smile. "It weren't nothing at all. I'm just glad I could help."

"Yes, thank you, George," Eir said. "We are grateful to you."

Grul was lying on the table beside the bed, breathing softly. He was covered in so many bandages, Maya could barely see any of his black feathers.

"How is he?" she fearfully asked.

"Recovering," her mother said. "George did a fine job removing the bullets. Now, Mia, are you sure you don't know where Greta is?"

"Loki is gone too," Vonni added. "Were they together?"

Maya avoided the question. "How long have they been gone?"

"Four days," Vonni answered.

"Four days?" Freya had promised to come right back. Even with the time difference between Utgard and Earth, this was taking too long. Should she tell her family the truth?

"The last time we saw her was the night you were attacked," her mother continued. "We fear the hunters may have taken her. But they claimed not to have seen her."

"You captured the hunters?"

"A few," Vonni said. "We're keeping them in the barn for now. But we can't hold them much longer. Others will notice them missing."

"We should have killed them all, after what they did to Mia," Gwyn muttered.

Vonni shook his head. "I don't know what it's like in Asgard, but here on Earth we don't do things like that."

Eir stroked Maya's head. "Rest now. Your sisters are

returning to the mine. I'm going out to search for Greta. I'll be back soon."

Maya felt guilty for not telling her family what she knew of her younger sister. As she lay back, she closed her eyes, realizing that if Freya didn't come back soon, she would have to tell them the truth.

26

FREYA WAS PUT IN CHAINS AND CARRIED BACK TO THE keep by a large Dark Searcher. She looked for her brother among the Searchers escorting her, but he was being kept well away from her.

They landed at the front of the keep, and without anyone saying a word to announce their arrival, the massive doors swung open to receive them. Freya looked up into the darkening skies and wondered if this would be the last daylight she would ever see.

She was carried through the main floor of the keep and then down into the lower levels. The sounds of the Dark Searchers' footfalls on the rough stone stairs were the only things to disturb the overwhelming silence.

At the very bottom of the steps, she was dragged down

a darkened corridor. Torches spit and burned along the wall, offering little light, and the sound of dripping water matched the breathing and heavy tread of her escort.

Freya wanted to ask about her brother. She wanted to ask if Odin would be informed of her presence in the keep. But she was too frightened to speak. Was Kai being punished with her? He had committed no crime, but would they recognize this? What about Archie? Were he and Orus still at the top of that mountain, waiting in the deepening cold for her to return?

At the end of the corridor the group of Searchers stopped. A large metal key was pulled down from a hook on the wall and inserted in the lock of a thick iron door. The lower half of the door was solid. The upper half contained a large window with bars. The hinges creaked as the door was opened.

Freya was shoved inside. Without ever speaking a single word to her, the Dark Searchers locked the door and drifted away.

Freya looked around her small cell. No outer windows. She was deep underground in the lowest level of the keep. There was no bed, no straw, nothing for her to sit on. It seemed the cell had been designed to terrify the occupant.

It worked.

After the Searchers left, Freya heard a sound in the corridor. She ran to the barred window in the door and tried to peer out. Had they found Archie? Was he being brought down to her? A lone Dark Searcher appeared out of the darkness, moving steadily toward her door.

With her senses working overtime, she didn't need to see who it was to know.

Dirian.

The Dark Searcher paused before her door. The only sound he made was his heavy breathing.

Freya took a step back, and her heart leaped when he reached for the key. Her eyes darted around her tiny cell. They had taken her sword from her, and there was nothing she could use as a weapon against him. She was at the mercy of this Dark Searcher, but Dirian had none.

The key entered the lock.

Freya panicked as the door was slowly pushed open. "Get out!" she shouted, hoping desperately other Searchers would hear. "Stop!"

Dirian continued into her cell.

It was only now that Freya realized just how large he truly was. Standing in his full armor, cloak, and visored helmet, he took up most of the free space in the cell.

"Stay back!" Freya warned. "There's a war coming. Odin needs all his warriors. You can't kill me—not without his consent."

Her words bounced off him like rain. He made no attempt to mask his emotions. She could feel his burning rage. Dirian hated her and held her personally responsible for his disgrace—and he wanted her to know it.

Freya tried the only weapon she had left to her—her reasoning. "I know you hate me." She backed into the corner of her cell. "But what happened to you is not my fault. You killed me during the Challenge. Even after everyone told you to stop. Your disgrace is your own fault, not mine!"

Dirian inhaled deeply. For the very first time, she heard him speak.

"I killed you once," he rasped with a sound more growl than voice. "But you didn't have the sense to stay dead—that was your mistake. You will not rise again after I am finished with you."

Slowly and methodically, Dirian drew his two swords and opened his one remaining wing. He advanced on Freya.

With the Dark Searcher taking up most of her cell, there was no getting around him. She would have to fight.

"You may kill me again," Freya challenged. "But you'll know you've been in the fight of your life!"

Freya opened her own wings and flew at Dirian with all her might. She dove in close, hoping to break his visor like she had at the Challenge. But Dirian was ready for her. He easily blocked her attack.

She tried again, reasoning that the closer she pressed to him, the less chance he had to use his swords. The attempt was brave but futile. When she tried to punch him as hard as she could, his first blade cut into her left wing. The second blade sliced into her side.

Freya couldn't keep from crying out. The back of Dirian's gauntlet knocked her across the cell, and she collapsed to the floor.

"You will not hasten your death, little one," he rasped. "Soon you will understand the depth of my humiliation."

She lay in the corner, fighting to catch her breath. Her wounds were searing hot, and her eye started to swell shut. Freya knew that without her sword she could never defeat him. But she wasn't going to make it easy for him either. She lunged again, hoping to find his blind spot like she had in the Challenge. But Dirian was prepared for her. He caught hold of her arm and wrenched it back.

"Not again," he growled.

Freya strained and pulled away from him, rubbing the tendons in her arm.

Dirian stood before her and started to laugh. "Is that all you've got, Valkyrie? A couple of small cuts and you give up?"

Oh, Azrael, Freya thought. She had no more options. Should she call him for help? But if Azrael appeared in Utgard, it would start the war. She couldn't allow that. She was on her own and would face whatever end Dirian had for her.

"Azrael can't help you now . . . ," Dirian boomed, as if he had read her thoughts.

"Go on, Dirian," she panted. "Kill me, but you'll always

be in disgrace!" Freya launched at him, using all her strength. But to no effect. Dirian unleashed his rage and anger and let his blades do the talking for him.

"Dirian, stop!"

Agony was blinding Freya, but in her misery, she was sure she recognized the voice. As Dirian's sword cut again and then again, she heard him let out a grunt of pain. Suddenly he was knocked away from her.

Both she and Dirian fell to the floor together. Freya forced herself to look up. Thor stood above Dirian, clutching his hammer. That would have been the only thing powerful enough to stop the murderous Dark Searcher.

"Take him out of here," Thor barked. "And get a healer down here now!"

Freya was barely conscious as Dirian was carried out. She felt Thor kneel at her side.

He turned her over. "Oh, Freya, you little fool, what have you done?"

27

"MAKE HER WELL ENOUGH TO TRAVEL," THOR commanded. "We'll be leaving for Asgard at first light."

Freya was lying on a narrow cot as a Dark Searcher healer treated her deep wounds. She felt compassion from him, and it surprised her. He was dressed as all the others, and carried his twin blades, but he was gentle and almost caring as he lifted her head and offered a potion to take the pain away. She was fast learning that not all Searchers were pure evil.

A line of Searchers stood guarding her with their weapons drawn. They weren't so compassionate.

"Tell me why," Thor demanded. He and his brother Balder were seated opposite her. "Valkyries are forbidden in Utgard—especially now that we are on the brink of war. Why are you here?"

Freya was helped into a seated position by the gentle Searcher. Every part of her body hurt, but especially her side, where Dirian's blade had cut deepest. "I needed to find my brother," she grunted softly.

"Brother?" Thor repeated. "What brother?"

"Kai. He's my twin. He's the young Dark Searcher with the white wings. You came here for his Searcher Ceremony."

"He's your twin?" Balder asked.

"We were separated at birth," Freya said. "I've felt him my whole life. I wanted to see him before the war started. If either of us fell in battle, I'd never know him. I couldn't bear that."

"You risked your life just to meet your brother?" Thor demanded.

Freya's eyes passed from Thor to Balder and back again. "Wouldn't you do the same for each other? I don't understand why Odin commands all the male babies born to Valkyries be taken from their mothers and delivered here to become Dark Searchers. Why can't we know each other? We would serve him just as well. But our families wouldn't be broken."

"Odin commands as Odin commands," Thor said.

"That's no answer," Freya remarked.

Thor's face went red. "What?"

"Brother, calm yourself," Balder said. His green eyes turned to Freya. "Are you questioning our father's reasons after Thor just saved your life?"

"No," Freya insisted, lowering her head to them. "It's just that you have your brothers. You know what it is to care for your whole family. Why are Valkyries and Dark Searchers denied that?"

"The reasons for Odin's decisions are known only to him. It is our place to obey. You are in so much trouble, Freya," Thor said. Then his eyes softened. "I have watched you for a long time, and I applaud your independent spirit. But this time you've gone too far. Not even I can help you now. You must face our father and answer for your crimes. I fear he will not be lenient."

Balder rose and looked sadly at her. "By the time Odin has finished with you, you'll wish Dirian had killed you—permanently."

Thor faced the Dark Searchers. "Take her back to her cell until it's time for us to leave."

Freya was carried back to her cell, and she found a cot had been placed inside. The healer Searcher helped her lie down. "Rest now," he rasped. "You face a great trial; you will need all your strength."

"Thank you." Freya settled herself onto the bed. "Wait." She reached for the Searcher's hand. "Did you know your mother was a Valkyrie? That all the Searchers are the sons born to them?"

The Dark Searcher considered for a moment before pulling free of her grasp. He walked to the cell door, and Freya was certain he wasn't going to answer. Before he passed through, he turned back, shaking his visored helmet.

"No, child, I didn't. I doubt any of us knew that."

Saying no more, he left and locked the door behind him.

A sound at the door roused Freya from sleep. She opened her eyes to see her cell door swing open. She was about to scream when a voice spoke.

"Freya, it's me. You must stay silent."

It was a relief to hear Kai's voice. Freya sat up as her brother entered the cell.

"Hurry." He tossed her Dark Searcher outfit and golden sword to her. "We don't have much time. The moon is rising and they are preparing for my Searcher Ceremony."

Freya was too stunned to speak. She let her brother haul her to her feet and help her dress in her Searcher armor and cloak. She winced as the buckles were tightened and closed around her wounds.

He fastened the golden sword around her waist. "The healer is guarding the outer door to the cells; we must hurry. I know a secret way out of here."

"But, Kai, if they catch you . . . ," Freya started.

Kai paused. "I heard Thor and Balder talking. They believe Odin will execute you. I can't let that happen. Freya, I have spent my life feeling different from the Searchers around me. When you told me you felt the same with the

Valkyries, I began to wonder if this is the reason for it. Part of me has always been missing. I never knew what that was. But now I know it's you. I have a family. I need to understand what that means and . . ."

"And?" Freya asked.

"I need to meet my mother."

Perhaps it was the healer's potion dulling her senses, but Freya could hardly believe what her brother was saying. He caught hold of her hand and drew her out of the cell and down the darkened corridor.

The healer Searcher was standing at the end of the corridor with a torch in his hand, which he offered to them. He said nothing as Freya and Kai walked past, but she could feel he was happy for them.

"This way," Kai whispered.

They descended deeper into the bowels of the keep. Kai navigated his way confidently through the confusing twists of his home as though he had done it many times before. Soon they entered the dark maze of tunnels running beneath the keep.

They emerged through the tree in the woods. Freya removed her helmet and inhaled the sweet aroma of freedom. The sky above them was dark gray as heavy, leaden storm clouds obscured the stars. But the air had never seemed sweeter.

"Here," Kai said, offering Freya a vial. "The healer said this will help you fly despite your wounds."

Freya didn't hesitate. She opened the vial and drank the bitter liquid. Her head started to spin, and if Kai hadn't caught her she would have fallen. But within minutes, with her brother's arms around her for support, Freya recovered.

"Can you fly now?" Kai asked. "We mustn't linger. They will be expecting me for my ceremony. If I don't arrive, they'll discover the truth."

Freya nodded. "I can fly, but we must find Archie. I left him and Orus at the top of a mountain."

"And we nearly froze to death, thank you very much!" Archie emerged from his hiding place in the trees and ran up to her. "I think I've got frostbite!"

Orus cawed and flew to Freya's shoulder.

"Archie?" Freya threw her arms around her best friend and held him tight. "How did you get here?"

"Kai found us," Archie explained. "He told us what happened. Are you okay?"

"I'll live," Freya replied.

Archie started to chuckle and shake his head. "You do have a talent for getting yourself into trouble, don't you? Dirian? Really? You thought you could beat him barehanded?"

"I didn't have much choice," Freya said. "He attacked me."

"And he'll do it again if we don't get out of here," Kai insisted. "We must go. Archie, Freya is wounded. I will carry you again."

"Wait," Freya said. She looked around. "What about Loki?"

"He's gone," Kai said. "They are searching for him, but Thor believes he is long gone. We will find our way to Bifröst without him."

"But he was going to get us through the gate!" Freya said.

"When they discover us missing, they will secure the gate. Frogg will not allow anyone to leave. I know another way out of Utgard. It will be dangerous, but if we succeed, no one will know how we left."

"Take us there," Freya said.

Kai caught hold of Archie, leaped up into the air, and flapped his white wings. Orus returned to his hiding place in Freya's cloak as she flapped her wounded wings and flew up into the sky behind her brother.

28

BACK ON EARTH, MAYA HAD BEEN CONFINED TO BED and ordered to rest. But she couldn't sleep. Freya and Archie should have been back by now.

"Something's wrong. I know it," she told Grul. "I have no choice—I must tell Mother."

"She'll be furious," Grul warned. He was still wrapped in bandages and nestled in a soft towel on the bedside table.

"Better that than letting something happen to Freya." Maya's eyes landed on her armor, lying on the floor beside the bed. It was dented almost beyond recognition.

"Look at those bullet strikes. I was lucky to survive."

"We both were," Grul agreed as he picked at the bandage on his wing. The raven stopped. *"Are you sure you want to do this?"*

Maya nodded. "What choice have we got?"

She climbed slowly to her feet and attempted to open her wings. They were wrapped in thick bandages. George had done a fine job setting the bones, but the pain in her right wing reminded her that it was broken.

She crept downstairs, dreading facing her mother. Maya found her in the dining room, sounding desperate and panicked. "I've tried everywhere," Eir was saying. "I can feel no trace of her. Something must have happened. The hunters who shot Mia may have taken her. I'm going back into the barn. They will tell me the truth, or I will tear it out of them—"

"Mother, stop," Maya interrupted. "They're not here. Loki, Greta, and Archie—they've . . . they've gone to Utgard."

"What do you mean they've gone to Utgard?" Eir was stunned. "Why would they do that?"

"*Here we go,*" Grul warned. "*Get ready for the explosion!*"

"She had no choice. . . . She . . . she had to find Kai." Maya paused. "Her twin brother." Her sisters erupted into gasps of confusion and surprise, but Maya saw her mother's face freeze into recognition.

"Mother." Maya attempted to soothe Eir. "Greta has felt Kai for most of her life, though she didn't understand what she was feeling. Now she does. When they bumped into each other during the battle at the Ten Realms Challenge . . . she knew. Just like you with Vonni."

Eir said, "But she can't go to Utgard! They'll kill her if they catch her there."

"Greta knew the danger," Maya insisted. "I tried to stop her, but she wouldn't listen. Nothing was going to keep her from finding Kai."

"*Loki is with her,*" Grul offered. "*Surely he wouldn't let anything happen to her.*"

"Loki?" Eir cried. "He'd be the one to hand her over! I must go to her!"

"You can't." Vonni stepped in. "All I've heard since Greta got here was how Utgard was about to declare war on Asgard. You can't go—not now."

Brundi rose carefully from her chair. "It's been too long. You wouldn't find her. All we can do is hope that Loki brings them back safely."

"But Loki—" Eir protested.

"I've told you," Brundi cut in sharply. "Loki has been a dear friend to me and this family. Even if he doesn't like Greta, he wouldn't let anything happen to her because of me."

Eir was shaking as she wrung her hands and started to pace. "Oh, Mother, I hope you are right."

29

FREYA, ARCHIE, AND KAI HEADED BACK TOWARD THE frost giants' city. It was illuminated with a golden glow that shone high into the dark storm clouds. From the distance, it was stunning. When they reached the city center, Kai led them down to the ground.

"It's beautiful here," Freya said, staring in wonder. "Where does the glow come from? Asgard doesn't shine like this at night."

"It's dwarf magic," Kai said. "It's enough to light up the city so there's no need for torches. With the confused way homes are built here, Utgard would burn down without it." Kai became serious. "Mind yourself when you're on the ground. The frost giants don't look down."

"We know," Archie said. "We nearly got drowned earlier."

The streets were clogged with the huge frost giants as they went about their business. Keeping to the Dark Elf trails, Freya, Archie, and her brother wound their way through the congested city.

"Over there." Kai pointed.

Across the wide street was a frost giants' inn. The sign said ODIN'S HEAD, and there was a picture of the frost giant king sitting at a banquet table with Odin's head on a platter before him.

"Does Odin know about this place?" Archie asked.

"I don't know," Kai said. "This inn has been here a very long time. But with tensions running high, they just changed their sign. The giants all love it."

"They would," Archie said.

Giants stood outside the inn, holding enormous tankards of mead. They were toasting their king and getting very drunk.

"Come," Kai said. "That inn rests up against the outer wall of Utgard. There's a tunnel through the wall in their basement."

"We have to go in there?" Archie cried.

Kai nodded. "I have used the tunnel many times to get out of Utgard unseen. Now, be on your guard," he warned. "I fear it won't take much to trigger disaster."

They walked carefully with their heads down so as not to draw attention to themselves. They were almost at the inn when Archie bumped into a troll.

The creature turned around and knocked him to the ground.

"Hey, watch it!" Archie cried.

He rose and shoved the troll back.

The troll sniffed the air. His round, bulbous nose moved closer. A filthy hand reached out and tore Archie's hood off. "Dead human," he spat.

"What is a dead human doing in Utgard?" A Dark Elf stepped in. Her pale-green face was unmasked and pinched into a deep scowl as her black eyes blazed. "And dressed like a Dark Elf. I won't tolerate it!"

"He's with me." Kai's voice was commanding. He made a show of resting his hands on the pommels of his blades. "He is my slave—a gift for my Dark Searcher Ceremony. Do you have a problem with him?"

The Dark Elf looked Kai up and down. "Yes, child Searcher, I do have a problem. I will not allow this human to dress as us." Her eyes hardened on Archie. "Remove your cloak and mask this instant."

Freya stepped forward and, doing her best Dark Searcher impression, growled and moved her hand to her sword.

"I wouldn't annoy him if I were you," Kai warned, indicating Freya. "He has a short temper."

"I don't care if you are Dirian himself! The human removes the elf cloak right now or I will remove it for him."

They hadn't noticed the crowd of elves and trolls that

had gathered around them, sensing a fight. A young Dark Elf made a grab for Archie's cloak. Freya swooped in, caught hold of the elf's hand, and wrenched it away.

The elf screeched in rage, and the next thing they knew he had called others to his aid.

Freya was swarmed by elves, kicking and punching her— though they reached no higher than her midsection and were doing no harm to her, until one managed to hit her in her wounded side. She swatted him into the gutter.

"Dark Searchers mustn't hit elves!" A large troll grabbed Freya from behind and gripped her wounded arm. Freya howled in pain.

There was a shocked intake of breath from the crowd. As the troll kept hold of her, a Dark Elf snatched off Freya's hood and another wrenched off her helmet.

"Valkyrie!" the troll roared.

"Valkyrie!" the crowds echoed. "There's a Valkyrie in Utgard!"

Freya let out another howl and drew her sword. "Go!" she cried to Kai and Archie. She swung her sword in a wide arc to keep the crowds at bay as they backed into the main street.

"Gee, look out!" Archie cried.

Freya turned just in time to see a frost giant's bare foot coming down above her. She threw herself flat to the ground and pointed her sword upward. The giant's foot came down straight onto the sharp blade and stopped just before crushing her.

The giant screeched, and as he hopped in pain, he squashed a troll and stepped on two of the Dark Elves before losing his balance and falling into another frost giant—who he took down with him.

The crowds of Dark Elves, dwarfs, and trolls panicked and ran for shelter as the giants fell like massive trees toppling in the forest.

This was the distraction they needed. "Come on!" Kai ordered as he caught Freya by the hand and hoisted her up. "This is going to get ugly!"

The sound of the two frost giants hitting the ground was like an explosion. "Valkyrie!" the bare-footed giant cried. "A Valkyrie attacked me! Call the king! Odin has declared war and sent his Valkyries to Utgard!"

"The Valkyries are attacking!" panicked a dwarf.

"Invaders in Utgard!" cried a Dark Elf.

Kai shook his head. "Rumors spread faster than lightning. Hurry up before they claim all of Asgard is here!"

Kai grabbed Archie and flew toward the entrance of the inn with Freya close behind. They maneuvered around the drinking frost giants, who swatted at them in the air as though they were irritating flies.

As they entered the inn, giants were rushing out to see what all the noise from outside was. Ducking between legs and darting around full skirts, Kai led them to the rear of the inn. He landed and put Archie down.

"We have to run from here," he called.

Freya caught hold of Archie's hand. "Stay with me and don't let go!"

Archie looked up and around at the huge frost giants pushing to get out. "Now I know how a mouse feels!"

"This way," Kai called.

They ran up to a door at the back of the inn. It had a gap between the bottom of the door and the floorboards just high enough for them to squeeze through. Kai lay flat on his stomach and crawled under. The others followed, and they emerged into a small back room. Frost giants were playing cards around a large table. Kai put his finger to his lips and motioned for them to follow him around the room, keeping as close to the wall as possible.

When they were halfway around, a frost giant burst in. "The Valkyries are in Utgard! They're on the rampage and attacking everyone. Sound the alarm!"

The giants stood and cast their chairs back. One missed Freya and Archie by a hairbreadth. The ground shook as they roared and charged through the door.

"Quickly!" Kai called as he caught hold of Archie, opened his wings, and flew across the room. "Frost giants have powerful senses—it won't take them long to trace us here!"

Freya followed her brother. They ducked under another door and then flew down a deep set of stairs.

"Down here!" Kai led them through a dimly lit hall until they reached another door. They crawled under it and into a storeroom filled with casks of mead. "Follow me. The tunnel is at the back!"

Suddenly the door burst open and three frost giants charged in.

"There she is!" one boomed, pointing down at Freya.

"Gee, run!" Archie cried, catching her by the hand.

They only managed a few more steps before a giant threw himself to the floor and snatched up Freya and Archie. "Gotcha!" He rose to his feet, holding them in his massive grip. "Why have you attacked Utgard?"

Freya and Archie were trapped. The giant's fingers wrapped tighter around them and started to squeeze.

Archie cried in pain.

"*Let them go!*" Orus cawed as he swooped at the giant's head.

"Stop!" Freya begged. "I'll tell you, if you loosen your grip. You're hurting my friend."

The giant roared with laughter, and the sound nearly deafened them. "Hurting a dead boy! Don't make me laugh!"

Kai buzzed toward his head, stabbing his swords into the giant's cheeks. "Release them!" he shouted.

The blades did little more than sting the angry giant. But it was enough. He staggered back as his friends came forward to try to swat Kai—but they kept missing him, which meant all they were doing was hitting the wounded giant.

Kai darted forward, his sword aimed at the giant's chin. It worked! The giant cried out and opened his fists to try to catch him.

Freya and Archie fell from his hands. Freya opened her wings and caught Archie before they hit the floor.

"This way!" Kai shouted as he flew away from the giant and toward a load of stacked casks.

Freya and Archie followed close behind. They landed on the floor and ran behind the first cask. The giants were shouting and racing after them, tossing the casks aside as if they weighed nothing.

"In here," Kai called as he darted behind a barrel against the wall and disappeared into a tiny hole. Freya and Archie followed close behind.

But just as they slipped through the opening, the barrel was torn away and a giant reached for Freya. He missed her legs and only managed to catch hold of her bottom flight feathers. But it was enough. He wrenched her back.

"*No!*" Orus cawed. "*Archie, help her!*"

With only seconds before Freya was dragged from the hole, Archie caught hold of her golden sword and pulled it from its scabbard. He swung it back and tried to cut her feathers, but the sword's magic wouldn't allow him to strike her.

"*Not her feathers, you idiot!*" Orus squawked. "*The giant, stab the giant!*"

Archie swung around toward the giant. He saw his mark and managed to stab the golden sword into the giant's hand.

The frost giant screeched and snatched his hand back, taking with him a handful of feathers from Freya's wings. But Archie and Kai caught hold of her and dragged her deeper into the tunnel.

Angry shouts followed them as they dashed through the dark tunnel. They ran as fast as they could, taking what felt like hundreds of sharp turns, until the sounds of the angry giants faded. They nearly choked on the stale air and the dust from moldy, damp earth, but they pressed on. Eventually the air became cooler and fresher. Up ahead, they saw the dull light of the exit.

"We're under Utgard's outer wall," Kai announced.

The ground beneath them rose, and they crawled out of a narrow hole in the thick stone wall. Snow was falling heavily, depositing a thick layer on the frozen ground.

Freya took deep breaths, drinking in the fresh air. She opened and flapped her wings. There was a large gap along the bottom of one wing where some of her long flight feathers had been yanked out.

"Can you fly?" Orus asked.

"I hope so." She straightened the remaining feathers.

"There is no time to preen," Kai warned. "They'll soon discover where we've come out. We must go."

Kai, with Archie, was first into the sky. It was a lot harder for Freya, with her wounds and damaged feathers, but she managed to take off behind him. The storm was rising, turning the thickly falling snow into a blizzard, obscuring the way ahead.

"Where is it?" Freya demanded as they circled in the sky. "It should be here!"

Bifröst was nowhere to be found.

"Freya, over there," Orus cawed. *"What's that? It looks like a fire in the sky."*

Freya followed Orus and saw the flash of bright flame in the dark-gray sky. She beat her wings and flew closer. It was coming from a large black dragon.

"It's Loki!" she called back. "Kai, this way!"

Freya chased the flame like a beacon, and soon they saw the huge dragon soaring before the entrance to Bifröst.

"Hurry!" the dragon roared. "Before Bifröst shifts again!"

Freya had never been so happy to see the shimmering colors of the Rainbow Bridge. She flew into the blazing colors and saw Kai entering beside her. The dragon followed up at the rear.

Halfway across the bridge, Freya stopped. She was

panting as she turned and faced the opposite direction. "Bifröst, open the passage to Midgard!"

Freya and her brother launched into the air and flew the length of the bridge.

In moments, they exited Bifröst high in the skies above Earth.

30

AS ANOTHER DAY CAME AND WENT, THE FAMILY argued about launching a rescue mission to Utgard. Tempers flared as they weighed the dangers of starting the war with the frost giants against the need to find Freya.

Eir was still furious at Maya for not talking sooner. But her mother's anger was nothing compared to the guilt Maya felt for not stopping her sister. If anything happened to Freya, she would never forgive herself.

Just after supper, George came running into the dining room. "Vonni, everyone! Come quick. Some of the men have broken out of their restraints. They've taken Brundi and Gage as hostages."

The Valkyries reached the barn together. The barn doors were closed and the men on the inside were shouting.

"You heard me," a voice challenged. "Release us right now or we'll kill the old woman!"

Tash was standing outside the barn. "They've got my brother and Brundi!" she panicked. "They've got a pitchfork and say they'll hurt them."

Maya raised her head and closed her eyes, seeking out Gage in the barn. Her grandmother was calm but furious. The little boy was frightened, but they were both very much alive.

"Gage is fine," she reassured Tash. "He's a little frightened, but Brundi is with him."

Tash ran over to Eir and knelt before her. "Please, ma'am, please, can you save my brother? You have all these powers; don't let them hurt him. He and Brundi are all I have left. I swear I'll do anything you ask. Just save my brother!"

The senior Valkyrie took hold of Tash's hand in her own gloved hands. "Do not fear, child. We will do everything in our power to free my mother and your little brother. Gage is very special to all of us."

Eir moved closer to the barn and called the Valkyries forward. "Remove your coats and open your wings. We do not have a moment to waste with these foolish humans. Let them see who we are and what they're up against. We will make them surrender their hostages, and then we will fly to Utgard!"

31

FREYA FELT HER EXCITEMENT GROWING AS THEY headed back to Idaho. Her brother, Kai, was flying by her side, carrying Archie. She could sense his anticipation as he took in all the sights of Midgard.

Loki soared ahead of them. He'd changed shape again and was now an eagle that was leading them home.

They headed through the clouds and into the clear skies. The sun was just starting to set and casting blazing pinks and reds in the sky.

"You know the rest of the way from here," Loki squawked. "Tell Brundi I will be back shortly."

"Where are you going?" Freya demanded.

"I must return to Utgard to see what's happening," Loki said. The eagle winked one of its golden eyes. "Try not to miss me too much." A short time later they were gliding over the property lines of Valhalla Valley. Even before they reached the house, Freya sensed something was wrong. Her mother's and sisters' fury was running wild.

They saw a crowd gathered outside the barn. Tash was crying, and the residents of the ranch looked terrified. They stood behind a line of Valkyries in place to attack the barn, their swords held high.

"What's happening?" Archie cried.

"I don't know," Freya called. "But it's not good!"

They touched down just as her mother charged forward and wrenched the barn doors open.

"Kai, stay here with the others." Freya drew her golden sword and ran to join her sisters and uncle.

A large group of men stood in the middle of the barn. They were preparing for a fight. Freya spotted Gage, being held by one man, while two more men were holding tight to Brundi and pressing a pitchfork to her back. It all became clear when she recognized one of the men she'd left at the top of the mountain.

"You will release your prisoners now!" Eir threatened, brimming with rage. Vonni was right beside her, bare-handed but ready to fight.

"One more step and I'll kill the old woman!" the man warned. "We're in control here. You'll give us back our weapons and surrender to us."

"Surrender to you?" Eir challenged. "You expect us to surrender to you? You fool! Do you not know who we are?"

The man's determination didn't waver. "I don't care who or what you are. You take one more step and I'll kill her."

"And that"—Vonni's voice grew deep and threatening—"will be the last mistake you ever make. Release my mother and you may survive this."

Gage was looking at Freya and Archie. His lips were trembling and his face was flushed with fear. "Archie, help me . . . ," he whimpered.

At this, Eir turned immediately and saw Freya. She lowered her sword and took a step closer. "Freya, by Odin, where have you been? Maya said you went to Utgard to get—"

In that instant, the men struck. They charged toward Eir and Vonni.

"Mother—look out!" Freya screamed.

But before they could do anything, Kai flew into the barn with both his black blades flashing. He landed among the men, and with one of his blades, he wrenched the pitchfork away from the hunter threatening Brundi. He took out the other with a swipe of steel. Kai then spun and, in a movement too fast to follow, brought down the hunter holding Gage.

Freya charged in and caught hold of Gage. She pushed him toward the open doors. "Go outside with Archie and find your sister. Don't look back!"

"Come with me, Gage," Archie called, drawing him to the barn doors.

Freya turned back to the fight. A hunter was charging at Kai with the pitchfork in his hands. "Die, you winged freak!"

With one sword, Kai easily deflected the pitchfork. His second blade slashed down, hitting it out of the attacker's hand. He glanced back at Freya. "So this is a living human? They're so weak."

"I'll show you weak!" The man charged again, but he didn't stand a chance against Kai's Dark Searcher skills. He fell to the ground, beaten.

The air was filled with the sounds of Valkyrie howls and flashing swords as the fight heated up.

"Give me a sword!" Brundi demanded. "Let me fight!"

"Mother, get out of here!" Eir shouted back. "Keep the humans outside safe!"

"No. This is my battle!"

"Mother, go!" Vonni ordered her out of the barn as he caught hold of a man and threw him the length of the building.

From the barn door, Brundi watched her family fight for the world she had created in Midgard.

The hunters stood no chance. Soon there were only three men left standing. They huddled together in a horse's stall, begging for mercy. With the fight was over, Angels of Death arrived to claim the others. Nodding to the Valkyries, they collected the men and left silently.

"Wow, Kai." Freya turned to her brother. "You've got to teach me some of those moves."

"Me too!" Archie said. "Crixus would be blown away if he saw me doing that with two swords."

"It's easy," Kai said. "Anyone can do it."

"Anyone who'd trained their whole life as a Dark Searcher," Freya corrected.

"Then I shall train you."

They became aware of everyone staring at them. "Is that him?" Gwyn took a step closer.

"It must be," Skaga answered.

"Kai?" Eir whispered, disbelieving. "Is this really my Kai?"

Freya nodded and looked at her brother. She elbowed him in the side. "Go on, Kai. I told you about her. That's our mother."

Kai looked uncertain as his eyes locked upon his mother for the very first time. He cleared his throat. "So . . . are you really my mother . . . ?"

Eir nodded as tears sparkled in her pale eyes. "My beautiful Kai!" She crossed the distance between them in two long strides and wrapped him in her winged embrace.

Kai stood frozen as his mother held him. Arms at his sides, he was unprepared for the show of emotion. But soon he relaxed and embraced his mother awkwardly.

As her mother and brother were reunited, Freya approached her sisters. "So what do you think of our brother? Kai's my twin. We were separated at birth."

{ 329 }

"We heard." Kara nodded. "We've been frantic about you, especially when Mia said you'd gone to Utgard."

"You told them?" Freya turned to Maya.

"I had to," Maya cried. "You've been gone for days! We thought you'd been captured by the Dark Searchers."

"*She was,*" Orus cawed. "*Dirian nearly killed her again!*"

"Dirian?" Eir immediately returned to Freya's side. "What happened? Tell us everything."

"It's a long story," Freya said. "It involves a few angry frost giants, Dark Elves, and trolls."

"*Don't forget Thor and Balder,*" Orus added.

Freya nodded. "They were there too—I think I might be in trouble with Odin . . . again." She looked at her sister. "But, Mia, your wings. What happened?"

Maya shrugged. "Broken again. I had a run-in with those men just after you left for Utgard. They were going to burn down the house. I stopped them, but they shot me—and Grul."

"*Grul was shot?*" Orus cawed. "*Where is he?*"

"In the house, resting," Maya said. "He's in the dining room."

"*Freya . . .*"

"Go on, Orus," she said. "Go to Grul."

Orus flew off Freya's shoulder. "*It's not that I care, really . . . ,*" he protested as he disappeared out of the barn.

Freya turned to her uncle. "Is it all right for Kai to stay here?"

Vonni was staring at his nephew in silence. Everyone had been telling him that he was a Dark Searcher. This was the first genuine one he'd ever seen. "Of—of course. But what about the war? Won't they miss him?"

"They don't know he's here. Kai is free of the Dark Searchers. He'll have to hide in the mine with you during the war."

Kai came forward. "I will not hide from battle!" he said indignantly. "No Searcher ever would. I helped you get away from Utgard because your life was in danger. You must stay here until it's safe to return to Asgard and face Odin. But I am going to rejoin my brothers. I will serve with them and, if called to, fight beside them."

Kai looked as his mothers and sisters. "You will also. We must defend Asgard. If it falls, there is no hope for the other realms. Including this one."

The Valkyries looked at each other.

"He's right," Skaga said. "It is our duty. We cannot remain here. We'll complete the work on the mine, but then we must return." She turned to Freya. "Kai is also right about you. If you are facing Odin's wrath, it is better for you to remain here until it's safe to come back."

"I have to stay here?" Freya repeated. "For how long?"

Her mother nodded. "However long it takes to cool Odin's temper. It will give us time to plead your case."

Vonni stood beside her. "Our home is your home—you

know that. You are welcome to stay as long as necessary. I know Mims will be thrilled."

"If we have to stay, Gee," Archie said, "at least you can teach Mims what it is to be a Valkyrie."

Freya looked at her mother and sisters. In her haste to reach her brother, she hadn't thought about the full outcome of her actions. Finding Kai had cost dearly. It had cost her . . . her home in Asgard.

32

AFTER SECURING THE PRISONERS, THEY LEFT THE BARN
and were greeted by loud applause. Gage ran forward and
hugged Kai tightly, clinging to the white feathers on his wings.

Kai didn't know what to do and stood with his hands
above his head, looking distinctly uncomfortable. "Release
me, small human."

"It's all right, Kai," Freya said. "Gage is a hugger." She
reached forward and ruffled the boy's red hair. "Are you all
right, little man?"

Gage nodded.

Tash came to save Kai from her little brother. "Um, I, uh,
saw what you did in there. Um . . . thank you for saving my
brother." She stumbled on her words, and Freya was sure she
saw a blush come to Tash's cheeks.

She wasn't surprised. Kai was as beautiful as Vonni. But it was Kai who surprised Freya. "I, ah . . . there is, uh, no need to thank me." He stammered and struggled over his words and quickly turned away to walk over to the barn. He leaned heavily against the side of the barn wall and dropped his head.

"Are you okay?" Freya went to check up on him with Mims and Archie.

Kai looked back over to Tash. "Yes, fine—just a weird feeling. My stomach twisted when I talked to that girl. Maybe Midgard doesn't agree with me?"

Archie grinned. "Is Tash the first human girl you've ever met?"

Kai nodded. "No living humans can survive in Utgard."

"Boy, are you in for a lot of surprises, then." Mims laughed. "All the girls on the ranch will think you're really cute."

"I don't understand," Kai said, catching his breath.

"You will," Archie answered.

"Where's that grandson of mine?" Brundi pushed through.

Freya introduced Kai and stood back, watching her brother try to deal with another long-lost relative smothering him in an embrace.

"Do you think he'll be okay?" Archie asked. "He looks really uncomfortable with all this attention."

"He'll be fine. All Kai's known in his life is training and fighting, duty and honor in the Dark Searchers' keep. He's got to learn that there are other feelings too. It must be over-whelming for him, but he'll get used to it."

"It's strange to me, too," Archie admitted. "Look around you. Did you ever think you'd see your family mixing with humans like this?"

Freya and Mims gazed over at the people around them. Freya's Valkyrie sisters were talking with the ranch hands, their wings on full display. Maya was holding Grul and Orus in her arms and talking to George, the ranch vet.

Her mother, Vonni, and Sarah were fussing over the baby and introducing him to Kai. Everyone was mingling, and despite their vast differences, they were becoming a large, close family.

Vonni raised his voice and called everyone to attention. "We are truly blessed to have everyone here." His eyes found Kai. "I am overjoyed to welcome Kai into our family. But now that we're all back together, we must return to the mine. The war draws ever closer. We must not delay. After supper, it's back to work for all of us."

As evening fell, the surviving intruders were pulled from the stall and lined up along the wall of the barn. The Valkyries stood before them, their faces stern.

Mims was watching with Freya, Archie, and Kai. "Are they going to kill them?" she asked fearfully.

"Of course. They attacked you and must be destroyed to remove the threat." Kai spoke coolly.

Freya looked at the hard expression on her brother's face. His Dark Searcher training ran deep. She hoped he would one day learn compassion.

"I hope not," Archie frowned. "There's been enough killing already."

"Death is the only way to silence them," Kai added.

"There is another way," Freya said. "I've never seen it done, but Maya told me about it."

"What's that?" Archie asked.

"Erase their minds," Freya explained. "Valkyries have the power to erase a bit of someone's memory, or their whole life. It's the only way to keep the men from talking about what they've seen here."

"All Midgard residents," Maya was announcing, "please return to the house and wait for us. We can't have you near us when we do this or you may have parts of your mind erased."

She walked over to the barn door, clutching Grul close to her chest. "I think you'd better go too, Archie." Her eyes landed on Kai. "And you. We don't know if this might affect you and Vonni."

"Yes," Vonni agreed, approaching them. "Let's go into the house and let these ladies do their work."

"Freya, Mims," Eir called, "you too. You're too young for this."

"But I want to see," Freya protested.

"Me too!" Mims said.

"Not yet," Brundi said. "You'll have plenty of time to learn it later. Now, do as your mother says. We'll be out shortly, and then we'll go to the mine."

"I don't know about you, but I for one don't want my mind erased," Orus cawed. *"I'm saving up my insults for when Grul is recovered, and I'd hate to forget them."*

Freya walked toward the door but looked up at the raven on her shoulder. "Will you ever admit that you care for Grul?"

"Me? Care for that bird brain?" Orus spat. *"Never."*

They were walking toward the house when the first soft notes of beautiful voices flowed from the barn.

Vonni paused to listen.

"Come on, Dad." Mims caught hold of her father's arm and pulled him away.

The music from the barn was beautiful and beckoning. It was hard to drag everyone away from it. Freya suddenly realized the danger. She caught hold of Kai's arm as well as Archie's and dragged them toward the house.

"No, Gee, I want to hear," Archie said dreamily.

They were still protesting as Freya pushed them up the steps to the house. Once they were safely inside, Archie shook his head. "Wow, that was powerful."

Kai was standing back and humming softly. "I should like to learn that piece."

Vonni nodded. "Me too. Maybe when this is over, they'll teach it to us."

Brundi soon returned to the house and announced that it was now safe to go outside.

"How are they?" Freya asked.

"As innocent as newborns. It's as if they're starting over. They won't be troubling anyone ever again."

As they waited for the others to emerge from the barn, Gage ran to the front door and threw it open. He charged onto the porch. "Everyone, look—they're coming!"

"Gage, stop. Who's coming?" Tash chased after her little brother.

Gage pointed up into the sky. "Them—the black angels!"

Freya also felt the presence of something approaching the house. She and Archie ran out onto the porch.

"I don't see anything." Vonni was staring up into the dark sky.

"But I can feel them," Kai said darkly. He looked at Freya. "It's the Dark Searchers. They've found me!"

33

FREYA DREW HER SWORD AND LEAPED DOWN FROM THE
porch. "Vonni and Mims, go get my mother and sisters. Tell
them Dark Searchers are coming. Then stay in the barn—we
don't want them to see either of you. If we're lucky, they
won't sense you in there. Everyone else, stay in the house!"

"This is not going to be good," Orus cawed. *"They must be furious to come all this way to get Kai. This will be our worst battle yet."*

"No, it won't." Kai stepped away from his sister. "Not if I
surrender. The war is coming; they can't afford to lose fighters." He looked back at Freya. "You should go into the barn
too. Let me face them alone."

Freya shook her head. "This is my fault. I was the one to
lead Archie and Orus into Utgard. I won't let you take the
blame for what I did."

"Don't be foolish," Kai insisted. "Archie, get her away from here."

Freya stood between Kai and Archie, looking strong and determined. "Don't even think about it, Archie. I won't hide. Not from them."

"I'm not asking you to," Archie said. "I'm ready to fight too."

Kai pulled away. "Are you mad? They'll hurt you. Don't you understand that? I can't let that happen. If I surrender, maybe they'll leave you alone."

"Oh, no you don't, little brother." Skaga drew her sword. "We haven't trained all our lives for nothing. We will fight and we will win."

"You must know that Dark Searchers never lose. They will kill you all. I can't be the cause of that."

"They won't kill us," Freya said darkly. She stepped away from her family and gazed up into the night sky. "Azrael, please come. We need your help!"

"Freya, no!" Eir cried, arriving from the barn. "You can't call him. This is our fight. We can't involve the Angels of Death."

"It is too late for that, dear lady," Azrael said as he and a large group of angels landed at the ranch. They were dressed in blazing-white battle armor over their tunics. In their hands they held white feathered helmets and had swords at their waists. "I have been involved since the very beginning."

The Angel of Death approached Brundi. "Brünnhilde,

I was the village elder who hid your son from the Midgard Serpent. It was me who removed Vonni's wings."

Brundi inhaled sharply. "You?"

Azrael nodded. "Your cause was just. You fought for your children. I had to help. But now I fear my efforts may have been in vain."

He focused on Freya. "I've been waiting for your call. We will stand with you and, if necessary, fight beside you." Azrael drew his shining sword. "I started this; it's time I finished it."

"There!" Freya cried as she watched the skies and saw the stars blotted out by a dark mass.

They heard the sound of wind passing over feathers and the flapping of large, powerful wings. Twelve large Dark Searchers landed on the ground before them in front of the line of Angels of Death. In full battle armor, their dark cloaks billowed in the cold night wind and contrasted vividly with the floating softness of the angels' white.

Beside them, Thor landed heavily, carrying Balder. The brothers' faces held dark scowls. "Azrael," Thor shouted. "What are you doing here?"

"I am stopping an injustice."

"There is no injustice. Freya is a criminal and has led Kai astray. Utgard is in chaos because of her! The frost giants are on the rampage, and the Dark Elves are screaming for blood. She and Kai will come with me to face my father. He will decide their fate."

Azrael stood before Thor. "I don't think so," he said, shaking his head. "It is true that Freya can be a bit high-spirited, but she has a good heart. She has not dishonored Odin. Please return to Asgard; the Valkyries will be along shortly."

"What about Kai?" Balder asked.

"Kai will decide his own fate. You'll not take him back to the Dark Searchers against his will," Eir said as she stood before Thor. "He's my son. It nearly destroyed me when he was taken from me the first time. I won't let that happen again."

"Yes," Kai called firmly. "I will decide my fate." He approached Thor and bowed respectfully. "And I choose to remain with the Searchers—"

"Kai, no!" Freya cried.

"I'm not finished," Kai said. "Yes, I wish to return to fight beside my brothers. But I will never be denied my family again."

"Are you trying to bargain with me?" Thor said.

"What choice have I got?" Kai said. "All our lives, my brothers in the Dark Searchers have been kept away from Asgard and treated like outcasts, only venturing there when Odin needs us. We didn't know that our mothers are Valkyries. We were pitted against them and told they were our enemies. But no more! I have found my family, and you won't harm them—not because of me."

"Freya has filled your head with fantastical stories. Surely my father would have told us that you were related if it were true," Thor said.

"Kai speaks the truth!" Vonni called from the barn doors. He trotted over to Thor and the Dark Searchers. "You all have family. They are the Valkyries!"

He started to pace before the line of Searchers. "I have fought in countless wars over the ages and am not unfamiliar with battle. I will fight you if I must. But I ask you to listen to me now. I am Giovanni Angelo—son of the Valkyrie Brünnhilde. Were it not for my mother's actions, I would be one of you." He paused, pulled off his sweater, and presented his bare back to the line of Dark Searchers.

"Look at me," he demanded. "Look at the scars where my wings once were. They were removed to keep me safe." He turned back toward them. "Use your powerful senses. You know I am one of you. I am a Dark Searcher, and I will fight to the death to protect my family!"

Vonni reached for one of Kai's swords and raised it. "So who's first?" He turned on Thor. "I know all the myths about you, Thor, and I know how powerful you and that hammer are. I used to imagine how wonderful it would be to meet you if you were real. Well, now I know you are very real, and I still feel the same. But I will fight you if I must. This is my family—including Kai—and you won't take them away from me."

"Dad, no!" Mims ran over to her father and faced the line of Dark Searchers. "Leave us alone. Just leave us alone and go back to where you came from!"

She stood defiantly with her father. Thor took several steps forward and grasped her chin in his large hands. "You called him Dad? Is this man truly your father?"

Mims nodded. "I know he's a Dark Searcher, but he's good. I have a little brother too—he's got black wings, just like all the other Dark Searchers—but he was born here on Earth to my human mother."

There was a collective intake of air as the Searchers stared at her.

"Please," Freya begged Thor. "Listen to us. Dark Searchers don't have to be our enemies. They are our brothers. I don't know why Odin separated us. Kai is my twin. Just look at him and you can see it. Look at Giovanni—he is my mother's twin."

Freya appealed to the Searchers. "One of you is Vonni's older brother. Brundi is your mother. Can't you feel it? We're all connected. We're family!"

Azrael lowered his sword. "Thor, we speak of injustice, but here is the greatest injustice of all: families destroyed for no reason. It is time Odin reconsidered his order of separation."

The Angel of Death faced the Dark Searchers. "Search your hearts. Don't each of you yearn to know where you come from? Who your mother is? Or if you have sisters?"

One by one, the Dark Searchers lowered their swords.

"Dark times are coming." Vonni addressed them now. "Wouldn't it be better if we all worked together and not against each other? If war comes, Odin will need every fighter he can get to defeat the frost and fire giants."

"We're all on the same side," Freya insisted, joining her uncle.

One of the Dark Searchers started to move forward. Freya's senses told her that he was the healer. Gasps were heard as the Searcher reached up and removed his helmet. He was Brundi's age, with long black hair tied back and dark-blue, penetrating eyes. He was a beautiful sight to behold.

"I have wanted to know my origins for an age," the healer rasped in his broken voice. "Now I know the truth." He turned back to the other Searchers. "They speak true. Valkyries and Dark Searchers are one." He walked over to Vonni. "I will stand with you and, if I must, die with you. But I will never raise a weapon to my sisters again."

"You will fight against Odin?" Thor demanded.

"We don't have to fight at all," Freya insisted. "Don't you see? All we're asking for is the right to know each other. Where is the crime in that?"

As she spoke, another Dark Searcher crossed the line and stood beside Vonni. "I too will stand with my brother." He removed his helmet, and everyone gasped. The resemblance between Vonni and the Dark Searcher was striking. The Searcher turned back to Brundi and bowed his head deeply. "My mother."

Brundi's hands went up to her mouth as she recognized her firstborn son. "Kris?" she cried as she stumbled forward to embrace him.

One by one the Dark Searchers put away their weapons and stepped forward.

Azrael leaned closer to Thor and Balder. "Where is the injustice in that? Truly, what crime have they committed?"

Thor lowered his hammer when the Searchers all moved to the side of the Angels of Death and the Valkyrie family. "There has been no crime committed here," he admitted.

"But tell me, Angel," he continued. "What am I supposed to tell Odin?"

34

"FREYA, ARCHIE, AND KAI," THOR COMMANDED AS HE and Balder stood away from the others, "we cannot linger a moment longer. We must return to Asgard. You three have caused a lot of trouble in Utgard. We must explain to my father what has happened."

"It wasn't our fault," Orus cawed. *"They started it, not us!"*

"Actually, a troll started it—" Kai corrected.

"It doesn't matter who started it," Thor interrupted. "We must let Odin know."

"What about them?" Freya gestured to the Dark Searchers and Valkyries.

Thor nodded. "Your words tonight made a lot of sense, and I will implore my father not to separate Valkyries and Searchers. But that's not what is important right now."

"The war is," Freya said darkly.

Balder nodded. "We will need all our fighters if we are to defend Asgard. The Dark Searchers and Valkyries cannot remain here."

"What about Vonni and his family?" Archie asked.

Thor's eyes settled on Vonni. He was standing with Sarah and Kris, his brother. "It is best if he remains here. He can fight and he is brave to stand up to me. But he has never gone against a frost giant."

"We're preparing a deep mine for the family to hide in," Freya said. "We hope the gold inside will shield them if the giants invade Midgard in the war."

Thor raised an eyebrow. "Was it only to hide them from the frost giants?"

Freya dropped her head. "And Odin," she admitted. "We were certain he would kill Vonni and maybe even Mims and the baby if he knew the truth."

"Do you think of Odin as a barbarian?" Thor challenged. "That he would kill children?"

"No!" Freya said quickly. "But Odin insists his rules are obeyed. Brundi broke the rules and Vonni and the family are the result. We thought he'd be furious."

"She's right, brother." Balder nodded. "Odin will be furious when he learns the truth."

"But not enough to kill," Thor said. "Right now our father has a lot more to concern himself with than a small family here in Midgard."

Suddenly screeching pierced the sky. An eagle touched down and shimmered into Loki. His face was covered in a film of sweat and his clothes were in tatters.

"Loki! What are you doing here?" Thor demanded.

"It's Dirian!" Loki gasped. "He called the Dark Searchers to his side. Those who wouldn't join him were killed. Dirian has found a way to keep them dead—they can't rise again." He turned to the Searchers. "You're all that's left of Odin's loyal Searchers. If you'd stayed in Utgard, you'd be dead too."

"This can't be!" Thor shouted. "We were just there!"

"I swear by all I believe, it's true!" Loki continued. "Dirian and his Searchers waited until you and your hammer left, and then they made their move. They were the ones who forged the alliance with the frost and fire giants and stirred up the Dark Elves, dwarfs, and trolls. They convinced them all to join their cause. Dirian has accused Odin of sending a Valkyrie to Utgard to spy on them. He's the one leading the attack against Asgard."

"Dirian is the traitor?" Balder cried.

Loki focused on Freya. "His hatred for you has driven him mad. He is out for your blood."

"No, this isn't Freya's fault," Azrael called, coming forward. "I should have worked it out sooner. Dirian is an opportunist—I have no doubt he's been plotting against Asgard for some time. He's using Freya's appearance in Utgard as the trigger, but she is not the cause."

"It doesn't matter what started it," Loki insisted. "Light Elves have been pouring into Asgard to align with Odin's forces. I tried to find Odin to tell him, but then heard Heimdall was closing Bifröst—I was the last to get across."

"We're trapped in Midgard?" Kris growled as the Dark Searchers gathered around.

"It's far worse than that," Azrael said as he called his angels together. "It has started. We must all prepare."

"You don't mean . . . ," Freya cried.

Azrael's face was ashen as he turned to her and nodded. "War in the realms has begun."

A GUIDE TO THIS WORLD

Norse mythology is old. It's not just old; it's really, really old! It's also known as Scandinavian mythology and was created, retold, and loved by the Vikings. The Vikings, or Norsemen, settled most of Northern Europe and came mainly from Denmark, Norway, Sweden, Iceland, the Faroe Islands, and Greenland.

As you get to know the Norse myths, you might notice there are some similarities to the ancient Greek myths (including flying horses—but not my sweet Pegasus). Here's a simple comparison.

In Greek mythology, you have the Olympians and the Titans. The "younger" Olympians, in fact, came from the "older" Titans, and yet, there was a war between them and the Olympians won.

In Norse mythology, you have the Aesir and the Vanir. The "younger" Aesir came from the "older" Vanir, and yes, there was a war! But the difference is, in Norse mythology, neither side won—they called a truce.

Here's a big difference. In Greek myths, you have the place called Olympus. But in Norse myths, there are in fact nine worlds, or "realms" as they are sometimes called. In each of these realms, you have some really weird and wonderful creatures. And you know what? *We* are part of those nine realms. We're in the middle bit. And instead of Earth, our world is called Midgard.

Now, some of you may think you don't know Norse mythology at all. You do, but what you have learned may not be correct.

What's the biggest mistake I hear all the time? Okay, here is a really big one. I mean *big*. He's huge. He's green and has a bad temper. Yes, I'm talking about the Hulk. He is *not* part of Norse mythology. Neither are Iron Man, Hawkeye, Black Widow, nor many of the other characters from the Avengers movies. But no matter how many schools I visit, the moment I mention Thor or Loki, the students immediately think that the Hulk and the other characters are part of Norse mythology.

Trust me, they're not.

Don't get me wrong: I love the Avengers and Thor movies as much as anyone. But they are the creation of Marvel, Paramount, and Disney. The real Norse myths are much older and have a much richer history.

So, as you enter the world of Valkyrie and Norse mythology, I would like to introduce you to some of the characters you may meet along the way.

Some will appear in this book; others will appear in the

later books in this series. But I also encourage you to go to your local library or bookstore and check out more books on Norse myths. Believe me, with all the heroes and monsters you'll meet, you will soon love them as much as I do!

—Kate

NAMES AND PLACES IN NORSE MYTHOLOGY

YGGDRASIL—Also known as the Cosmic World Tree, Yggdrasil sits in the very heart of the universe. It is within the branches of this tree that the nine realms exist. Yggdrasil is supported by three massive roots that pass through the realms. It is said that the fierce dragon Nidhogg regularly gnaws on one of the roots (when he's not eating corpses— don't ask). The Well of Urd, where Odin traded his eye for wisdom, sits on another root. Water from that well is taken by the Norns, mixed with earth, and put on the tree as a means of preventing Yggdrasil's bark from rotting. They also water the tree. It is said that a great eagle sits perched atop the tree and is harassed by a squirrel, Ratatosk, who delivers insults and unpleasant comments from the dragon Nidhogg, who resides at the base. Yggdrasil gives the nine realms life. Without it, they and we would cease to exist.

AESIR—This is the name of the group of younger gods, like Odin, Thor, Loki, Frigg, and the Valkyries. These are warrior gods who use weapons more than magic.

VANIR—This is the name of the older gods. Not much is known about them, but there are some familiar names. Freya and her twin brother, Freyr, are two well-known Vanir who were traded to Asgard in a peace exchange after the war. The Vanir are more earthen/forest-type gods who deal with land fertility and use a lot of magic.

ODIN—He is the leader of Asgard, the realm of the Aesir. A brave, strong, and imposing warrior, he presided over the war with the Vanir. He has many sons, most notably Thor and Balder. Odin carries a powerful spear, Gungnir, and wears an eye patch. It is said that Odin journeyed to the Well of Urd, where he exchanged his eye for wisdom. Each night Odin can be found in Valhalla, where he celebrates with the fallen heroes of Earth's battlefields. His two wolves sit loyally at his side.

FRIGG—The devoted and very beautiful wife of Odin, she is the mother of Balder and is known for her wisdom. Sadly not a lot more is known about her, other than that she knows everyone's destiny. In later mythology, she is often confused with Freya and their deeds are mixed.

THOR—The son of Odin, he is known as the thunder god and is often compared with Zeus from the Greek myths. Thor is impossibly strong, with flaming red hair and a raging temper. He is known for being a fierce but honorable warrior. Thor is a sworn enemy to the frost giants, but calls Loki (who is part frost giant) a friend. They had many adventures together. Thor is also known for his mighty hammer, Mjölnir, which was created by the dwarf brothers Sindri and Brokkr on a mischievous bet with Loki. After its creation, they gave it to Thor, as he was one of the few strong enough to wield it. (By the way, Loki lost the bet and the two dwarfs sewed his mouth shut.) Thor is actually a married man—his wife is Sif, and they have three children. Note: We use the name Thor every week, as Thursday was named after him. Just think: Thor's day.

BALDER—Son of Odin and Frigg, he is known as the kindest of Odin's sons. Balder is a devoted brother to Thor and can calm his brother's fearsome temper. Sadly, within the mythology, Balder died, and it is widely believed that Loki caused his death and was responsible for keeping him dead.

LOKI—He is the trickster of Asgard. His origins are a little unclear, but it's said that both of his parents were frost giants. He is by turns playful, malicious, and helpful, but he's always irreverent and self-involved. Loki likes to have fun! He enjoys getting Thor into trouble, but then he helps Thor out of the same trouble. Loki is a shape-changer and appears in many disguises. For all his troublemaking ways, it is written that Loki is tolerated in Asgard because he is blood brother to Odin.

HEIMDALL—Ever vigilant watchman of Bifröst, Heimdall has nine mothers but no father. He is a giant of a man and amazingly strong. Heimdall requires less sleep than a bird, and his vision is so powerful he can see for hundreds of miles, day or night. His hearing is so acute that he can hear grass or wool grow. It is written that he carries a special horn, Gjallarhorn, that he will sound at the start of Ragnarök when the giants storm Bifröst.

VALKYRIES—Choosers of the slain, the winged Valkyries are an elite group of Battle-Maidens who serve Odin by bringing only the most valiant of fallen warriors from Earth's battlefields to Valhalla. There, the warriors fight all day and feast all night, being served food and mead by the Valkyries. In early mythology, the Valkyries could decide who would live or die on the battlefield, but later this was changed to only collecting them for Odin. The Valkyries arrived on the battle-fields riding blazing, winged horses, and their howls could be heard long before their arrival. It is written that the Vanir goddess Freya, who was traded after the war, was in fact the very first Valkyrie. Again, within the mythology, she gets to keep half the warriors she reaps—but it's not written what she does with them. The other half go to Odin.

FROST & FIRE GIANTS—Throughout the mythology, the frost and fire giants often appear, and there are many stories about Thor's encounters with them. Fearsome, immense, and violent, they each live in their own realms. Frost giants are from Utgard in Jotunheim, and the fire giants come from Muspelheim. Though there are some peaceful giants, most seek to conquer Asgard. To offer an idea of size, there is one story in which Loki, Thor, and two humans venture to Utgard to meet the frost giant king, but get lost in a maze of tunnels. It is later discovered that these tunnels were, in fact, the fingers of a frost giant's glove.

DWARFS—Both good and bad, dwarfs play a large part and fill an important role in Norse mythology. They are the master craftsmen and architects of the building of Asgard. It was dwarfs who created Thor's mighty hammer, Mjölnir, and Odin's spear, Gungnir. There are many stories of the dwarfs and their amazing creations.

LIGHT & DARK ELVES—These are the two contrasting types of elves. Dark Elves use dark magic, cause a lot of trouble, and can be very dangerous; they are hard to look upon and seek to do harm. Whereas the Light Elves are fairer to look at than the sun, use their magic for good, and help many people.

MIDGARD SERPENT—Also known as Jormungand, the Midgard Serpent is the son of Loki and his giantess wife, Angrboda. The Midgard Serpent is brother to the giant wolf Fenrir and Hel, Loki's daughter and ruler of the underworld. It is written that Odin had Jormungand cast into the ocean, where he grew so large he could encircle the Earth. There is a ongoing feud between Thor and the Midgard Serpent. It is written that Jormungand is big and powerful enough to eat worlds.

RAVENS—Ravens play a large part in Norse mythology, and Odin himself has two very special ravens, Huginn and Muninn, who travel through all the realms and return to Odin at night. They sit on his shoulder and tell him everything that is happening in the other realms. They are known for their wisdom and guidance.

VALHALLA—Odin's great heavenly hall for the heroic dead has a curious problem. In the mythology, there is a question of where Valhalla actually is. Most say it was part of Asgard, but others suggest it is in Helheim, the land of the dead. One thing is clear: Valhalla is a wondrous building where the valiant dead from Earth's battlefields are taken. Here they are served and entertained by the Valkyries who delivered them there. They drink and feast with Odin and continue their training until the day comes when they are called back into service to fight for Asgard during Ragnarök.

BIFRÖST—Also known as the Rainbow Bridge, this is a magnificent, multicolored bridge that links Asgard to Midgard and some of the other realms. It is said to have been created by the gods using the red of fire, the green of water, and the blue of air. Bifröst is guarded by Heimdall the watchman.

THE NORNS—There are three Norn sisters who dwell at the Well of Urd at the base of Yggdrasil. The oldest is Urd, the middle sister is Verdandi, and the youngest is Skuld. These are the goddesses of destiny, similar to the Greek Fates. Urd is able to see the past, while Verdandi deals with current events. Skuld is able to see everyone's future. It is said that they are weavers, weaving people's destiny. If a thread is broken, the life ends.

RAGNARÖK—Also known as the apocalypse of the Norse gods and the end of everything, Ragnarök (in the mythology) is said to have been started by a very insane Loki and his wolf son, Fenrir, along with the frost and fire giants. They took on Asgard, and during the war all the gods were killed. Odin was killed by Fenrir, who was then killed by another of Odin's sons. Thor and the Midgard Serpent fought a battle to the death in which they managed to kill each other. Heimdall was the last to fall at the hand of Loki. It is during Ragnarök that Odin called on the warriors of Valhalla to fight for Asgard—but there were no winners. And it was from the ashes of Ragnarök that a new world was formed from the survivors—the world that we inhabit today.

DARK SEARCHERS—The Dark Searchers did not actually exist in Norse mythology. They are my creation because, in all my research, I couldn't find a mention of Odin's police force. So I created them for that purpose.

AZRAEL & THE ANGELS OF DEATH—Now, some of you may already know that Azrael and the Angels of Death don't come directly from Norse mythology. That's very true. But as they are known all over the world in almost every culture, and since they do similar jobs to the Valkyries and have wings just like the Valkyries, I thought it would be fun to mix things up a bit. To avoid confusion, I set it up so that the Valkyries only deal with the most valiant warriors reaped from Earth's battlefields, who are then taken to Valhalla—thus staying true to Norse mythology. Azrael and his Angels of Death deal with everyone else—thus staying true to many other cultures.

ACKNOWLEDGMENTS

*No man is an island, entire of itself; every man is a
piece of the continent, a part of the main. If a clod be
washed away by the sea, Europe is the less, as well as if
a promontory were, as well as if a manor of thy friend's
or of thine own were: any man's death diminishes me,
because I am involved in mankind, and therefore never
send to know for whom the bell tolls; it tolls for thee.*
—John Donne

You might wonder why I have put those wonderful words
in the acknowledgments of this book. But there is a reason.
Just like "no man is an island," no book is created by one
person alone. It takes a whole collection of people to create
what you are holding in your hands right now.

From my amazing agents, Veronique Baxter and Laura
West, to my great editor, Fiona Simpson, and cover designer
Karin Paprocki, and so many more people whose names I will
never know but wish I did. They all work together to make it
possible for you to read the story I tell.

And what book would be complete without its readers?

ACKNOWLEDGMENTS

YOU, my friends, are as much a part of this story as my agents and editor. Because it's you who really matter to me. You inspire me to keep going. And for that, I sincerely thank you.

For those of you who know me, there are others I need to acknowledge, and I hope that you, dear reader, will acknowledge them too. The animals around us—those whom we share this world with. Be they horses, dogs, cats, frogs, dolphins, whales, sharks, or all the others . . . they all need our help and protection. I ask each of you to do all you can for them.

Please . . .